Dedicated to my husband

Your love shines like the beam from a lighthouse.

Illuminating the way home as I sail on life's turbulent seas.

Thank you for loving me.

Traditional Family Secrets

Robin Wainwright

Published by Robin Wainwright, 2024.

Chapter One

Crescent Bay, California – Lighthouse

It was the end of August, and the lazy days of Summer were winding down in Crescent Bay. The flow of tourists had trickled down to a few die-hard vacationers who were desperate to make one more summer memory before autumn arrived.

Shaun Morrow said goodbye to his last tour group of the day and began locking up the lighthouse keeper's cottage.

On the second floor, Shaun unlocked a door that led out to the cottage's Widow's Walk, a flat, railed observation deck on top of the cottage. Shaun sighed with contentment as he leaned against the wrought iron railing and stared at the sea. He loved his life. The village of Crescent Bay employed him to operate tours at the old lighthouse. Plus, his job allowed him to pursue his other passion, the preservation and restoration of old buildings, with lighthouse preservation as his specialty.

He had come to the village of Crescent Bay to do precisely that, preserve their lighthouse so that future generations could enjoy this unique town's history. Little had he known that his acceptance of that job would lead to a fascinating and dangerous ghost hunt and the love of his life. His contented grin deepened when he thought of his wife, Maggie.

Maggie was everything he had always dreamed of in a life partner. She was independent, intelligent, had a sharp sense of humor, a nurturing soul, and was sexy as hell. Plus, she was patient with Shaun's eccentricities.

Past girlfriends had told Shaun that he was often distracted, frustrating, and scattered. Shaun knew they were right, but there wasn't much he could do about those traits. Shaun's brain had always run on multiple tracks, and his inner focus had often made him miss social cues. And yet, Maggie loved him as he was with all his quirks.

A dog's excited yip caught his attention, and he looked away from the ocean. He spied Maggie leading their two dogs, Anne Bonny and Jack Rackham, toward the lighthouse. She saw him on the Widow's Walk and waved.

"I'll be right down. I need to lock up," Shaun bellowed. Maggie gave him a thumbs up. Shaun sprinted through the cottage, checking windows and doors, ensuring that everything was turned off. Then, locking the front door, he cast a sunny smile toward Maggie. The two little dogs barked and jumped, yanking at their leashes, trying to get to Shaun.

Maggie said, "Stad," which meant *stop* in Irish. Both dogs stopped barking and plopped down on their rumps, waiting quietly for Shaun to acknowledge them. Shaun knew the routine, so he ignored the dogs while he greeted his wife with a loving kiss and a hug.

Maggie savored her husband's touch and then knelt to unhook the dogs' leashes. She could feel the dogs' bodies quivering, but they both sat as still as possible as they waited for Maggie's next command. "Dul," Maggie said, which was Irish for *go*, then she sat back and smiled as both of the little dogs began leaping up on Shaun, making him laugh. He knelt to pet their soft fur, avoiding their doggy kisses.

"Hi, my little pirates," Shaun said affectionately. Anne Bonny rolled over onto her back, and Shaun obliged her with a belly rub. Anne Bonny was Shaun's dog and was named after a rumored distant relative of Shaun's who had been a female pirate. Shaun had given Jack to Maggie as a wedding present during their honeymoon in Ireland. Maggie had decided it was only proper to name her puppy after a fellow pirate, Jack Rackham, Anne Bonny's lover.

Following some humanly indecipherable signal, both dogs decided their greeting ceremony was complete. So they moved off in unison to smell the grounds around the lighthouse.

Shaun smiled at the little dogs and then moved toward Maggie to pull her into his arms. "I've missed you," he said.

"I missed you too. That's why we decided to come down and pry you out of the cottage," Maggie said.

"The last visitors just left; I was locking up," Shaun said.

"Funny, it looked to me like you were daydreaming," Maggie said with a gentle smile.

"Perhaps," Shaun agreed, "but I was daydreaming about you."

"Aw," Maggie said, "you're a sweet talker."

"Sometimes, but it's also the truth. I was thinking about how lucky I am that I took the job here in Crescent Bay because it led me to you."

Maggie's heart gave a little tug, and she rose onto her tiptoes to kiss Shaun. "That was my lucky day, too," Maggie agreed.

Maggie rested her head on Shaun's shoulder, and they stood in the late afternoon sunshine watching their two dogs romp and play around the grounds of the lighthouse. Then, sensing their scrutiny, the two dogs paused in their exploration and raced back to their owners, yipping with tales about all they had discovered.

"Are you ready for dinner?" Shaun asked them, and their barking doubled in excitement for the offered meal.

"Stad," Maggie said in a commanding tone, and both dogs dropped to their rumps and sat while Maggie reattached their leashes. Then, she handed Anne Bonnie's leash to Shaun, and they began walking home.

"By the way, Daniel has been trying to get a hold of you and said that you weren't answering your phone. I told him I'd swing by the lighthouse and see what you were up to," Maggie said.

"Oh," Shaun said in surprise, and then he fished his cell phone out of his pocket and showed her the blank screen. "I guess it died on me. Did he say what he wanted?"

"He said that 1906 Renovation has a new job, and he wanted to know if you'd be available for some consulting," Maggie said. 1906

Renovation was a family-owned company that belonged to one of Shaun's best friends, Daniel Bradshaw.

"Sure," Shaun said. "Sally can cover for me at the lighthouse. If it's somewhere interesting, do you want to come with me?" he asked.

"Why, so I can watch you wander around with your tools, taking notes while you talk to yourself?" Maggie teased.

"That's only during the day. The nights are getting longer, and who knows what may happen after the sun goes down," Shaun said with a suggestive wiggle of his eyebrows that made Maggie laugh.

"We'll see," Maggie said.

"If nothing else, you could join me for a couple of days once I get settled in," Shaun said.

"Let's see where they are sending you first," Maggie said. "It was a hectic summer, and I could use a break before the autumn tourists begin arriving."

Usually, the walk from the lighthouse to Maggie's business, the Foghorn Tavern, took about fifteen minutes, but the time was easily doubled when they walked the dogs. Maggie and Shaun smiled indulgently and answered questions about the dogs' names and breed while the two dogs did their best to look adorable. They were standing outside the village's main coffee shop, Java Junction, when a male voice hailed them.

"There you are, Shaun," the voice said. Shaun looked up to see Michael Tuitt walking toward them. Michael was a good friend and coworker at 1906 Renovation. "Daniel has been trying to reach you," Michael said when he moved to stand by their side. "Hello there, you little privateers," Michael said as he knelt to pet and give belly rubs to the two dogs.

"Maggie told me," Shaun responded. "My phone died on me."

"No worries," Michael said as he stood up. "Are you available tonight? Daniel and I could come by the tavern for dinner, and we can give you the details then."

"Sounds like a plan," Shaun said. "6:30, okay?"

"6:30 it is. And this is a weird one. I think you'll be intrigued. We'll see you then," Michael said with a grin. Then he turned and began to walk away.

"Wait, why will I be intrigued?" Shaun yelled after him, but Michael just looked over his shoulder, gave them a wink and a saucy wave, and kept walking.

"Argh," Shaun complained. "He knows that is going to drive me nuts."

Maggie nodded in agreement, and there was a twinkle in her eye.

"You know what he's talking about, don't you?" Shaun asked.

"Perhaps," Maggie said with a secretive grin.

"But you're not going to tell me either, are you?"

"Nope," Maggie said. "You'll have to wait for Daniel."

Shaun studied her face, deciding if he should push for more information. Mysteries drove him crazy, but he recognized the sparkle in Maggie's eye, which told him he wouldn't be able to pry any more information out of her. He gave a disgruntled sound and then shrugged in defeat. "Alright, I'll wait, but you know I hate not knowing."

"I do," Maggie said as she leaned in to kiss him.

Chapter Two

Crescent Bay, California – The Foghorn Tavern

The Foghorn Tavern was the central gathering place for the village of Crescent Bay. The Tavern included a family restaurant and a large comfortable bar. As with most of the businesses in Crescent Bay, the Foghorn Tavern spotlighted the town's nautical heritage. Its walls were finished in dark wooden planks, and the lighting was designed to resemble flickering lanterns. The bar design was reminiscent of an Irish pub with subdued lighting, large comfortable booths, and a fireplace. Maggie owned the tavern and lived in a spacious apartment on the second floor with Shaun and the pups.

Maggie and Shaun walked through the tavern's front door and were met by Maggie's assistant, Suzy, who was bursting with questions.

"One second," Maggie said as she held up a hand signaling that Suzy should pause, then she turned to Shaun. "Will you take the pups upstairs? It looks like I'm needed down here."

"Will do, but it will cost you," Shaun said with a mischievous grin as he puckered his lips. Maggie laughed and planted a loud smooch on her husband's lips.

"Thanks. Don't forget to set an alarm for dinner," Maggie said, and Shaun nodded.

Shaun's inquisitive mind often took him on wild mental adventures that occasionally caused him to miss appointments. Over the years, he had learned to set multiple alarms to pull himself back to the material world.

"Will do. See you at 6:30," Shaun said as he stole one more kiss before heading to their apartment.

Maggie watched Shaun weave through the bar with the two little dogs prancing beside him and smiled. She loved being married to Shaun Morrow, and that thought was surprising to Maggie. Before

Shaun, Maggie had been happy living a single independent life. She slept with whomever she desired and planned her life without considering anyone else's wishes. Maggie's attitude had been shaped by a rough childhood that included her father divorcing her mother during Maggie's high school years. The divorce forced Maggie into the caretaker position for herself and her emotionally dependent mother. Maggie's father's abandonment had taught Maggie to be fiercely independent. She had sworn that she would never rely on anyone else for anything. Then Maggie fell in love with Shaun. It wasn't that Maggie was dependent on Shaun, but she often took Shaun's feelings and desires into consideration before making decisions, which was a big change.

The saving grace of her childhood had been her close friendship with Sarah Gnome. Sarah's parents, Sinthia and Tom, had opened their home to Maggie and had practically adopted her. She had found peace in their presence.

Maggie turned away from Shaun's retreating form and dove into the responsibilities of being a small business owner. Time slipped by with surprising speed, and Maggie was buried in the minutia of running her restaurant when a deep male voice spoke to her.

"Table for six, please," the voice said. Maggie automatically responded with, "Do you have a reservation?" before she glanced up from the guest register to see the face of Daniel Bradshaw grinning at her.

"I don't, but I do know the owner," he said, smiling as Maggie came around the podium to hug him.

Daniel Bradshaw had come to Crescent Bay to supervise the restoration of the village's lighthouse. He had fallen in love with and married Heather Moore, the owner of Java Junction. Heather was standing behind Daniel, and she smiled when Maggie moved to hug her.

"Free hugs? I'm next," another male voice said, and Maggie looked up to see Michael and her best friend Sarah Gnome standing in the tavern's open door.

"Nope, I claim a home-field advantage," Shaun said as he walked into the lobby. Maggie laughed when Shaun spun her around and dipped her backward for a kiss.

"Well, since we're all here, let's eat!" Michael said.

Maggie led the small party to the tavern's back room, where a large booth was set up for their group.

"I'll be right back," Maggie said. "I just need to check in with Suzy and let her know I'm off the clock."

Maggie moved away, and Sarah shook her head, "Like she's ever off the clock when she's here."

"True," Heather said as everyone opened their menus.

The meal progressed with the usual banter and jokes that close friends share, and when Suzy placed a plate in front of each couple, the assembled friends groaned. The plates were filled with portions of Mario's Molten Mountain. A decadent dessert created by Maggie's head chef Mario. It consisted of a huge mountain-shaped piece of chocolate cake, so dark it was almost black. Arranged around the base of the chocolate mountain were large scoops of rich French vanilla ice cream drizzled with melted dark chocolate.

"Seriously?" Sarah asked as she patted her full belly.

"Well, if you can't eat it —" Michael stated as he slid the plate closer to himself.

"I didn't say that," Sarah said as she moved the plate back.

Over a post-dessert cup of coffee, Daniel began to explain Shaun's next assignment.

"This one's a little odd, but I think you'll find it interesting," Daniel said. "It is a lighthouse in the town of Bountiful."

"Wait a minute," Shaun said, "Bountiful is not on the coast."

"That is correct," Daniel said with a smile.

"Okay, I'm already intrigued," Shaun said.

"I knew you would be. The lighthouse was relocated to the estate by Mr. Madeira," Daniel said.

"You're kidding me," Sarah said in shock. "He had an entire lighthouse dismantled, transported, and then reconstructed on his estate."

"He did," Chris said.

"Some people have more money than brains," Maggie said.

Daniel smiled in agreement before continuing, "Mr. Madeira passed away and left his property to the State with the stipulation that the lighthouse remain intact. The State would like to open the lighthouse up for tours, but it needs some repairs."

"And that's where we come in," Shaun said, and Maggie could imagine him mentally rubbing his hands together in anticipation.

"I'm in," Shaun said. "When do I leave?"

Chapter Three

Bountiful, California – The Madeira Estate

Shaun was filled with excitement as he drove the winding mountain road toward the town of Bountiful and the Madeira estate.

Shaun had spent the previous day making sure that his shifts at the Crescent Bay lighthouse were covered and trying to convince Maggie to join him on his adventure. He had received her promise that she would consider it after he had scoped out the location.

The mountains he drove through were covered in the dried grasses of late summer. As the elevation increased, the temperature dropped enough for Shaun to turn off the car's air conditioner and lower his window. He grinned as he put his hand out the window and cupped his palm so he could play with the wind currents caused by his car's passing. One of his favorite things about living in California was that you could change your natural environment via a short car ride. He had started this morning's journey on the humid sands of Crescent Bay, and now he was rising above the clouds into a land filled with the smell of green growing things.

Shaun followed Daniel's directions to the tall wrought-iron gates of the Madeira estate. He rang the buzzer on the little box by the gate, and after identifying himself, the large gates swung aside to let his car through. Shaun craned his neck, trying to catch a glimpse of the lighthouse, but he couldn't see it through all the thick foliage. The driveway seemed to go on forever, a long curving black paved path, and Shaun marveled at the type of wealth necessary to have such a large estate. He drove around yet one more bend in the road to see the heart of the Madeira estate unfolded before him. Shaun stopped his car as he paused to take it all in.

The main house reminded Shaun of an old English manor house. The house was rectangular, with what looked to be multiple wings and four floors. Shaun thought the house was too large for just two people to live in, but Daniel had told Shaun that the Madeiras had never had children, so they must have rambled through the large house alone.

Shaun's breath hitched when he spied the lighthouse that rose from behind the manor. It was painted in broad red and white stripes. Shaun was surprised to see someone standing on the gallery that surrounded the lamp. Shaun watched the figure for a full minute, but the figure didn't move. *Weird*, Shaun thought when he broke his trance and refocused to drive the rest of the way down the long driveway to the front door. He was unloading his luggage from the car's trunk when the mansion's large dark-wood front door opened, and a slender older man tottered out to the top of the front porch.

"Hello," Shaun called as he closed his car's trunk and walked up to shake the man's hand. "I'm Shaun Morrow from 1906 Renovation."

"Yes, I was told to expect you, Mr. Morrow. I'm George Byrne, and I'll be your liaison while you're here," George said.

"Nice to meet you, Mr. Byrne," Shaun said.

"Please call me George," the old man said, and Shaun smiled in response.

"Thank you, George; please call me Shaun. Let me grab my bags, and you can show me around," Shaun said.

"Actually, sir, you will be staying in the cottage. Please drive around to the back of the manor," George said as he indicated a narrow service road that bent around the side of the manor. "I'll meet you there."

"Oh, will do," Shaun said, feeling a little embarrassed that he had assumed he'd be housed in the main building. Shaun piled his suitcases into the trunk and drove around to the back of the manor.

Shaun parked his car in front of a small two-story building built to resemble a lightkeeper's cottage with whitewashed walls and a thatched roof. Shaun unloaded his luggage for the second time and then paused to stare at the lighthouse behind the cottage. Shaun could see that although the lighthouse was magnificent, it needed some maintenance.

He squinted up at the figure he had spied standing on the wrought iron galley encircling the lighthouse lamp room and realized it was a statue. A scuffling sound caught his attention, and he turned to watch George make his slow and painful way from the manor to the cottage.

"This way, sir," George rasped out when he reached Shaun's car and turned to walk the two steps to the cottage's front door. George pulled a large brass key out of his pocket and unlocked the front door before he turned to hand the key to Shaun. "This is where you will be staying while you're here," he said as he stepped out of Shaun's way and motioned him to enter.

"Did Mr. Madeira have this cottage built after the lighthouse was relocated?" Shaun asked, and George shook his head no.

"This was Mr. Madeira's art studio. After the lighthouse was relocated, he remodeled the cottage to look like a lightkeeper's cottage."

"An art studio?" Shaun asked in confusion.

"Yes. Although Mr. Madeira made his fortune in architecture, his real passion was sculpting and painting," George said. "If you follow me, I'll give you a quick tour of the cottage."

The front door had opened onto a cozy living room with a bookcase framed fireplace and overstuffed furniture. Shaun smiled when he saw that the bookcases were full of books he could explore.

"The living room," George said. Then he moved through the room toward an arched doorway in the right wall with Shaun trailing behind him.

"The kitchen," George said. The kitchen was small and reminded Shaun of a kitchen in an extended-stay hotel suite. Functional enough to make something edible but not meant for more than a small meal. That was okay because cooking was not one of Shaun's passions.

George continued through the kitchen, down a short hallway, and past two doors, one closed and one open. When Shaun peeked into the open door, he saw a small bathroom with a toilet and sink.

The hall ended at a pair of large wooden doors made of dark wood carved with intricate geometric patterns. George paused before the doors and glanced over his shoulder to see if he had Shaun's attention before swinging the doors open dramatically.

Shaun stepped through the doorway and stood in awe as he took in the scene before him, Mr. Madeira's art studio. The wall opposite the door was glass, topped by an arched glass ceiling. The sweeping view through the windows showcased the lighthouse and the forest beyond.

"Beautiful," Shaun whispered, and George merely nodded his head in agreement. Shaun wrenched his eyes away from the view to inspect the room. Minutiae of an artist filled the floor; easels, paints, and a large draped statue.

"I don't imagine you'll be spending much time in this room, but the state said we were to give you access to the entire property. That includes the manor," George said as he fished another key out of his jacket and handed it to Shaun. "But, be warned, the manor is equipped with a security system, and I arm it each night before I go home," George said, and Shaun could hear the challenge in George's voice. George had probably been in Mr. Madeira's employ for most of his adult life, and the passing of his employer was a significant change for the older man.

"Thank you, I can't imagine I'll need to get into the manor when you aren't here," Shaun said, noticing the tension in George's shoulders ease.

George nodded in acknowledgment, and Shaun crossed the room to look at the lighthouse. A monument on a raised section of grass sat near the lighthouse's base. "What's the monument for?" Shaun asked.

"That's Mrs. Madeira's final resting place."

"What?" Shaun said, shocked.

"When Mrs. Madeira passed away, Mr. Madeira thought she would want to be buried next to something she loved. So, he had her buried there. He spent time every day at her grave, taking her flowers and speaking to her. It was heartbreaking to see," George said.

"Is Mr. Madeira buried there too?" Shaun asked.

"No. Mr. Madeira left directions that he should be cremated and sprinkled in the ocean when he passed away."

"Is the state going to have to move the graveside?" Shaun asked.

"They can't. That was one of the stipulations in Mr. Madeira's will. In order for the state to take ownership of the estate, they had to agree to leave Mrs. Madeira's grave alone and maintain the lighthouse."

"Seems like a good deal for the state," Shaun said, and George agreed.

"Now, if you want, I can show you the upstairs," George said as he turned slowly and began his way back toward the kitchen.

Thinking about the pain George had experienced walking up the two low steps in front of the cottage, Shaun shook his head no. "I don't think that will be necessary."

"If you're sure," George said, and Shaun nodded his head that he was. "Okay then. I'm here until about six o'clock when the construction workers leave. I have to watch them to ensure that none of them get sticky fingers." Shaun struggled to keep a smile off his face because he understood that George was warning him that he'd also be keeping an eye on him. "Is there anything else I can do for you, Mr. Morrow?"

"Yes, would you be willing to give me a little more history about the lighthouse and the Madeiras, perhaps over a cup of tea," Shaun suggested. He had noticed a wee bit of an Irish lilt in the older man's speech, and he was hoping they could bond through the shared ritual of afternoon tea.

"That sounds lovely," George said with a small smile. "Unpack your things and meet me in the manor's kitchen when you're done. A servant's entrance is around the back of the manor, just across the lawn from the cottage; it leads right into the kitchen."

"Thank you, George," Shaun said as he walked the old man out of the cottage.

Shaun stood in the living room with his luggage and wondered how he was supposed to get upstairs, and then he remembered the closed door next to the bathroom. He opened the door to discover a set of tight dark steps leading upward. He lugged his suitcases up the cottage's narrow staircase to the second floor and found that the upstairs was designed as a loft. Floor-to-ceiling windows and an arched roof mirrored the architecture of the studio below. An enclosed bathroom with a deep tub for soaking took up one-third of the floor space. The view was even more stunning on the second floor.

After Shaun unpacked his luggage into a beautiful wooden armoire, he walked to the window facing the lighthouse. He wondered how someone could sleep in this room if the lamp in the lighthouse was functional. He fingered the curtains and discovered that they were blackout curtains. Still, Shaun was glad he had a sleep mask for when he slept.

Shaun walked down the stairs and out of the cottage to cross the lush lawn that stretched between the cottage and the manor to knock on the back door. George answered the door and led Shaun through a sizeable modern kitchen into a small alcove with a cafe table and four chairs. Shaun thought that this must have been where the servants ate.

"I have some Earl Grey or a fine Irish blend from Lyon's. Which would you prefer?" George asked.

"I've never cared for Earl Grey. However, the Lyon's sounds wonderful," Shaun said, and he thought he saw a flicker of approval dance across George's face.

"Good choice. I'll return shortly with the tea."

Shaun glanced out the windows and marveled at how beautiful and serene the estate was. No matter which direction Shaun looked, he saw beautiful green grass, lush plants, and trees. The Madeira estate was very park-like in its design.

George returned carrying a tray with two cups, a teapot in a cozy, and the bits and pieces necessary to dress one's tea. George had even put some biscuits on a silver tray.

"How do you take your tea?" George asked.

"Milk, no sugar," Shaun said.

George nodded, poured some milk into one of the cups, and topped it off with tea in what Shaun knew was the Irish manner. George poured tea with the expertise of a long-time tea drinker, and Shaun thanked him when he handed him the cup and saucer. Shaun took a sip of the hot tea and then closed his eyes in appreciation. When he opened them, he saw that George was watching him with a small smile curving his lips.

"Thank you. It's been a long time since I've had a good cup of tea," Shaun said, and he noticed that his voice had taken on a faint Irish accent, mirroring George's.

"You're welcome," George said as he doctored his tea. "Where do your people hail from?"

"I was raised in Upstate New York, but my grandparents are from Bray, in County Wicklow," Shaun said.

"Ah," George said with a knowledgeable nod of his head. "My ancestors came from Cork," George said. "Have you been back to the mother country?"

"I have. I was blessed to have parents who wanted me to experience my heritage. My wife and I honeymooned in Ireland," Shaun said.

"It's a beautiful place that still pulls at my heart," George said, and Shaun nodded in understanding. "So, now you're here to restore our lighthouse," George said.

"I am. I've always loved the history and romance of lighthouses, and I've been lucky enough to preserve a few of them."

"It's a good thing to preserve history for future generations. But unfortunately, so few Americans understand that fact. They don't understand how easy it is to lose something that they can never regain, all in the name of progress," George said as he glanced out the window at the lighthouse. "Take that lighthouse. It stood on the cliffs of Sand Dollar Cove for over 200 hundred years, saving the lives of innumerable sailors. It was operational until they decided to demolish it. The city didn't want to spend more money on its upkeep. So, they fired the lighthouse keeper and would have torn it down if it wasn't for Mr. Madeira."

"Really? They still had a lighthouse keeper? I'm surprised it hadn't been automated like so many of its brethren," Shaun said.

"In the short term, it was cheaper to pay one man to tend the light than swap out the internal mechanisms for an automated system," George said.

"Wow, so who tends the lamp now?" Shaun asked as he looked out the window at the lighthouse.

"No one. When Mr. Madeira had the lighthouse transported to the estate, he hired someone to put in the automation necessary to turn the light on and off. It's always been a little temperamental, but I'm sure the technology has improved since then," George said.

"That's part of why I'm here. I'm glad Mr. Madeira was into lighthouses; otherwise, this gem would have been destroyed," Shaun said.

"He didn't do it for himself; Mr. Madeira did it for his wife. Didn't anyone tell you the tale?" George asked.

"Not in detail," Shaun said.

"Ach, well then," George said as he sat back into his chair and took a deep breath. Shaun smiled when he recognized the motions of a natural storyteller settling in to spin a yarn.

"You see, Mr. Madeira spent his youth building his fame as an architect. He met his future wife, Teresa, working in the steno pool in his office.

"Teresa was a sweet girl, but she came from a humble background that hadn't prepared her for what was expected of the wife of a wealthy man. Nevertheless, Mr. Madeira was patient with her, and their love for each other was evident to everyone who saw them.

"As Teresa matured into her new role, she created a national charity focused on preserving and restoring lighthouses."

Shaun glanced up at the lighthouse standing in the middle of the manor's backyard, and George nodded his head. "Yep, like that one right there. Teresa tried to save it, but the land was too valuable, and the local city council voted for its destruction. Her failure to save the lighthouse broke Teresa's heart. She moped around the manor for weeks, depressed that she had failed. Teresa's depression upset Mr. Madeira. So he decided to save the lighthouse by buying and transporting it to where it now stands. He even created a special sculpture to honor the brave lighthouse keepers." George gestured to the lighthouse and the pale sculpture poised on the gallery.

"Did it help her depression?" Shaun asked.

"Unfortunately, no. Mrs. Madeira had fallen into a deep darkness that she seemed unable to escape," George said. "During the day, Teresa prowled the lighthouse, and most who saw her reported that she appeared to be crying. At night, she could be seen as a silhouette staring out her bedroom window toward the lighthouse as its light swept the estate."

"Why do you think this affected her so intensely?" Shaun asked.

"I don't know for sure, but maybe she didn't know how to deal with failure," George said.

"Maybe," Shaun said hesitantly as he looked up at the beautiful old lighthouse. He found it hard to believe that someone could react so dramatically to failure. Still, he found many things people did confusing, so he supposed it was possible.

"In time, she might have been able to rise from her depression, but she suffered a fall before she could. It was a wet morning, and she was walking on the lighthouse's gallery when she slipped and fell. One of the groundskeepers found her lying near the lighthouse's base and called an ambulance. She has in terrible shape. The doctor said that she was lucky that the lighthouse was shaped like a wedge with the bottom wider than the top."

"Why was that lucky?" Shaun asked.

"Because she only fell about ten feet before she hit the side of the tower and tumbled down the side of the lighthouse instead of plummeting straight to the ground. She spent the last years of her life completely paralyzed and bedridden. Mr. Madeira was so loving and attentive during those years. It broke our hearts to see how tenderly he took care of her," George said.

"I heard that he had a hard time accepting her death," Shaun said.

"It's true. After Mrs. Madeira died, Mr. Madeira fell into denial. He would talk to us as if she was still alive, stating that Mrs. Madeira had done this or Mrs. Madeira had done that. It was a little disturbing, but we figured it was his way of coping with her death. We hoped it would pass in time," George said.

"Did it?" Shaun asked.

"Unfortunately, no. It progressed to Mr. Madeira speaking to Mrs. Madeira out loud. He would insist that Teresa was in the room and that she was tormenting him. He would scream and fight with something we couldn't see," George said as he looked down into his now-empty teacup.

"We don't like to talk about how it was near the end of Mr. Madeira's life. He was such a great man; it was hard to watch his decline," George said, and Shaun was surprised to see George's eyes swim with unshed tears.

"I'm sorry that happened," Shaun said. "That must have been difficult."

"It was," George said as he covertly wiped his eyes and straightened his spine. "Would you like a tour of the manor?"

"I would," Shaun said.

"Why don't we go around to the front so that you can see it the way it was meant to be seen for the first time?" George said.

Shaun followed George out of the house and around to the large front entrance. George pushed open one of the two wooden front doors and gestured for Shaun to enter.

Shaun stepped into the foyer, which featured an intricately tiled mosaic floor and two curved staircases flowing gracefully from the first floor to the second. The gleaming wood of the staircase was carved into intricate patterns, cherubs, and woodland creatures. Centered above the floor's mosaic was a magnificent chandelier that glittered with what looked to be hundreds of crystal drops.

"Waterford crystals," George said when he noticed Shaun staring at the chandelier.

"Wow," Shaun said, and George laughed to himself.

"Wait until you see the rest of the manor," George said with a smile as he motioned that Shaun should proceed him into a room to the right.

George led Shaun through rooms filled with beautiful architecture, furniture, and art pieces. Mr. Madeira's paintings and sculptures were scatted throughout the manor. They were of such a high quality that it was hard to tell them apart from the artwork Mr. Madeira had purchased.

A handful of workers from the State were installing barricades and Plexiglas to protect the manor and its contents from future visitors. George pointed out where the workers had installed cameras and occupancy sensors.

"It's necessary, I guess," George said sadly. "You just can't trust folks to respect other people's property."

"I'm going to give you a special treat," George said as he grabbed the knob on a small cabinet door at the end of the second-floor hallway. "A tour of the third and fourth floors."

George explained that the manor's first and second floors would be open to the public, but the third and four floors would be off-limits. The second floor could be reached via either the staircase or a small elevator that Mr. Madeira had installed as his health had declined. Since the state couldn't figure out how to make the third and four floors accessible to everyone, those floors would remain closed. George seemed content with that arrangement. The third floor had been Mrs. Madeira's private domain, and the fourth floor had been used primarily for storage and the servant's quarters. Shaun grinned when he saw the spiral staircase hidden behind the small door.

The third floor was darker than the first two floors as no windows opened directly into the corridor, and all the doors were closed. George reached out and flipped a light switch which gave a dim illumination. Still, it wasn't until George began opening doors that the hallway lost its intimidating air.

"These were Mrs. Madeira's quarters," George said. "Before her accident, she used these rooms as an office and for her various projects." George opened a door at the end of the hall, and when Shaun entered the room, he saw a hospital bed and various pieces of medical equipment. "This was where Mrs. Madeira passed away," George said. As he turned to look away, Shaun saw George raise a shaky hand to swipe at his cheek to hide his eyes tearing up.

Shaun walked to the window directly across from the hospital bed to give George a little privacy. The lighthouse was framed in the center of the window, and now that he had a higher vantage point, Shaun could see the sculpture of the lighthouse keeper more clearly. The life-sized, off-white statue was poised with one hand resting on the railing that surrounded the gallery. The statue's other hand held a spyglass pointed directly into Mrs. Madeira's bedroom.

"Isn't it magnificent?" George asked when he joined him at the window. "I think it's Mr. Madeira's finest work."

Shaun nodded, but something about the statue raised the hair on the back of his neck. Leaning forward for a closer look, he realized that the statue was holding his spyglass up to a blank white surface. Why did the statue have no face? He couldn't imagine how anyone could get a restful night's sleep knowing that the faceless statue was staring into their room.

George walked Shaun through the rest of the third and fourth floors, and when they were back in the foyer of the first floor, Shaun thanked George for the tour.

"It's a beautiful home, thank you for showing it to me," Shaun said.

"It was a pleasure," George said. "Well, my day is done, so if you'll excuse me, I need to ensure that the State's crew is gone and lock up the manor."

"Have a nice evening George. I'll see you tomorrow."

"You too," George said, but then he paused and lay his hand on Shaun's arm. "I feel better for having met you. Thank you for coming here and preserving Mr. Madeira's legacy."

Moved by George's sincerity, Shaun nodded and said, "It's an honor."

Shaun exited through the servant's entrance and walked toward Mrs. Madeira's gravesite. A slight rise supported a cement slab with a roughhewn piece of granite placed at its head. The front of the rough rock had been ground to a smooth mirror-like finish and then engraved with the image of a lighthouse surrounded by crashing waves and a quote. The quote read:

A lighthouse protects others from the dangerous ground on which it is built.

The quote seemed dark to Shaun. *Did Mr. Madeira blame the lighthouse for his wife's injury and eventual death?* Shaun wondered.

Shaun tilted his head back to look at the top of the lighthouse and the statue of the faceless lighthouse keeper. Then, checking his watch, he saw that he had about two hours of sunlight left in the day. So he retrieved a clipboard and pencil to take notes as he did a quick visual inspection of the lighthouse.

Although Shaun was excited about seeing the inside of the structure, he made himself wait until he had walked the outside, noting places where the mortar needed repair and the surface repainted. When he entered the lighthouse, it took a moment for his eyes to adjust. It was bright outside, but the inside of the lighthouse was dimly lit by narrow windows. The windows marked the ascent of the spiral staircase, which wound around the inside walls. Shaun clicked on a flashlight and shone it around the room. The well which had held the clockwork mechanism to spin the lens was empty, and Shaun shook his head at what he felt was a desecration of history. He would have preserved as much of the old mechanism as possible. Now, instead of an educational resource, the State was left with a large empty building. Shaun wondered if the State would be interested in recreating the original mechanical structure. He made a note on his clipboard to research the expense and viability.

Shaun began the long climb to the watch room, where the lightkeeper would have tended the lamp and kept an eye on the sea. The steps were in good shape, and he noted a few places where the mortar could use some reinforcing. Shaun kept climbing slowly, but he was panting when he pushed open the door into the watch room. He couldn't imagine his knees' condition if he had to climb those stairs multiple times a day for years. He marveled at the strength of the men whose job it had been to do that climb repeatedly.

He paused to examine the electric-powered automation equipment that had replaced the clockwork mechanism. It was an older system, but it had been well maintained. The automation system included a photoelectric cell that would turn the lamp on depending on the darkness of the surrounding area. Shaun was looking forward to seeing the beam projected by the bulb through the rotating lens. The lenses that graced most modern lighthouses were Fresnel lenses that consisted of prisms that focused the bulb's light into a far-reaching beam. The lenses were created in 1822 by French physicist Augustin-Jean Fresnel. Fresnel lenses were classified into orders based on their size and focal length. The lens in the lighthouse at Crescent Bay was a first-order lens and stood over seven feet tall. The Madeira lighthouse lens was a 3 ½ order Fresnel lens consisting of two perfectly round disks, made up of smaller and smaller concentric circles, held together with a band of gleaming brass. The lens measured about 43 inches tall, and its surface was a riot of rainbow colors. Shaun thought it was one of the most beautiful things he had seen.

Shaun walked to the door to the gallery, the walkway that encircled the outside of the lighthouse. The gallery door opened away from the manor toward the forest. When he pushed open the door, Shaun smiled at the expansive view of the Madeira estate's acres of unspoiled forest. The smell of hot pine filled the air, and Shaun closed his eyes to savor the wild scent. Then, forcing himself to refocus on the task at hand, Shaun leaned down to closely inspect the metal of the gallery for any cracks or faults that would make it dangerous to walk on. Satisfied that it was safe, he carefully stepped onto the metal grate. He moved slowly around the gallery, inspecting the places where the gallery joined the old brick of the lighthouse and the sturdiness of the railing that kept a person from accidentally falling to their death. That thought made him think about how Mrs. Madeira had slipped and fallen. If Mrs. Madeira was familiar with lighthouses, she should have known how dangerous it was to walk on a lighthouse's gallery and taken precautions. Shaun wondered if Teresa's depression had overwhelmed her and caused her to jump from the tower. The stigma of suicide might have caused Mr. Madeira to concoct a story that said she had slipped instead of jumping.

Shaun worked his way around the gallery, so focused on searching for safety concerns that he completely forgot about the statue of the lighthouse keeper until it popped into view. Shaun clutched his chest and laughed at the scare. Then he paused to inspect the statue. The stone was a pale off-white that closely matched the color of the lighthouse's masonry work, but the statue was unsettling. Instead of fully formed facial features, the blank surface had the merest suggestion of eyes, a mouth, and a nose. Yet, the rest of the statue had been carved in exquisite detail. Shaun looked in the same direction as the statue and verified what he had thought earlier; the statue was training its spyglass into Mrs. Madeira's bedroom. Had Mr. Madeira made the statue faceless to represent all the different lighthouse keepers' legacies Mrs. Madeira had saved?

The sun was rapidly descending, and as the dark shadows grew, Shaun realized he was the only person on the estate. He was isolated from anyone else for miles around. Then, a loud click startled him, and he laughed, understanding that the automated light had turned on. A whirling followed the clicking sound as the Fresnel lens began to spin. He stood in awe as the light swept a bright beam of light across the vast estate, and a feeling of peace descended on him. He loved lighthouses and all they represented. They were a beacon of safety for those who sailed an often turbulent sea.

Patting the statue's shoulder, Shaun clicked on his flashlight in preparation to descend the staircase when a light turned on inside the manor. Shaun froze and squinted, searching for motion in the newly illuminated room on the third floor. Then a light in the adjacent room clicked on, and the next, until all the windows on the third floor shone brightly. The last room to illuminate was Mrs. Madeira's bedroom. Shaun focused on that room, trying to see any movement inside, even contorting to view through the statue's spyglass. Then the lights began to turn off one after another in the order they turned on. The last room to go dark was Mrs. Madeira's bedroom. Shaun stayed still, scanning the manor for any signs of life, but the manor remained dark and still. Shaun considered his options.

Shaun decided to check the external doors and windows of the manor. If he found anything open, he'd call the police.

After descending the lighthouse stairs, Shaun worked his way around the outside of the manor. He pushed on windows and turned doorknobs, looking for anything suspicious. At the front door, Shaun peered through the window next to the door and saw a blue light slowly flashing next to the manor's alarm panel. He assumed that meant that George had set the alarm before leaving for the night. Shaun continued moving around the manor, checking windows until he returned to the lawn that grew between the cottage and the manor. The manor appeared to be securely locked and empty. He looked up at the dark windows on the third floor and strained his ears, listening for movement. He realized that none of the ordinary night sounds were present. There was no chirping of insects or rustling made by small critters as they moved through the undergrowth. The only sound was a quiet whooshing sound as the light from the lighthouse continued to sweep across the estate.

Shaun had an eerie feeling of being watched, and his gaze moved from the manor to the thick forest surrounding the estate. "I'm just spooking myself," Shaun announced to the night in an attempt to end the odd silence. Shaun decided that if someone were inside the house, they would trip the alarm and thus call the police themselves. Shaun turned away from the manor to enter the cottage.

Chapter Four

Bountiful, California – The Madeira Estate – Artist Cottage

The sounds of a jaunty sea shanty filled the air as Shaun struggled to disentangle himself from the thick comforter and piles of pillows. He made a mad grab for his cell phone, and when he saw the caller ID, he cringed. It was Maggie; he had forgotten to call her last night. Preparing himself for the worst, he swiped to answer the call and put a loving note into his voice, "Good morning, beautiful."

"Morning is right," Maggie said, and Shaun winced.

"I'm sorry. I meant to call you last night, but something weird happened," Shaun said.

"Why am I not surprised?" Maggie asked, and Shaun's shoulders relaxed when he recognized the teasing tone in her voice.

"This place is a little unsettling," Shaun admitted.

"So, tell me what happened," Maggie said as she poured a cup of coffee and sat down to listen to Shaun's tale.

"Rich people are weird," Maggie pronounced. "Imagine spending money to relocate a lighthouse to your backyard in an attempt to lift your wife's spirits. That's just stupid."

"Why is that stupid?" Shaun asked. "It sounds romantic to me."

"Not at all. Imagine fighting to save a historic building, failing, and then having your spouse move that building into your backyard. It would be a continuous reminder of your failure," Maggie said.

"I don't think Mr. Madeira saw it that way," Shaun said. "I think he was trying to support his wife by saving the building."

"That may have been how he saw it, but I doubt that Mrs. Madeira saw it the same way," Maggie said.

"Maybe," Shaun said hesitantly.

"Okay, think of it this way. Remember that large Fresnel lens you found in that storage shed in Florida?" Maggie asked.

"The third-order one? Yes, it was beautiful," Shaun said a little sadly.

"Remember how you felt when it broke during shipping? Now imagine if I had the pieces of that lens mounted and placed on a platform outside our bedroom window. How would that make you feel?" Maggie asked.

"It's not the same thing," Shaun said. "That lens was destroyed."

"What if Mrs. Madeira was focused on saving a lighthouse's history by keeping it in its original location for the public to enjoy? Wouldn't transplanting it to a private estate be the same as destroying it?" Maggie asked.

"I guess so," Shaun conceded. "But, I don't think Mr. Madeira moved the lighthouse to be cruel.

"People are often unintentionally cruel," Maggie said. When Shaun remained silent, a soft smile curved the edges of Maggie's lips. Shaun's soul was romantic, and her practical side had just stomped all over the fantasy that Shaun was spinning about the Madeiras. Feeling guilty, Maggie changed the subject, "Would you still like me to come up?"

Shaun brightened, "Definitely. When?"

Maggie chuckled at Shaun's enthusiasm. "I spoke to Mario and Suzy, and they have agreed to cover for me. Sarah says she'll watch the dogs," Maggie said, and then she stopped when Shaun laughed. "What?" she asked, confused.

"So, you're saying we can have a couple of nights without the kids," Shaun teased, and Maggie laughed.

"I guess so. I can head up after the lunch rush this afternoon if that works for you," Maggie said.

"I'd love that. Give me a call on my cell when you get here. I love you," Shaun said.

"I love you too. See you soon," Maggie said.

Shaun practically sprung from the bed, happy that Maggie would be joining him shortly. Downstairs while searching for a cup of tea he realized he'd have to drive into Bountiful for supplies before Maggie arrived.

Shaun hated doing anything productive before his first caffeine hit kicked in, but he had no choice this morning. When the doorbell rang, he was deciding between beginning his workday or heading into town.

"Good morning," George said when Shaun swung the front door open. "I hope I'm not disturbing you, but I thought you might be interested in a cup of tea before you began your day."

"George, you're a lifesaver," Shaun declared. "I completely forgot to swing by the store yesterday."

George smiled. "Good. I left a large pot of Irish Breakfast tea steeping in the breakfast nook. Would you care to join me?"

"I would," Shaun said, and George stepped aside as Shaun closed the cottage door.

"Did you sleep well?" George asked as they walked toward the manor.

"I did," Shaun said.

"The light from the lighthouse didn't disturb you?" George asked.

"No, between the blackout curtains on the windows and my blindfold, I had no problems," Shaun said.

"That's good, then," George said.

"I did have something strange happen," Shaun said as George opened the servants' entrance and motioned for Shaun to precede him.

"What's that?" George asked.

"I was up on the lighthouse gallery, standing next to the statue, when a series of lights on the third floor came on," Shaun said. "No one was supposed to be here after you went home, were they?"

"No, the house was empty. Something probably triggered those new occupancy sensors that the State installed," George said.

"I completely forgot about those," Shaun said. "I'm glad I didn't call the police."

"Me too. We've had so many false alarms that the security company is threatening to charge the State each time they come out to the manor. After the last false alarm, the security company turned off the occupation sensor's automated calling feature. If you ask me, it's their fault for making those sensors so sensitive anyway," George said.

George placed a little milk in the bottom of Shaun's cup and then topped it off with strong fragrant tea. "I appreciate that you are looking out for the place, Shaun, but you don't have to worry. After I've set the alarm, the security service will be notified if anyone opens any doors or windows."

Handing Shaun his cup, George asked, "What are your plans for the day?"

"My wife Maggie will be joining me for a couple of days, so I'll need to go grocery shopping. Plus, I want to begin a more thorough inspection of the lighthouse for damage and needed repairs," Shaun said.

"Your wife Maggie, you say. How nice. Have you been married long?" George asked.

"A couple of years. Maggie owns a tavern in Crescent Bay," Shaun said.

"Would that be the Foghorn Tavern?" George asked, and Shaun nodded. "I've had the pleasure of spending some time in that establishment. It reminds me of the pubs in Galway." George's expression softened, and Shaun thought that he looked wistful.

"How long has it been since you were in Ireland?" Shaun asked.

"It's been about five years. I still have family in Cork, and once the manor has been handed over to the State, I plan to retire there. I never married, and so I never had any children. There's not a lot holding me here." Shaun's face must have given away his feelings because George stopped what he was saying to clarify. "Now, don't go feeling sorry for what I don't have. I had a wonderful life living in this beautiful house and working for the Madeiras."

"How long did you work for the Madeiras?" Shaun asked.

"My whole adult life, must be about 50 years now," George said.

"That's amazing. A person rarely stays in a job that long," Shaun said.

"Mr. Madeira never treated us like we were employees. He treated us more like family. It's because of his generosity that I can retire in Ireland. He left me a large bequest that should see me through what's left of my golden years."

"That's wonderful," Shaun said.

"It 'tis. Would you like another cuppa?" George asked as Shaun emptied his cup.

"As much as I'd love a second cup, I need to start my day. Thank you for the tea; it was a lifesaver," Shaun said.

"One second," George said as he pulled a notebook out of his pocket and used a pen to scribble something onto a page. He tore the page out and handed it to Shaun, "It's the alarm code. Just in case."

Shaun felt honored that George trusted him. "Thanks, George." He said as he tucked the paper into his wallet.

The drive from the Madeira estate to downtown Bountiful was a pleasant one. The meandering two-lane mountain road was shaded by ancient trees, creating a lush green canopy over the blacktop. Bountiful was an old mining town that promoted its history to attract tourists. As a result, the main street was lined with quaint and kitschy shops filled with mass-produced tourist-ware and local artists' work.

Shaun parked in front of the small general store and smiled when he entered the building. Tourist kitsch was prevalent, but it was primarily displayed in the front of the store to encourage impulse buys. The rest of the store was broken into two sections, one for campers and the other geared toward local citizens. Shaun walked by the camping supplies and began to fill his basket with what he considered necessities. He grimaced when he saw that the store's tea selection consisted of Lipton or Celestial Seasons. He placed a box of tea featuring a large buffalo into his basket. The store's wine selection was more varied, and Shaun smiled as he added a couple of bottles of Maggie's favorite wine to his supplies. He was wandering toward the front of the store when a book on display made him pause. The cover of the oversized paperback featured a picture of the Madeira lighthouse. Unfortunately, the book's title, *Lighthouses of Horror!*, was printed in a horrible red font that looked like dripping blood. Shaun reached for the book, flipped to the table of contents, and sighed when he saw that book included a chapter on the lighthouse at Crescent Bay. He added the book to his basket and went to check out.

"Good morning," the lady behind the counter said. Her name badge read Alice.

"Good morning," Shaun replied.

"Looking at your cart, I'd say you're here for a while," Alice said as she typed Shaun's purchases into an old-fashioned cash register.

"I am. I'm doing some work on the Madeira lighthouse," Shaun said

"Really?" Alice asked, and then she paused to hold up the book. "You don't buy into all this haunted stuff, do you?" she asked, and Shaun shrugged. "Well, I can tell you that the locals don't. Mr. Madeira was a wonderful benefactor for many artisans and businesses here in Bountiful. It upsets us that folks are trying to say that his home is haunted."

"And yet, you're selling this book," Shaun pointed out.

"I don't get to choose what we put on the shelves; I'm just a clerk," Alice said a little defensively.

"So, does your boss think the Madeira lighthouse is haunted," Shaun asked.

"No, but he knows that the scary stuff sells, plus it's written by a friend of his," Alice said. She turned the book to the back cover exposing a photo of a man wearing a cowboy hat and sporting a long white beard standing in front of the Crescent Bay lighthouse. The paint on the lighthouse walls was peeling, and the ground around the base was covered with tall weeds. Which told Shaun that the picture had been taken before he had arrived to begin renovating the lighthouse.

"I see," Shaun said. He debated telling Alice that he worked at the lighthouse in Crescent Bay, but Alice continued before he could decide.

"Don't get me wrong, Peter is a good author; I just wish he'd write about something other than ghosts." Shaun nodded and decided that the moment had passed. He paid for his groceries and returned to his car. After placing his bags in the trunk, he paused to look at the other stores, and a divine scent wafted by him. It was the smell of baked sugar.

Shaun followed his nose to a store called Bountiful Baking. Shaun could see brown loaves of bread, cakes with brightly colored frosting, and other treats through the large glass windows. He decided to limit himself to one loaf of freshly baked bread.

When he left, his bags were packed with two loaves of bread, some delicate tea cakes, a couple of scones, and a raspberry tort. He hoped that Maggie wouldn't kill him for putting so much temptation in her path. Still, once the lady at the counter had begun offering him samples, his willpower had crumpled.

As he returned to his car, Shaun mentally put on blinders; he couldn't afford more distractions. Feeling guilty, he pulled a still-warm loaf of French bread from the bakery bags. As he pulled out of town, he tore off a large chunk of French bread and bit into it with gusto.

Maggie took her time driving the gently curving road from the beach to the mountains and the Madeira mansion. Pop music played quietly on the radio. Maggie smiled as the stress of running her own business fell away from her shoulders, and peace descended. She let her mind drift as she enjoyed the changing scenery and cooler temperatures.

The various shades of green reminded her of their honeymoon in Ireland and the feeling of a connection she had felt the moment her feet had touched the Irish soil. She smiled as she remembered Shaun's joy as he shared his ancestral homeland with her. Ireland's warm and welcoming people had left a lasting impression on her soul, like the stunning landscape painted in lush greens and ancient structures.

Thanks to Shaun, she had enjoyed many adventures. Some of their adventures were mental vacations as Shaun spun tales about whichever piece of trivia had sparked his curiosity that day. Still, some were actual trips like this one. Although Maggie had heard of the Madeiras and their mansion, she had never thought she would spend time on their estate.

Maggie pulled up to the large iron gates that blocked the driveway to the mansion, took out her cell phone, and tapped in Shaun's number. The phone rang a couple of times and then went to voice mail. Maggie wasn't surprised; in all likelihood, Shaun had probably forgotten to charge his phone again. Maggie pushed the call button on the intercom box outside the double gates.

"Hello?" a man's voice asked.

"Hello," Maggie responded. "My name is Maggie Foley. I'm here to meet my husband, Shaun."

"You mean Shaun Morrow?" the man asked.

"Yes," Maggie said, and after a short pause, the gate began to swing back out of her way.

"Come on in, Mrs. Morrow. I believe Shaun is currently in the lighthouse," the man said.

"Thank you," Maggie said with a small smile. It wasn't worth correcting the stranger about her last name being Foley. The voice on the intercom sounded like an older man, and the older generation had a hard time understanding why a woman wouldn't take her husband's name. When she and Shaun had talked about it, they had decided against it. Shaun said that he didn't own her and that her history wouldn't be erased because they married. Maggie smiled to herself as she thought about what an enigma Shaun was. He valued the past but didn't feel bound by its outdated traditions and expectations.

She drove up the long winding driveway and gasped in shock when she saw the mansion. The building was intimidating. Maggie parked her car and was walking up the steps to the manor's door when it opened. An older gentleman walked out to meet her.

"Hello, Mrs. Morrow. My name is George Byrne. I am the caretaker for the estate."

"Hello, Mr. Byrne. It's nice to meet you," Maggie said. "Shaun spoke highly of you. Thank you for making him feel welcome."

George's cheeks blushed, and his demeanor shifted from stiff formality to a gentle smile. "It has been a pleasure. It's nice to meet someone who values and preserves the past. You can call me George if you wish."

"Thank you, George; you can call me Maggie," Maggie said as she returned his smile.

"Well, Maggie, I believe Shaun is looking forward to your arrival. He is probably in the lighthouse. If you drive around the manor, you will see a cottage. That is where you will be staying during your visit."

"I'll do that then. Thank you," Maggie said as she began to head back to her car.

"It's coming up on tea time. Perhaps you and Shaun can come to the manor for a cuppa after you get settled. Then if you like, I can take you on a tour of the manor," George said with a hopeful tone.

"I'd like that. Thank you, George," Maggie said. George nodded and smiled as he turned to go back into the manor.

Maggie slowly pulled around the far side of the manor and was delighted by the thatched-roofed cottage sitting in front of the white and red striped lighthouse. Because of her time with Shaun, she could tell that the lighthouse needed some maintenance. *Shaun must be in heaven*, she thought.

Maggie knocked on the cottage door, and when she received no reply, she tried the doorknob and found the door unlocked. She opened the door and called out but received no response. With an indulgent smile, Maggie moved her luggage from the car's trunk into the cottage's living room. Shaun's focus could be as sharp as a laser when working on a project, but he forgot everything outside that focus. Things like locks, appointments, food, water, and sleep fell by the wayside when the history bug bit Shaun. Maggie considered exploring the cottage alone but decided she'd wait for Shaun to give her a tour. She stepped out of the cottage, closing the door behind her but leaving it unlocked. She couldn't be sure that Shaun had the keys with him or if he'd left them somewhere inside the cottage.

She looked up at the lighthouse and was startled to see someone standing on the gallery. At first, she wondered if it was a ghost as the figure was pale white, but when they didn't move, she realized it was some sort of statue. "Yeah, that's not creepy at all," Maggie said to herself as she walked over to the lighthouse door.

She pulled the heavy door open and looked into the dim interior. "Shaun?" Maggie yelled, and from a distance, she heard Shaun reply.

A light appeared near the top of the circular staircase, which wound around the inside walls of the lighthouse, and Shaun's head popped into view as he looked out of what must have been the watchman's room. "Maggie?" the voice drifted down.

"Yep," Maggie called back. Then, she watched as Shaun carefully but quickly made his way down the stairs to envelope her in a big bear hug followed by an enthusiastic smooch. "Why didn't you call me?" he asked.

"I did, but it went straight to voice mail," Maggie said, and when Shaun looked at his phone, he saw that he had no reception inside the lighthouse.

"Sorry, no reception here, I guess," Shaun said as he showed Maggie his cell phone.

"It's okay. George let me in," Maggie said.

"So, you've met George. What do you think?" Shaun asked.

"He seems like quite a character. He invited us to tea," Maggie said.

"George makes a wonderful cup of tea." Shaun gave her another kiss before he released her. "I missed you," he said.

"You've only been gone a couple of days," Maggie said.

"A minute away from you is too long," Shaun said with a twinkle in his eye.

Maggie laughed. "Shaun Morrow, you have more than a little of the blarney in your blood."

"Guilty," Shaun said with a laugh. "Let's get you unpacked, and then we'll have tea with George. Then, hopefully, he'll feel up to giving us a tour of the manor."

"Is George okay?" Maggie asked in concern.

"I'm sure he is, but I think his joints bother him a bit. He didn't mention it, but it was obvious that he was a little creaky when he gave me the tour."

"Maybe we should skip it then," Maggie said.

"He was so proud yesterday as he showed me around the manor. I think turning down George's offer might hurt him more than his joints. So we'll just take it slow and not put too much stress on him."

Shaun led Maggie across the lawn to the servant's entrance at the back of the manor, and Maggie smiled as Shaun rambled on about what he had discovered in the lighthouse. She wasn't listening closely to the details he shared about mortar, paint, and other necessary repairs. Instead, she was enjoying the cadence of his voice and enthusiasm for the project.

Shaun opened the door and gestured for Maggie to precede him into the manor. George appeared and smiled at them.

"Awk, good. Are you all settled in then, Miss?" George asked.

"I am, thank you. Shaun tells me that you know how to make a proper cup of tea," Maggie said.

"That's kind of him. I'll show you where you can rest your feet while I get our tea," George said.

Maggie was more of a coffee drinker, but she had learned to appreciate the ritual of tea time. There was something soothing about taking a break in your day to enjoy a slow brewed cup of tea and some biscuits.

George joined them at the round table with a fully loaded tea tray and preceded to regale them will tales of his time at Madeira Manor. George enchanted Maggie. His pride in the manor was evident in his demeanor and choice of words.

Maggie was so engrossed in the tales that George was spinning about the glory days of the Madeira Manor that she was surprised when she saw that her teacup was empty.

"Would you like another cup?" George asked Maggie, and she shook her head no.

"It was delicious, but I think I best cut myself off so I sleep tonight," Maggie said.

"As you wish. Sleep is even more elusive as you age, so I understand. Would you like a tour of the manor?" George asked.

"If you have time," Maggie said, allowing George to say no if he didn't feel up to it.

George pulled a pocket watch out of his jacket and clicked it open to check the time. Maggie grinned to herself. Of course, a man like George would have a pocket watch instead of a cell phone to tell time. "I have enough time for a quick tour," George said as he stood up slowly and stretched. "I'm not sure these old bones will enjoy the rainy weather in Ireland, but I think the pints will take the edge off." George turned and led the way into the front foyer with a chuckle. On the way, George stopped to show her the kitchen, scullery, and a small bedroom where he had stayed as the manor's butler.

When they walked into the entryway, Maggie's breath stopped. The large double staircase with heavily carved dark mahogany wood banisters was dramatic and intimidating.

Seeing Maggie's reaction, George smiled and said, "It is a wonder, is it not?" Maggie could only nod her head in agreement. Then, she moved forward to gently caress the carvings of winged cherubs, birds, and foliage.

"It's beautiful," Maggie said. She looked up, saw the crystal chandelier, and wondered about the type of wealth it must have taken to build such a showplace.

"Mr. Madeira lived here alone with his wife?" Maggie asked, and George nodded.

"Mr. Madeira imagined he'd have a large brood of children to inherit his estate, but unfortunately, it was not to be," George said.

Maggie wandered over to a towering set of closed doors to the left of the staircase. The doors mirrored the architecture of the staircase, made of mahogany and carved with whimsical cherubs, flora, and fauna. "What's through these doors?" Maggie asked.

"That would be the formal parlor," George said as he walked by her to grasp the two doorknobs and push the doors open in a grand gesture.

An oversized fireplace and mantel dominated the room. The ceiling rose above the room at what Maggie estimated to be around fifteen feet. A large crystal chandelier hung above, giving the room a soft glow. Maggie thought about the housekeeping staff responsible for dusting and removing cobwebs from such a dizzying height. Only the wealthy could afford to build and maintain structures like this one. The furniture consisted of overstuffed couches and chairs upholstered in heavy red damask arranged in small conversation areas throughout the room. Visually the room matched those of the manor houses she and Shaun had toured in Ireland, but it didn't feel like a home. Instead, it felt like a sterile museum re-creation.

"Let's finish this floor, and then we'll take a tour of the second floor," George said. George led them to a set of matching doors on the opposite side of the parlor, and when he opened them.

Maggie gasped in delight, "A library."

The library was identical to the formal parlor, except these walls were lined with dark wooden bookcases filled with books. Maggie wandered over to one of the bookcases, and she had to put her hands behind her back to keep from stroking the spines of the ancient tomes.

"Mr. Madeira was an avid collector," George said.

"It's wonderful," Maggie said. She imagined curling up on one of the overstuffed chairs with a good book and a glass of whiskey in front of a roaring fire.

"It is," George agreed as he pulled out his pocket watch to give it a quick check. "The workers should be finishing up for the day, but I think we can squeeze in a quick tour of the upstairs."

Maggie and Shaun followed George as he slowly walked to the base of the staircase. George's limp was evident, and Shaun and Maggie shared a concerned look.

"George, would it be okay if we used the elevator? I haven't had a chance to ride in it, and it looks like a beautiful one," Shaun said.

"Of course," George said with a gracious smile. Maggie tucked her hand into Shaun's and gave it a gentle squeeze. She appreciated him giving George a way to save face and not struggle climbing the tall staircase.

The elevator was nestled between the right staircase and the servants' hall. It was a beautiful art nouveau-inspired contraption with shining brass metal covering its mesh doors and inner walls. Once everyone was inside the elevator, George closed the screened door and pressed the second-floor button.

"Mr. Madeira installed this elevator when it became too painful for him to climb the stairs," George said.

With a little bounce, the elevator reached the second floor, and George opened the gate. The rooms on the second floor consisted of an office, a lavatory, and Mr. Madeira's bedroom suite. The rooms were huge, and Maggie imagined that her apartment above the tavern could have fit into Mr. Madeira's office with room to spare. The furnishing echoed the style downstairs with overstuffed furniture in heavy red brocades. It projected an impression of wealth but no warmth. Maggie shivered in reaction, and Shaun looked down at her in concern.

"We should have brought you a sweater," Shaun said.

"I'm sorry, Miss, but it's almost impossible to keep rooms of this size warm. Even when Mr. Madeira was alive, we had to keep a fire blazing in the fireplace and the central heater blowing," George said.

"I can imagine," Maggie said as she wandered over to a large window overlooking the backyard and the lighthouse.

"Excuse me, George," a male voice said, and Maggie turned around to see a large man in construction clothes in the doorway.

"Yes," George said.

"We're done for the day, but we're having a problem with the front gate. It's not opening, and my gate code isn't working," the man said.

George looked a little annoyed at the interruption. Then, turning back to Maggie, he said, "I'm sorry, but we'll have to continue the tour tomorrow if that is okay with you, Miss."

"Of course," Maggie said with a smile.

As Shaun and Maggie walked back to the cottage, Maggie realized something. "Wait, the elevator only goes to the second floor. So how do they get to the third and fourth floors?"

"There is a stairwell," Shaun said, and then he grinned. "It's behind a hidden panel."

"Hidden?"

"Yep. It's behind a panel at the opposite end of the hall from the elevator. George said that after Mrs. Madeira passed away, Mr. Madeira had the stairwell enclosed to be out of sight. So, he wouldn't be reminded of his loss."

"Like I said, rich people are weird," Maggie said, making Shaun chuckle.

George stood aside as he watched the automated gate slowly roll closed behind the last truck of construction workers. He wasn't sure why the gate had malfunctioned; it had worked when he had typed his code into the keypad by the gate.

The gate closed with a solid metallic clang, and George turned away from the keypad to examine the growing shadows. Dusk was gathering, and George thought back to his childhood. His mother had always admonished him to be indoors before the gloaming. That was when the dark fae rose to torment their human neighbors. The memory brought a sharp pang of longing for his long-deceased mother. Closing his eyes, George sent up a silent prayer for his mother's soul. Then shrugging off his melancholy, he turned and began his slow, painful trek back to the manor.

Total darkness had fallen by the time George rounded the last bend in the road, and the manor came into view. The beam from the lighthouse swept in a continuous circle spotlighting the surrounding forest and turning the manor into a dark silhouette. He paused to stare at the manor and was surprised to feel a shiver down his spine. His eyes turned to the forest, examining the shadows for a source of his unease. Then he chuckled and shook his head. What was he looking for? The dark fae? Still chuckling at his actions, he looked back to the manor and paused. A faint glow emanated from the third floor. George shook his head wearily and cursed modern technology. He'd have to check that the manor was empty before heading home.

George rode the elevator to the second floor and then walked down the hall to the cupboard, which enclosed the stairwell leading to the third and fourth floors. The stairs were dimly lit from above, and George began his slow, painful ascent to the landing on the third floor. Stepping out into the hallway, he saw that all the doors to the various rooms were open. Pausing to listen for footsteps, he was not surprised when the manor remained quiet. He should search the rooms to ensure that no one had entered while he was at the front gate, but he was hesitant to move farther down the dimly lit hall. "Silly old man," George admonished himself. "Get a move on so you can go home and have some supper." George forced his feet to move down the hallway, pausing to look into the rooms he passed.

The sweep of the light from the lighthouse created an odd kind of heartbeat as it swept the manor and poured through the windows. Once George had ascertained that a room was empty, he would close the door behind him, shutting off the pulse of the lighthouse beam, and move on to the next. Soon the only room left open was the one at the very end of the hallway, Mrs. Madeira's bedroom, where she had taken her last breath. George crossed himself in a reflexive gesture that he hadn't used since he was young and stepped into the bedroom. The light from the lighthouse blasted into the room, momentarily blinding George, and he covered his eyes in reflex. When the light moved on, George lowered his hand and blinked as his eyes adjusted. The room was sparsely furnished with an armoire, a couple of chairs in front of the fireplace, and Mrs. Madeira's empty hospital bed. The light from the lighthouse swept through the room again. George squinted his eyes, and when the beam moved on, he saw a wispy figure standing at the window. At first, George thought his eyes were playing tricks. The figure he saw must be an optical illusion, merely shadows cast by the moving lighthouse beam onto the sheer curtains. Still, when the figure looked at him, he knew what he saw was not an illusion.

George struggled to breathe as his head shook from side to side, rejecting what his eyes were seeing. "Mrs. Madeira?" George finally managed to croak out. The apparition's lips moved, and although George couldn't hear the voice, he knew she had said his name.

"Yes, it's me, ma'am. George." He said as he slowly and cautiously began to advance on the specter. George's mind was in turmoil, trying to understand why Mrs. Madeira's spirit was still in residence. Was she looking for her husband? George wondered. Maybe she didn't realize he was waiting for her on the other side. The idea of her wandering the halls of the empty manor searching for her loving husband made George's gentle heart ache.

George stopped when he was about seven feet from the ghost, he had expected her to fade away as he advanced, but she had become more solid. He could see her clearly now. She was colorless, painted in shades of white and shadow. Her eyes locked with his, and she mouthed his name again as a confused look crossed her face.

"Yes, ma'am," George repeated. "Are you looking for Mr. Madeira?"

George watched in horror as Mrs. Madeira's head snapped back as if from a slap, and her jaw unhinged like a snake's. Her scream seemed to emanate from everywhere at once, and George turned to run as fast as he could. The scream chased him down the hallway and back to the stairwell.

Chapter Five

Bountiful, California – Madeira Manor – Artist Cottage
Artist

Maggie and Shaun were finishing a leisurely breakfast when the doorbell rang. With a shrug, Shaun stood up and moved from the kitchen through the living room with Maggie in his wake. When he opened the door, he saw a man dressed in work clothes holding a clipboard in his hand.

"Can I help you?" Shaun asked, and the man nodded.

"I hope so. I'm Mr. Heard, the foreman in charge of the construction crew," the man said.

"Nice to meet you, Mr. Heard. What can we do for you this morning?" Shaun asked.

"I was wondering if you've heard from George this morning," Mr. Heard asked.

"No. He's not in the manor?" Shaun asked.

"I don't think so. He usually arrives before the crew and opens everything up for us. But this morning, the manor is locked tight, and no one is answering the door. I called his home number and got his answering machine."

Shaun felt a wave of unease rise through his body, "George gave me a key to the manor and the alarm code. Why don't we walk over and check out the manor?"

In front of the manor, a group of workers lounged against their trucks, sipping coffee.

"What's up?" One of the men shouted, and Mr. Heard responded. "Not sure. Hang tight."

"Not a problem. We're on the clock," the man grinned, and Mr. Heard grumbled under his breath.

At the front door, Shaun peered through the glass and saw that the light on the alarm system was yellow. He shook his head because he wasn't sure what a yellow light meant, but he braced himself for the alarm to trip as he opened the front door. The front door swung open, but no alarm sounded.

"That's odd," Mr. Heard said. "George would never forget to set the alarm. He must be here somewhere."

"George?" Maggie yelled, making the two men jump and then chuckle at themselves. "Sorry," Maggie said with a small smile. The trio paused and listened for a response to Maggie's call, but the manor stayed eerily quiet.

"Do you think we should call the authorities?" Maggie asked.

"Probably," Shaun said. "What do you want to do, Mr. Heard?"

"My guys are on the clock, and we're on a tight schedule," Mr. Heard said in frustration. "But, I can't imagine George not showing up. So yeah, let's call the cops. Maybe they can swing by his house and check up on him. Can you take care of that while I get my guys started?" Shaun nodded and took Maggie's hand. They walked through the manor to the kitchen.

"What's up?" Maggie asked.

"I just wanted to make sure he wasn't in the kitchen."

"Shaun, if he were in the kitchen, he would have answered us," Maggie said.

"Hopefully," Shaun said.

"Hopefully?" Maggie asked in confusion, and Shaun watched her expression change as she understood what he was saying. "You mean he might have died? Shaun, that's horrible."

"It is, but he is an older gentleman, and these things can happen quickly." Shaun paused at the closed kitchen door and looked at Maggie. "Do you want to stay here just in case?" Maggie nodded and turned away as Shaun pushed through the kitchen door. "All clear," Shaun called back, and Maggie felt the tension in her shoulders ease.

Shaun and Maggie walked out of the servant's entrance and stepped into the early morning sunlight. Maggie's eyes searched the surrounding woods and the windows at the back of the manor. Still, nothing she saw gave her any clues about what may have happened to George.

"Hello, I'd like to file a missing person report," Shaun said into his phone. "No. He's an adult." Pause. "I understand that, but it's out of character for him not to show up for work." Shaun paused to listen, then responded, "Yes, we tried his home number, and there was no answer." Another long pause and Maggie could see Shaun's frustration mounting. "Seriously? 24 hours? The man is in his 70's and has gone missing." Pause. "No, he doesn't have Alzheimer's. Me? No, I just work with him. Alright, alright. Thank you," Shaun said as he hung up and growled.

"That didn't sound good," Maggie said.

"She said that she could take a report, but because he's an adult with no history of Alzheimer's or dementia, they won't do anything for at least 24 hours."

"That sucks," Maggie said. "What do you want to do?"

Shaun searched the surrounding space as though he was looking for some inspiration, and finding none, he shrugged. "I can't do anything, not for George anyway," Shaun said as the sounds of power tools signified that the construction workers had begun their day. "Want to join me in the lighthouse?" Shaun asked weakly.

"Oh, it's a temptation," Maggie said with a wry smile. She knew that once Shaun entered the lighthouse, he would be laser-focused on what was needed to return the lighthouse to its original glory. "But I think I'll spend a couple of hours in town window shopping and then have lunch with my handsome husband at Bountiful Harvest." Bountiful Harvest was the main saloon and restaurant for the town of Bountiful.

"Checking out the competition?" Shaun said.

"A girl has got to stay on top of her game, plus this way, I can write off my little vacation as a business expense," Maggie said.

"I married a brilliant businesswoman."

"You did," Maggie agreed. "Give me your phone." Shaun smiled as he watched Maggie set three separate alarms into his clock app.

"Three?" Shaun asked with a laugh.

"It's for your own good. I am not a woman who appreciates being stood up for a date, and I know you, Shaun Morrow. Once you get inside that lighthouse, everything else will cease to exist."

"Thank you for loving me," Shaun said as he took his phone back from Maggie and gave her a quick kiss. "Enjoy your adventure in town."

Maggie parked in front of Mountain Mystics Bookstore and smiled at the vivid window display of esoteric books and tools. She sighed with contentment when she pulled the front door of the bookshop open and was met with the intoxicating smell of herbs, oils, and incense.

"Good morning," a cheery voice rang out from further inside the store. Maggie saw a larger woman dressed in a flowing caftan in shades of purple stocking shelves. The woman reminded her of Sinthia Gnome, and she smiled back.

"Good morning."

"Can I help you find anything?" The woman asked.

"I'm just going to wander around if that's okay," Maggie said.

"Enjoy. If I can answer any questions, just let me know." Maggie nodded and moved over to look at the books on the tarot.

Maggie believed she had an ability for divination, and she enjoyed working with the tarot. She wasn't secure enough in her abilities to charge for her readings, but she enjoyed doing readings for her friends. She had become interested in the occult as a teenager when she discovered Sinthia Gnome hunched over her kitchen table with her tarot cards spread out before her. Sinthia had given her a reading, and Maggie had been hooked. Over the years, Sinthia shared her divination knowledge and some simple exercises to increase Maggie's psychic abilities. Maggie laughed when she saw a purple velvet tarot bag embossed with a grinning gnome. "Perfect," Maggie said.

"I'm sorry," the storekeeper said "were you speaking to me?"

"No, I was talking to myself. I just found the perfect gift," Maggie said as she held up the gnome tarot bag.

"Do you like gnomes?" The storekeeper asked. "If so, I have a whole shelf of gnome items." Maggie followed the storekeeper to a bookcase filled with gnome statues, mugs, pictures, cards, and more.

Maggie left the store with enough gnome merchandise to cover that year's Christmas and birthday gifts for all of the Gnomes in her life and a few gifts for herself.

A day without responsibilities was rare, and she was enjoying herself. Maggie strolled down the street, window shopping while relishing the warm sun on her skin. A delicious smell led her to Bountiful Baking. The logo on the window matched the one from the bag that had held their morning bagels. The bagels had been delicious, and Maggie decided she and Shaun could use a few more.

She returned to her car to unload her bags and was surprised when Shaun parked his car next to hers. Glancing at her phone to verify the time, she was bewildered. Where had the morning gone?

"You made it," Maggie said with a grin deciding not to rat on herself about her loss of time.

"And it only took two of the alarms," Shaun said as he dipped in for a quick kiss. "Your arms looked full. Did you find some good stuff?"

"I did. The little bookstore had a ton of gnome stuff, so I bought a few gifts. Plus, I got us some more bagels and a couple pieces of cheesecake for tonight."

"Yum. I'm glad we're going to lunch; I'm starving. My lady?" He said as he extended his elbow to Maggie in a grinning tribute to old-time chivalry. Maggie smiled back and placed her arm through his.

Maggie didn't really consider Bountiful Harvest competition for her tavern. But, it never hurt to check out how other businesses operated. Bountiful Harvest's decor leaned into the town's mining heritage. The tables were refinished cable spools topped with oak circles coated in a thick layer of epoxy which encased small mining implements. The walls were paneled in rough planks placed haphazardly to look like those lining a mining tunnel. Tintype photos of haggard-looking men in mining gear hung from the walls. The waiters and waitresses wore Levi's, pale blue button-up work shirts, and boots. The hostess wore an old-fashioned hard hat with a flickering flame in its lamp. It took Maggie a moment to realize that the flame was an LED. *Clever*, she thought.

"Good morning," the hostess said. "Welcome to Bountiful Harvest, two for lunch?"

"Yes, thank you," Shaun said.

Once seated, Maggie asked Shaun if he had any news about George.

"I spoke to the foreman on my way out. He said he hadn't heard anything."

Maggie toyed with her fork and wondered what could have happened to George. "I hope he's okay."

Shaun reached across the table to place a gentle hand on Maggie's, "Me too."

Chapter Six

Bountiful, California – The Madeira Estate

As their cars navigated the windy roads back to the Madeira estate, Maggie drove behind Shaun. The drive was beautiful. Maggie enjoyed the warm pine-scented wind blowing through her open car window. She smiled while thinking about what she and Shaun could do in the large soaking tub in the cottage. Then, turning off the main road to the lane leading to the manor's gate, she had to slam on her brakes when Shaun's car pulled up short. A pair of police cars were blocking the open gates, and as Maggie watched, a policeman approached Shaun's car. He spoke with Shaun, nodded, and moved back to his post before waving them through.

They parked in front of the cottage, and Shaun walked back to Maggie's car.

"It's George, isn't it?" Maggie asked before Shaun could say anything, and Shaun nodded. "Is he okay?" Maggie asked hopefully.

"I don't know. The policeman said we should unload and return to the manor entrance for an interview."

"Interview? Do they think we had something to do with George's disappearance?"

"I'm sure it's just procedure," Shaun said as he tried to reassure her. They unloaded the bags and then walked back to the front of the manor with heavy thoughts. A policeman was standing guard at the front door, and he watched Shaun and Maggie approach with a frown on his face.

"Can I help you folks?" he asked.

"Yes. I'm Shaun Morrow, and this is my wife, Maggie Foley. A police officer at the gate said we should report here for an interview."

The policeman nodded, "One minute, stay right here," he said, and then we opened the front door and disappeared inside the manor.

Maggie and Shaun stood quietly, waiting for him to return, glancing at the knots of police officers and construction workers standing idly in the early afternoon sunshine.

When he returned, the policeman spoke to Shaun. "Mr. Morrow, Detective Barnes wants to see you in the kitchen. I'm sorry, miss, you'll have to wait here," the policeman said when Maggie moved to follow Shaun into the manor.

"Why?" she asked in confusion.

"He'll talk to you next," the policeman said.

"Shaun?" Maggie asked, and Shaun smiled reassuringly.

"I'm sure it's standard procedure, right, officer?" Shaun asked him.

"It is. Detective Barnes will talk to you next, Miss."

"Okay," Maggie said as she stepped back from the door. Feeling awkward under the policeman's scrutiny, Maggie turned away and sat on one of the steps. She closed her eyes and sent out a quiet prayer to the universe for George. She hoped that he was okay.

In the kitchen, Shaun saw a man in a grey suit sitting at the round café table in what Shaun had begun to think of as George's chair. The man stood up and extended his hand. "Good afternoon Mr. Morrow. I'm Detective Barnes." Shaun shook the offered hand. "Please have a seat," the detective said as he indicated the chair across from his. "Can you tell me about the last time you saw Mr. Byrne?"

"Yes. My wife and I had tea with George yesterday afternoon around 4:00. Then, he took us on a tour of the manor. A construction worker asked George to help them with the front gate. Apparently, it wouldn't open. So that ended our tour," Shaun said.

"You didn't see him after that?"

"No. My wife and I went back to the cottage for the evening."

"I understand that you were hired to refurbish the lighthouse."

"Hopefully. I'm here to see what that would entail and draft a proposal."

"And your wife?" The detective asked.

"She came up to spend a couple of days with me." The detective nodded and wrote in his notebook.

"So, you and your wife didn't hear or see anything unusual last night?" the detective asked.

"No. Is George okay?" Shaun asked.

"The foreman said you have a key to the manor."

"I do. Is George okay?"

The detective studied Shaun's face and said, "I'm sorry, but George is dead."

"What?" Shaun asked in shock as his heart clenched. "How?"

"A construction worker found him at the bottom of the stairs leading up to the third floor. We think he fell."

"Damn," Shaun said as he rubbed his watery eyes. *The universe can be cruel*, Shaun thought. All George had wanted to do was make sure the manor was in good hands and then retire.

"How much longer are you scheduled to be here?" the detective asked.

"It depends on how quickly I can complete my assessment," Shaun said as he fished a business card out of his wallet. "If you need to get a hold of me after I'm done here, you can reach me at this number."

The detective took the card, gave it a quick glance, and then nodded before he stood up and offered his hand to Shaun, "Thank you, Mr. Morrow. I'd like to speak to your wife next. Please exit through the back door."

Shaun nodded and then walked out the back door to wait for Maggie.

When Maggie came out, her eyes were red from crying, and when she saw Shaun, she rushed into his arms. Shaun enfolded her in an embrace and gently stroked her hair as she cried.

"Poor George," Maggie said when she pulled away, and Shaun nodded. Then, hand in hand, they made their way across the grass to the cottage.

Chapter Seven

Bountiful, California – The Madeira Estate – The Artist Cottage

Shaun and Maggie shared a quiet and subdued evening. They were emotionally drained from the day's events and went to bed early.

In the night, Maggie woke to find herself snuggled close to Shaun. She carefully moved Shaun's arm from around her waist, slid from the warm bed, and rose to use the restroom.

On her way back to bed, Maggie shivered. Something was making her uneasy. She paused by the heavy drapes that covered the floor-to-ceiling windows and peeked around the curtain's edge to check outside.

Her eyelids slammed shut as the bright light from the lighthouse swept across her face. When the beam moved on, she stared down toward the lighthouse's base, blinking her eyes rapidly, trying to clear a large white mist from her sight, but the mist remained. It was surrounding the monument at the lighthouse's base.

The mist swelled and began to move. It slowly drifted outside the cottage toward the manor and out of sight. Maggie crept across the room to the windows facing the manor and watched as the mist passed through the servant's door and disappeared from view.

Maggie turned from the window, preparing to rush after the ghost, when she saw Shaun asleep in bed. She thought about waking him up, but she decided against it. The manor was locked up tight. So she was just going to peek in a couple of windows.

Maggie walked out the cottage's front door and across the lawn to grasp the doorknob of the servant's entrance, fully expecting it to be locked. But it turned in her grasp, and the door flew open. Maggie stood in shocked silence as she waited for the house alarm to begin blasting, but the night remained eerily quiet.

"What the hell," Maggie said to herself, and then she realized that the workmen had probably forgotten to lock up and turn on the alarm. Maggie smiled sadly; they were used to George taking care of those details.

Maggie took a tentative step into the small entryway and strained her ears for any sounds. There were no sounds of boards creaking under someone's feet or the soft sounds of doors or drawers being opened. *It's dead*, Maggie thought and immediately regretted it. *Enough*, Maggie thought as she pushed away the creepy thoughts and strode further into the house.

She froze when the overhead light clicked on in the dining room, then sighed. The occupancy sensors. Shaun had pointed them out to her when they had toured the manor. It would be difficult to sneak up on someone if the lights came on every time she entered a room. But on the plus side, the lit room was a little less creepy.

Maggie walked toward the front of the manor. The only lights on were the ones she tripped, so Maggie felt safe assuming that no one was lurking in the dark rooms she passed.

She stopped at the bottom of the double staircase as a shiver flowed over her. The light from the entryway only accentuated the inky blackness of the second floor. Her body rejected the idea of entering that darkness. Maggie took a deep breath and squared her shoulders, refusing to let those feelings stop her.

She walked up the staircase and stood poised on the second floor, still searching for signs of life, but the second floor appeared empty. She stood still long enough that the occupancy sensor clicked off and plunged the staircase into darkness. As Maggie's eyes adjusted, she noticed a glow at the end of the hall. She took a tentative step toward that light and gasped when she heard a click, followed by the hallway being flooded with light. Maggie looked at the motion sensor and growled softly at her cowardice; then, she marched down the hall to where she had seen the light. The doors of the rooms she passed were closed, and the cracks under the doors were black. But the bottom of the door at the end of the hall was illuminated. Maggie reached forward to grasp the small doorknob, tensing up, uncertain what lay behind the door. The door opened to show a spiral staircase leading up to the next floor. The staircase was lit by a light from above.

This must be where they found George, Maggie thought as she stared into the claustrophobic space. Maggie wiped an errant tear from her cheek as she whispered a silent prayer. *I'm so sorry, George. You deserved so much more. Wherever you are, I hope you're enjoying a pint. Sláinte.* Maggie stepped into the stairwell and closed the door behind her.

Third floor, here I come, Maggie thought as she began to climb the stairs to the floor above.

Pausing in the stairwell at the entrance to the third floor, Maggie stared down a long, well-lit hallway that showed six evenly spaced doors, three on each side. Maggie remembered that this floor had belonged to Mrs. Madeira and was where she had died. With that thought echoing in her mind, Maggie stepped out of the stairwell and into the hallway. The lights in the three rooms on the left were on, and Maggie slowly approached the first of those rooms. She peeked around the door and saw what looked like a home office. Maggie did a quick search, but the space was empty, so Maggie moved down the hall to the next room and repeated her search. Finally, Maggie approached the last lit room, and when she leaned in to peek around the door jamb, the first thing she spied was an empty hospital bed.

Maggie thought about Mrs. Madeira lying in that bed for years after her fall. Paralyzed and dependent on her husband and servants for everything. Maggie tried to imagine the horror of having her mind still functional while trapped in a body she couldn't control.

As she walked into the bedroom, those images were in her mind when she froze. The bed was no longer empty. A woman was lying in the bed, covered in a thin sheet that emphasized her body's emaciated condition. Tubes ran out from under the sheet connecting to various pieces of medical equipment. Sitting at her side was a grey-haired man holding the woman's hand as he whispered in her ear. Neither the man nor woman acknowledged Maggie's presence.

These must be residual spooks, Maggie thought to herself. Then she smiled because she wouldn't have known such a thing existed before Shaun. He called it the Stone Tape Theory. The theory states that when a high emotion or traumatic event occurs, it can saturate the environment creating a recording of the moment. These recordings can be replayed at a later time. Shaun told her about residual haunts in Gettysburg. People reported figures they thought were civil war reenactors marching across a field only to disappear between one moment and the next. Maggie watched the two specters and wondered what extreme emotions had been released in this loving exchange between a husband and wife. Could their love have been so deep at this moment that it has saturated the very walls with this image?

The man continued to speak to the woman in muted tones, and Maggie was startled when the woman's eyes swiveled from her husband's face to lock with hers. As the ghost's lips moved, a hushed sound reminiscent of wind rustling through fallen leaves reached Maggie's ears. The sound began to swirl around Maggie. A murmuring was woven within the strange rustling sound, and Maggie strained to understand it. The sound vortex sped up as the volume of the voice increased. The world tilted, and Maggie stumbled forward to grab the bed's footboard for support, and when she did, the voice rang through clearly, "It's a lie. It's a lie. It's a lie!"

Damn, this bed is hard, Maggie thought as she rolled over and a bright light popped on. "Shit," she grumbled as she flung her arm over her eyes. Lowering her arm, she squinted as her eyes adjusted. *Where the hell am I?* she wondered, and then it all came crashing back with such clarity that she found herself skittering across the floor as she rushed to get away from the bed. "Fuck, fuck, fuck," Maggie chanted as the memories came crashing back. Her eyes frantically searched the room for the ghosts she had seen, but the room appeared empty. She stood up and looked toward the bed, using a wall to balance. The bed was empty. Keeping her eyes on the bed, Maggie crept out of the room, backing slowly down the hall to the stairwell.

She grasped the handrail, preparing to rush down but stopped when she saw a dark shadow lying at the bottom of the stairs. "George?" she whispered, but the shadow didn't respond. She blinked her eyes, struggling to see more clearly, and when she looked again, she saw that she had been mistaken. The shadow was just that, a shadow.

With the method of George's demise foremost in her mind, Maggie moved quickly but carefully down the stairwell to the second-floor landing.

It felt like she was being watched, and Maggie fought not to run out of the house in terror. Instead, she retraced her steps and closed the door to the servant's entrance behind her.

She strode across the lawn to the cottage before daring to take one last look at the manor. The building was a large black shadow against the moonless sky. As Maggie opened the cottage door, the dark night was dimly illuminated. With dread, Maggie looked over her shoulder at the manor. A light was burning in Mrs. Madeira's suite. "Nope," Maggie said emphatically as she quickly closed the cottage door behind her blocking out the light and hopefully any of the ghosts that roamed the halls of the manor.

Chapter Eight

Bountiful, California – The Madeira Estate – Artist cottage

Maggie had managed to crawl into bed next to Shaun without waking him, and when she pushed back against him, he murmured in his sleep and wound a comforting arm around her waist. Shaun's presence had allowed Maggie to relax and drift off into a dreamless sleep. But now it was morning, and as she sat across from Shaun in the cottage's little breakfast nook, wondering how to tell him about her experience.

Shaun was telling Maggie about his plans for the day and when he paused to take a sip of tea Maggie jumped in.

"So, something strange happened last night," Maggie said, and Shaun froze with his teacup in the air as he looked curiously at Maggie, waiting for her to continue. "After we went to bed, something woke me up, so I went to the bathroom, and on the way back to bed, I looked out the window."

As Maggie shared her experience from the night before, the curious expression on Shaun's face melted into one of concern.

When Maggie finished her tale, she expected Shaun to jump in with questions or admonishments about her exploring on her own. So she was surprised when Shaun put his teacup down, rose from the table, and in a flat voice said, "Will you excuse me." Maggie sat in shocked silence as she listened to Shaun walk out of the cottage and close the door behind him.

Maggie was at a loss about what she should do. Should she follow him or sit and wait for his return? Finally, Maggie jumped to her feet. She had never been a person who waited patiently for the world to come to her, so Maggie went in search of her husband.

She found him standing over Mrs. Madeira's grave with his shoulders hunched and his hands in his pockets. Shaun didn't turn to look at her as she approached, but he did speak to her. "Maggie, please go back to the cottage," Shaun said.

Shaun's voice was odd, she had never heard him use that tone of voice before, and she wasn't sure how to respond.

"Please," Shaun repeated when she didn't move.

"I—," Maggie started, but Shaun's hand shot up, silencing her.

When he spoke, it sounded to Maggie as if he was forcing each word through clenched teeth. "Maggie, I need you to leave me alone."

"No," Maggie said, but she stepped back when Shaun spun around to face her. His face was flushed, and he looked pissed.

"I am struggling to not yell at you for doing something so dangerous. Why would you go wandering through an empty building looking for an intruder?"

"I wasn't thinking. I just kind of went for it. Besides, I didn't think it was a real person. I thought I was chasing a ghost."

"And that's better? After everything we've been through, you should know that ghosts are just as dangerous as the living. So why didn't you wake me up?"

Maggie shrugged because she didn't have any justification for her actions.

"You could have been injured while I was snoring away in the cottage. You're smarter than that."

That statement was like a slap, and Maggie's shame switched to anger. "I am smart! And I am a grown woman who doesn't answer to anyone for her actions."

"Why do you think I came out here?" Shaun asked, which pulled Maggie up short.

"What?" she asked.

"Why do you think I came out here?" Shaun repeated, and when Maggie didn't respond, he continued. "I came out here because of exactly that fact. I want to grab you and shake some sense into you because what you did scares me to my core. And yet, I'm not your boss. I'm your husband, and you're right. You don't answer to me. So how do I reconcile those two truths? How do I keep you safe and yet independent? That's why I came out here. I needed a moment to let my emotions run their course before I said something stupid." Shaun walked toward her and put gentle hands on her arms as he stared into her eyes. "I love you so much, and I would do anything to keep you safe, yet one of the things that attracted me to you was how strong and independent you were. I don't want to crush your spirit. Help me." Shaun said.

Maggie said nothing as she pulled Shaun into a long embrace. Then she stepped back, rested her hand on Shaun's cheek, and smiled gently.

"I love you too, and I am sorry I scared you. You're right; I should have woken you up to go with me. I promise to make wiser choices in the future. Thank you for loving me as I am and understanding why I do what I do," Maggie said.

"You do the same for me. I'm sure my quirks must drive you crazy, but you keep loving and supporting me. How could I do less for you? I fell in love with a powerful, strong, intelligent woman with a huge heart, and she is exactly the person I want to grow old with." Happy that the storm had passed, Shaun pulled Maggie in for one more hug.

They broke apart when the sound of men's voices drifted to them on the morning air. The construction workers had arrived to begin their day.

"We should probably tell Mr. Heard that the alarm wasn't set last night," Shaun said, and then, taking Maggie's hand, they went to find the foreman.

Shaun told Mr. Heard about the crew's failure to lock up and set the manor's alarm the night before. He lied and said that he was the one who had inspected the manor.

"I made sure that the doors were locked, but since the alarm company changed the alarm code after George's death, I wasn't able to arm it," Shaun said.

"I appreciate you locking up. I'll make sure it doesn't happen again," Mr. Heard assured them.

Satisfied that they had done what they could, Maggie and Shaun returned to the cottage to finish their breakfast.

They were surprised when a knock on the door interrupted their meal, and when Shaun opened the door, he saw Mr. Heard standing on the doorstep.

"I'm sorry to bother you, but I wanted to give you this," Mr. Heard said as he handed Shaun a slip of paper. "It's the new alarm code." When Shaun started to protest, Mr. Heard held up a hand to stop him. "I know that it's not your job to secure the manor, but I would appreciate it if you would act as a backup for my men, just in case they screw up again. They're pretty shaken up by George's death. I even had a couple quit because they felt uneasy in the house."

"I'm only going to be here for a week or two," Shaun said.

"That should be fine, we're almost done with our work in the manor, and then they'll change the alarm code again. We start on the cottage next. The lighthouse repairs we're leaving to your company if you win the bid. Anyway, I would appreciate it if you could do me this solid."

"Okay," Shaun agreed reluctantly. "But just in case someone forgets again."

Chapter Nine

Innkeeper's apartment – Foghorn Tavern, Crescent Bay, California

The next morning, dawn peeked under the curtains and danced across Maggie's closed eyelids. Maggie stirred, turned to look at the alarm clock, and groaned. She had returned to Crescent Bay late the night before and had made the mistake of cutting through the tavern instead of sneaking up the back staircase to her apartment. Once her employees saw her, she had been sucked into the minutia of business ownership. It was after midnight before she had managed to break away and crawl upstairs to bed. Maggie contemplated rolling over and falling back to sleep, but she knew that her mind would refuse to comply. Already it was scrambling from one to-do item to another. Finally, with a frustrated groan, she flung the covers off and headed to the bathroom.

Later, when Maggie's chef Mario arrived to begin his day, Maggie was hunched over a laptop in one of the tavern's booths.

"Good morning, Maggie. I didn't expect to see you down here until after the lunch rush."

"That was my plan, but my mind had other ideas," she said.

"Ah, I've had mornings like that. Late nights too. Is there anything I can do to help put your mind at ease?" Mario asked, and Maggie smiled.

"Thank you, Mario, but it's just the usual stuff."

"Okay, but if you think of anything, you know where you can find me," Mario said as he walked past her booth and pushed open the swinging doors to the kitchen.

Maggie checked the time and realized that her quiet morning was ending. She finished her coffee, shut down her laptop, and prepared to begin her day.

Maggie's morning was filled with the happy facade of a prosperous business owner. But beneath the mask, her mind was obsessed with her experience at the Madeira estate.

Late in the afternoon, the volume of customers at the Tavern tapered off to just a few locals. Maggie was preparing to take an extended break when someone called out her name. Maggie smiled when she saw Sinthia Gnome motioning for her to come over. Sinthia's curvaceous form was covered in one of the brightly colored dresses she preferred, and her long bright red hair fanned out behind her head in wild waves. Sinthia was sitting in a booth across from a slender older woman dressed in a dark purple dress. Her long beautiful silver hair was swept up into a large bun at the back of her head.

"Maggie, I'd like you to meet a friend of mine, Mrs. Bridget Kleyn. Bridget, this is the daughter of my heart Maggie Foley," Sinthia said.

"It's nice to meet you, Mrs. Kleyn," Maggie said as she looked into a pair of sharp steel blue eyes.

"You too, dear," Bridget said. "Sinthia has told me a lot about you."

"Normally, I'd say you can't believe everything you hear, but if Sinthia said it..." Maggie said and shrugged, making Sinthia laugh.

Maggie realized that Sinthia would be the perfect person to talk to about her experiences at Madeira Manor.

"Sinthia, if you have some time in the next day or two, I'd like to swing by your home and discuss something that happened," Maggie said.

The smile on Sinthia's face dissolved into a look of concern, "Are you okay, Maggie?"

"Oh, I'm fine. I just had something happen, and I need someone to talk to. There's no rush, though. You two enjoy your tea, and I'll give you a call tomorrow."

"No need for that," Mrs. Kleyn said. "Join us."

Maggie shook her head no and gave Sinthia a concerned look, "Thank you, but really it's okay. It can wait." Maggie insisted, uncertain if Mrs. Kleyn knew about Sinithia's interest in ghosts and such.

"Nonsense," Mrs. Kleyn said as she reached out to give Maggie's hand a reassuring pat.

"No, really. I don't want to interrupt your tea. I'll just give Sinthia a call tomorrow," Maggie insisted. But, Mrs. Kleyn was already sliding around the booth to make room. Maggie gave Mrs. Kleyn a weak smile and slid into the booth.

"So, what's up?" Sinthia asked.

Maggie struggled with a way to tell Sinthia that her issue had to do with the paranormal without outing her to Mrs. Kleyn. "You know the challenges we had while the lighthouse was being renovated? We're facing the same challenges with Shaun's new project."

"Are you having problems with spirits?" Mrs. Kleyn asked bluntly, and Sinthia laughed at the shocked look on Maggie's face.

"Mrs. Kleyn is one of *those* friends," Sinthia said, and Maggie felt herself relax. "Mrs. Kleyn is a necromancer," Sinthia said, and when Maggie looked shocked, she continued. "That's the official name, but I guess most would call her a medium. She specializes in communication with spirits and knows about my interests, so you can talk freely."

"Oh, good. I was tying myself into knots trying to figure out how to not out you," Maggie said.

"I could tell," Sinthia said. "So, what's happening."

Maggie's tale was interrupted by Suzy, who came over with a fresh pot of tea and a large mug of coffee for Maggie. Maggie smiled her thanks, and when Suzy moved off, Maggie told Sinthia and Mrs. Kleyn about her experiences at Madeira Manor.

"What do you think?" Maggie asked when she had finished.

"Do you often communicate with spirits?" Mrs. Kleyn asked.

"Not often, but I have had experiences in the past," Maggie said.

"Interesting," Mrs. Kleyn said as she shot Sinthia a look. "If you like, I could go up to the manor and see if I can communicate with the spirits."

"I wouldn't want to trouble you," Maggie said.

"Oh, it's no trouble. It's what I do. I have a couple more things I need to take care of here in town, but I could go up tomorrow night," Mrs. Kleyn said.

"Let me talk to Shaun first, okay?" Maggie asked.

"Of course. Just let Sinthia know after you speak to Shaun. She knows how to get a hold of me," Mrs. Kleyn said.

"I will," Maggie said as she slid out of the booth and stood up. "If you'll excuse me, I had a late night, and I think I need a nap before my night shift. It was good meeting you, Mrs. Kleyn. Thank you for offering to help."

"My pleasure, dear," Mrs. Kleyn said. "Go get some rest."

Exhausted, Maggie took a long nap. When she woke up, she checked in with her staff, walked the dogs, grabbed an early dinner from the tavern's kitchen, and then went back upstairs to give Shaun a call.

Shaun was intrigued about meeting a real-life necromancer, and his enthusiasm made Maggie smile. "She said she could come up tomorrow night. What do you think?"

"I think that'd be brilliant. Imagine watching a necromancer work. How cool is that?" Shaun asked.

"I'll let Sinthia know you want to accept Mrs. Kleyn's offer. What time should we plan on being there?" Maggie asked.

"The crew's spooked, and they've been leaving before sunset. So, if you arrive after 7:00, the crew should be gone."

"Sounds good. I'll firm up the details with Sinthia. How was your day?" Maggie asked, then laid down on her bed to listen to Shaun. Shaun went into great detail about the defects he had found in the lighthouse retrofit. Maggie smiled when Shaun began railing against crappy contractors who shouldn't be allowed to monkey with things they don't have the skills to fix competently. Maggie wasn't paying close attention to what Shaun was saying. She was just enjoying the sound of his voice.

After he wound down, Shaun remembered to ask Maggie about her day, and their roles swapped.

"I should probably head down and check on the crew," Maggie said after she finished recapping her hectic day. She paused when a wave of fear rolled through her making her body shake. "Shaun, promise me you won't go into the manor alone, no matter what you see tonight."

"Maggie," Shaun started, but Maggie interrupted him.

"I'm serious, Shaun. I have a bad feeling. Whatever walks in the manor can wait until Mrs. Kleyn arrives tomorrow night. Promise me," Maggie begged.

After a slight pause, Shaun responded. "I promise, Maggie. I'll stay out of the manor."

"Thank you," Maggie said as her shoulders relaxed. Shaun's inquisitive mind reacted to a mystery like a cat to catnip. But Shaun was a man of his word, so she knew Shaun would be safe. "I'd better go down and let the crew know I'm going to be gone tomorrow night. I'll see you then. I love you."

"I love you too. See you here tomorrow night," Shaun smiled as he disconnected the call and put his phone on the cottage's dining room table. Maggie had thrown a big wrench into his plans for the night. How had she known that he was planning on spending the night prowling through the manor? Standing up, Shaun walked over to the door to Mr. Madeira's art studio and pushed it open.

He stood on the threshold, facing the large glass wall, to watch the light from the lighthouse sweep over the surrounding woods. The statue of the lightkeeper stood forever poised on the gallery with his spyglass pointed toward the manor and Mrs. Madeira's bedroom. He thought of Maggie's experience in the manor and fought his desire to investigate. He had promised Maggie, and he would keep his promise. Then he smiled. He had promised to stay out of the manor but not the lighthouse.

He was filled with a sense of purpose and rushed back to his equipment bag and pulled out his flashlight. Leaving the cottage, Shaun followed the beam of his flashlight to Mrs. Madeira's grave at the lighthouse's base. He reread the inscription, and it still unnerved him. It felt like a futile prayer against the darkness.

A lighthouse protects others from the dangerous ground on which it is built.

Shaun tilted his head to look straight up toward the statue on the lighthouse's gallery. There was a mystery here, and it made Shaun's curiosity itch. Then, turning to look at the manor, he was startled when he saw that the lights on the third floor were lit.

Dammit, Maggie, Shaun thought, and then a smile slowly spread across his face. He reached into his pocket to pull out his key chain. He unlocked the door to the lighthouse. The inside of the lighthouse was awash in an undulating light that bled down from the lantern room 30 feet above. Shaun pointed his flashlight at the spiral staircase and began his ascent.

The lens made a quiet swishing sound in the lantern room as it spun on its bed of ball bearings. The room was cool, but Shaun was still unprepared for the blast of freezing air that surrounded him as he stepped out onto the gallery. He moved to stand beside the statue and stare at the illuminated windows in the manor.

Stepping behind the statue, he attempted to look through the statue's spyglass, but all he could see was an out-of-focus sliver of light. Smiling at his folly, Shaun made a mental note to add binoculars to his work satchel.

Shaun stepped away from the statue to squint at the lit windows in the manor. Searching for any sign of movement. A sudden rush of adrenalin poured through his body, making his muscles tense and his senses heighten, preparing him to fight or run. His eyes searched the surrounding area for why he suddenly felt like prey. Shaun's ears were filled with the sound of the rotating lens, which continued to spin behind him, unconcerned with Shaun's discomfort. That was when Shaun realized that the swishing sound of the lens's movement was the only sound he could hear. The night sounds of wind in the leaves, crickets chirping, and the crunching of little critters moving through the underbrush was missing. The stillness was unsettling. Shaun's eyes were jerked away from the shadowy forest by a sudden absence of light as the manor's third-floor windows went black.

Shaun watched the manor wearily. He blinked his eyes when he thought he saw an odd green glow emanating from the servant's entrance. Shaun watched in fascination as the green glow gained brightness, assumed a roughly humanoid shape, and began to drift across the lawn. Trying to keep the manifestation in sight, Shaun moved closer to the edge of the gallery. He grasped the handrail, and his wedding ring tapped against the metal bar. The quiet tap in the unnaturally silent night sounded like a gunshot, and both the manifestation and Shaun froze. Although the manifestation didn't have a face, Shaun felt its intense scrutiny moments before it rushed toward the entrance to the lighthouse.

Shaun's mind raced. How could he protect himself from whatever was approaching from below? He had seen how dangerous ghosts could be, and now he was trapped on a circular metal walkway 30 feet above the ground with no one else in earshot. He slapped his pockets, looking for his cell phone, and then remembered that he had left it on the dining room table.

A keening wail rose from inside the lighthouse, and Shaun pushed his terror aside as he struggled to assess his potential for injury. Sitting down on the walkway, he tied himself to the rail with his belt. If he plunged over the tower's edge, the belt wouldn't hold his weight, but it might give him time to stop his fatal descent. He wrapped his arms around the same railing, shut his eyes, and waited for the wailing ghost.

The screaming grew so loud that Shaun had to bend forward so that his hands could cover his ears, which turned Shaun into a shaking ball of fear at the feet of the statue. The wailing sound continued as a sickly green light bled through his clenched eyelids. Finally, Shaun's curiosity forced his eyes to open. The green light whipped around the statue in a wide circle, gaining mass with each scream. When the green energy rushed over Shaun's foot, it felt like it had been plunged into a bucket of flesh-burning dry ice. Shaun hissed as he snatched his foot out of the way. The wailing cut short, and Shaun held his breath as he felt the energy focus its attention on his huddled form.

"Please," Shaun begged for mercy as the energy pounced. The energy punched through him to speed back toward the manor leaving a cold stinging pain in its wake. Shaun curled up into a shaking ball as he began to sob. The manifestation had sucked out all of his body's heat and poured a feeling of total desolation into that void. It felt as if Shaun would never be warm and happy again.

The sight of his belt fluttering to the ground below shocked him back into his body. He stood with one foot on the railing's bottom crossbar, preparing to climb over the edge.

"Shit!" Shaun yelled as he pushed away from the railing to thump hard into the wall behind him and sink back to the floor. Fearful of what he might do next, he crawled on hands and knees around the gallery and back into the relative safety of the lantern room, closing the door firmly behind him. He couldn't remember unbuckling his belt or rising to climb onto the railing, but he knew that he had.

Shaun's body began to relax as his logical mind assumed control. Shaun knew that replacing emotion with cold logic was his way of dealing with fear, but that coping mechanism had always served him well.

First, he needed to get warm and then write down exactly what he had experienced before the facts could become colored by emotions. Finally, Shaun pulled himself to his feet. He began slowly and cautiously descending to the ground floor and back to the cottage.

Chapter Ten

Bountiful, California – The Madeira Estate

Maggie was surprised when Sinthia and Mrs. Kleyn had shown up at her tavern with Annie Martin in tow, but Sinthia had assured her that it would be okay. "Annie is Mrs. Kleyn's apprentice; this could be an invaluable learning experience."

"I think Shaun wants to keep this on the down-low," Maggie said.

"I can keep a secret, I promise," Annie had assured her. Maggie had searched Annie's earnest expression and nodded.

Now sitting in front of the closed gate, Maggie felt apprehensive. She pulled out her phone and called Shaun. "We're here," Maggie said when Shaun answered.

"I'll be right there," Shaun said.

Maggie, Sinthia, Annie, and Mrs. Kleyn sat in the dark car and waited for Shaun to drive down and let them in the gate.

Maggie stared at the moonlit landscape and shivered, "It's creepy. We're lucky the moon is out; otherwise, it would be completely dark."

"Thank you for letting me come," Annie said to Maggie.

"Yes, thank you," Sinthia echoed.

"You're welcome," Maggie said. Maggie would have said no, but she knew that Sinthia had a soft spot in her heart for Annie.

Annie had practically grown up in Crescent Bay. She had spent her summers with her grandmother Anastasia Pallas, a long-time resident of Crescent Bay and Sinthia Gnome's closest friend. When Anastasia passed away, she had willed her home to Annie, who moved in and became a full-time resident of Crescent Bay. Maggie thought of her as studious, with her dark brown hair pulled back in a ponytail and inquisitive green eyes. Plus, the fact that she worked in the library only added to that impression.

Car lights lit up the front gates, and Maggie stepped out to greet Shaun. In-ground sensors triggered the gate to roll open as Shaun parked his car.

Shaun walked to Maggie and gathered her into his arms. "I've missed you," he said.

"I've only been gone a day," Maggie said.

"Too long," Shaun insisted, making Maggie laugh.

"Hi Shaun," A voice called from inside Maggie's car, and Shaun waved hello to Sinthia, which is when he saw that Maggie's car was packed.

"Who else did you bring?" Shaun asked as he tried to see who was sitting in the back seat.

"It's Annie Martin," Maggie said.

"Annie? Why?" Shaun asked in confusion.

"Apparently, she is apprenticing with Mrs. Kleyn. She swore herself to secrecy, and Sinthia vouched for her." Shaun searched Maggie's face, and then he nodded. He knew that Maggie would have had a hard time telling Sinthia no.

"An apprentice necromancer?" Shaun said in wonder. "What do you know?" Maggie watched Shaun's face, and she recognized the look on his face.

"Please don't go peppering her with questions," Maggie begged.

"Ah, come on, Maggie," Shaun said.

"There's nothing wrong with asking questions," an older voice called from inside the car. Maggie looked back to see that Mrs. Kleyn had rolled down the car's window. "But, can we ask them somewhere warmer? My body doesn't care for the cold."

"Sorry," Shaun called back. Then he gave Maggie a quick kiss. "Follow me."

Getting back in their cars, they drove back up the driveway, and around the manor, to the cottage. Shaun opened the cottage door and ushered the group into the living room.

"Shaun Morrow, let me introduce you to Mrs. Bridgit Kleyn," Sinthia said.

Shaun extended his hand, "Mrs. Kleyn, it's good to meet you. Thank you for offering to help us."

"It's nice to meet you too, but please let me clarify. I'm not here for you. I'm here to help the spirits who may reside here," Mrs. Kleyn said as she shook his hand.

"Oh?" Shaun asked, startled by the woman's direct statement.

"Yes," Mrs. Kleyn continued. "Some spirits are confused about their current state of being and act out to get our attention. But the majority are merely interested in living their afterlives peacefully and are not our enemies. The problems occur when corporal humans brush up against a spirit and become scared, projecting many of our own fears onto that energy."

"I'm afraid I have to disagree respectfully," Maggie said, surprising Shaun. "We had a run-in with a ghost at the Crescent Bay lighthouse, and he was definitely our enemy."

"Yes, Sinthia told me about that," Mrs. Kleyn said.

When Shaun sent Sinthia a censuring look, Sinthia defended her actions. "I had to tell her, Shaun. I'm good at a lot of the occult stuff, but Mrs. Kleyn is an expert on spirits. You would have asked her if you had the chance."

After a slight pause, Shaun nodded, agreeing, "You're right."

"Anyway," Mrs. Kleyn continued impatiently, "as I was saying. Most spirits are not our enemies; that doesn't mean all, just most. I'll need to go into the manor and see if I can make contact before telling you what you're dealing with here."

"Before you do that, I should let you know that I had an experience last night," Shaun started, but Mrs. Kleyn held up her hand, signaling him to stop.

"I'd rather know as little as possible before I meet the spirit."

"Shaun?" Maggie asked, and Shaun turned a guilty gaze to her. "What happened?"

Shaun looked back to Mrs. Kleyn and then shook his head, "I'll tell you after this is over."

"Why didn't you call me earlier?" Maggie asked, and Shaun's heart clinched when he heard the betrayal in her voice.

"I didn't want you to worry—," he began.

"Worry? Shaun, what happened?" Maggie asked.

"Maggie," Sinthia said quietly, and Maggie turned her eyes to look at the woman she considered the mother of her heart. "Shaun is okay. Whatever he has to tell you can wait. Otherwise, it is going to taint Mrs. Kleyn's reading. You understand, don't you?"

Maggie struggled between her need to know what Shaun had gone through versus finding out the truth behind the mystery of Madeira Manor. "Okay," Maggie said in defeat, "But you aren't off the hook," she said as she shook a finger at Shaun.

"Understood," Shaun said. "Okay, so how do we want to go about this?"

"Annie and I will go through our opening meditation, and then we will walk over to the manor and see if anyone wants to talk to us," Mrs. Kleyn said.

"Alright, what can we do?" Shaun asked.

"Just stay quiet while we get ourselves focused," Mrs. Kleyn said. "Ready, Annie?"

Annie nodded, and the two women settled into the wing chairs in front of the fireplace. Shaun watched as the two women closed their eyes and breathed slowly and deeply. Shaun bit his tongue, his mind filled with questions he couldn't ask. Maggie watched Shaun's face and smiled fondly when she recognized his internal struggle.

Mrs. Kleyn and Annie's eyes opened at the same time, and they rose in unison

"Shaun, would you please let us into the manor?" Mrs. Kleyn asked.

"I disabled the alarm and unlocked the back door before coming down to the gate. Just close any doors you open behind you, and I'll rearm the alarm after you leave," Shaun said.

"Perfect," Mrs. Kleyn said in approval. "We'll be back shortly."

"Wait, what if something happens?" Shaun asked.

"We'll be fine, dear," Mrs. Kleyn said as she laid a gentle hand on his shoulder. Then she paused and looked deeply into his eyes before nodding. "You're a good soul. Don't worry. We walk with the Goddess, and she takes care of her children."

Uncertain how to respond, Shaun nodded and then watched as Annie and Mrs. Kleyn walked out of the cottage closing the door behind them.

"Wow," Shaun said as he turned to smile at Maggie.

"I know. She's intimidating," Maggie said, and Shaun nodded.

"Bridgit is a powerhouse," Sinthia agreed.

Shaun's curiosity wouldn't let him linger by the fireplace, so he wandered over to look out the window at the manor.

"So, what happened last night?" Maggie asked as she walked over to stand by his side.

"I didn't go into the manor," Shaun said defensively.

"Okay. Then, did something happen here in the cottage?"

"No," Shaun said hesitantly.

"You're starting to piss me off," Maggie said in an irritated tone.

"It happened in the lighthouse," Shaun said.

"You went up into that lighthouse? At night?"

"The third-floor lights came on in the manor, and I thought I'd be able to see more from up on the gallery. The haunting seemed to be tied to the manor, so I thought the lighthouse would be safe. I was wrong."

"I told you I'd watched that ball of light travel from the memorial at the lighthouse's base into the manor," Maggie insisted.

"You did, but since the lights inside the manor were on, I figured the ghost was inside the manor. I couldn't just sit here and do nothing," Shaun said, pleading for understanding.

"You two are well-matched," Sinthia interrupted, and Shaun and Maggie turned to face her. "You're both in love with a strong, courageous person who possesses a lot of curiosity. It's hard to stay angry at someone who you understand so intimately. Maggie would have done the same thing."

"True," Maggie said as she smiled ruefully. "Alright, tell us what happened."

When Shaun finished his story, Maggie stood in horrified silence at how close she had come to losing Shaun. She was about to demand that he leave with her immediately when Sinthia asked, "Do you have any residual effects?"

"I feel a little tired, but I didn't sleep much last night."

"I can imagine," Sinthia said. "Would you let me check your energy to ensure nothing was left behind?"

"I guess," Shaun said hesitantly. "What's involved?"

"You just have to relax while I run my hands over your aura to see if anything sticks out. "

"Okay," Shaun said as his curiosity rose, and Sinthia smiled.

"You can ask questions when I'm done, okay?" Sinthia said, and Shaun nodded in agreement. Then, Sinthia took Shaun's hand and pulled him away from the window into the center of the room so she could move freely around his body.

Maggie stood to the side, watching, distracted from her fear by watching Sinthia work. The Gnomes had practically raised Maggie, which meant that she had been exposed to what Sinthia's husband, Tom Gnome, referred to as woo-woo stuff. Nevertheless, Maggie greatly respected Sinthia's abilities and watched avidly as Sinthia closed her eyes and took a few deep breaths. Unconsciously, Maggie's breathing mirrored Sinthia's.

Sinthia's eyes opened, and with a gentle smile, she asked Shaun, "Ready?" With his nod of consent, Sinthia reached forward and began slowly weaving her hands through the air around Shaun's body.

At first, Shaun struggled to keep from smiling, feeling a little silly as Sinthia's hands danced around him. Then, an uncomfortable sensation fluttered through his chest, and Sinthia's hands paused.

"Did you feel that?" Sinthia asked, and Shaun nodded with a look of wonder on his face.

"What did you feel?" Maggie asked.

"An odd tugging feeling, but you didn't touch me," Shaun said.

"I didn't touch your physical body."

"Can I feel?" Maggie asked hesitantly. Maggie had no formal occult training but believed she could sense energy.

Sinthia looked at Shaun. "That's up to you." Shaun nodded, and Sinthia motioned for Maggie to come closer.

"Okay, quick class. First, you need to focus. You're going to close your eyes and take three deep breaths. Breathe in clean blue energy and breath out stress and negativity. See the nasty energy moving out of your body on your exhaled breath to pour onto the floor where it dissolves into nothingness."

"Like I do before a tarot reading," Maggie said, and Sinthia nodded in agreement. Maggie did as Sinthia directed, and when she opened her eyes, the room snapped into the heightened focus that Maggie associated with her trance state.

"Good," Sinthia said when she sensed Maggie's altered state. "What you're going to do is move your hand through the energy of Shaun's aura, searching for anything that catches your attention. Shaun, would you extend your arm?" Shaun did, and Sinthia gestured for Maggie to examine him. Feeling a little self-conscious, Maggie stepped forward and slowly moved her hand around Shaun's extended arm. Sinthia noted that Shaun's shoulders relaxed as his body recognized Maggie's energy. A little more of Shaun's natural shielding dropped, further exposing the abnormality that Sinthia had felt in his chest. To Sinthia, it looked like a piece of slimy seaweed that entered through his chest and exited his back.

Maggie stopped her examination and turned a disappointed face to Sinthia. "I didn't feel anything," she said.

"Nothing?" Sinthia asked incredulously.

"Nothing," Maggie insisted.

"No heat, no colors, or weird impressions?" Sinthia coached.

"I might have felt a little resistance, kind of a thickening of the air around his arm," Maggie said hesitantly.

"That's good. A lot of occult training is learning how to interpret your body's way of presenting the energies you interact with," Sinthia said. "I didn't feel anything unusual around his arms, but I wanted you to get a base reading of what his energy feels like. Now, do the same thing with the energy around his chest."

Maggie and Shaun shared a quick smile before Maggie focused on Shaun's chest. She moved her hand down from his neck across the front of his body, and then her hand froze, and she looked at Sinthia in surprise. "There's something there," Maggie said, and Sinthia nodded in agreement.

"What are you sensing?" Sinthia asked, and Maggie moved her fingers around the odd energy she had discovered hovering over Shaun's chest.

"It feels wrong, like it doesn't belong. I'm not sure how to articulate it," Maggie's fingers stroked and plucked at the aberration. Sinthia watched Shaun's face react to the uncomfortable sensation with an internal grin. Then, after a couple moments, she took pity on him and stopped Maggie's movements.

"Let's give Shaun a break," Sinthia said, and Maggie snatched her hand back when she saw the tight expression on Shaun's face.

"Sorry," she said.

"No, it's okay. It was just an odd feeling," Shaun said, reassuring her.

"So, what did you feel?" Sinthia asked Maggie.

"Like something was sticking out of his chest."

"Good," Sinthia said, turning back to Shaun. "Ready for another go? This might be a bit more uncomfortable."

"What are you going to do?" Shaun asked hesitantly.

"We will attempt to remove whatever is stuck through your chest. I can tell you more about it after we pull it." Shaun looked nervous, but he nodded his head, and Sinthia stepped next to Maggie.

"Now, see if you can grasp the energy in your hand, and when you do, you're going to gently pull it from his body," Sinthia said.

"I'm going to do what?" Maggie said as she stepped back and put her hands behind her back. "I don't think I'm ready for anything like that," she insisted.

"Unfortunately, about 90% of learning the occult is on-the-job training. You trust me, don't you?" Sinthia asked, and Maggie nodded her head. "Then let me show you what to do. This is a good skill to have. Take a moment to refocus, then reach back into his aura and grasp the bit of ick."

"Ick?" Shaun asked as he stared down at his chest, looking for the offending energy.

"Ick," Sinthia confirmed. Maggie repeated the breathing exercise to focus herself, and when she opened her eyes, Sinthia continued. "Now reach out and see if you can grasp it." Maggie reached forward tentatively, searching for the nastiness that she had felt before, and when she found it, she smiled as she wrapped her hand around it. "Good," Sinthia said. "Now, gently pull it out of Shaun's body." Maggie slowly pulled her hand away from Shaun's body and Shaun's breath caught. The sensation was nauseating, and Shaun struggled not to react so that he wouldn't interrupt what Maggie was doing. Maggie felt the negative energy detach from Shaun's body with a slight tug. She looked in wonder at the empty air below her clenched fist.

"What do I do now?" Maggie asked.

"You need to dispose of it responsibly, so you're going to cast it toward the ground and visualize it neutralizing and disintegrating into nothingness," Sinthia said.

Maggie threw her arm toward the ground as she opened her hand and visualized the offending ick being obliviated.

"Nicely done," a voice said from behind Maggie, and she turned to see that Mrs. Kleyn and Annie had returned.

"Thank you," Maggie said.

"How do you feel, Shaun?" Sinthia asked.

"It was a little uncomfortable when she pulled the ick out, but now I don't feel anything. What do you think that was?" Shaun asked.

"I think the spirit you interacted with left a leech in your aura which was feasting on your energy," Sinthia said.

"A leech?" Shaun said in disgust as he smoothed his shirt over where Maggie had pulled the energy away from his body.

"Perhaps not an actual leech, but that is what it was doing. It leeched off a little of your energy and channeled it toward the spirit. It may not have been intentional, but that is what it was doing," Sinthia said.

Mrs. Kleyn shut the front door and walked across the room to settle into one of the wing chairs. "Shaun, I'm ready to hear about your interaction with the spirit."

Shaun shared his story, and when he was finished, Mrs. Kleyn closed her eyes, leaned back into her chair, and said, "Hmmm."

Shaun struggled to be patient, but he was dying to know what Mrs. Kleyn and Annie had found in the manor. As he shifted from foot to foot, the wooden floor beneath his feet gave a gentle creak, and Mrs. Kleyn cracked open one eye to look at him. Shaun froze and offered her an apologetic smile.

Mrs. Kleyn turned her head to address Sinthia, "Whatever walks in the manor was not interested in speaking to us tonight."

"The space was empty?" Sinthia asked.

"Not completely," Mrs. Kleyn said. "We met George on the staircase to the third floor."

Maggie was startled by the sharp sting of tears in her eyes. She lowered her lashes, hoping no one would notice, but Mrs. Kleyn felt her energy shift. "Don't hide your tears, girl. There's no shame in grieving for those we've lost."

"Is George trapped here?" Shaun asked in a horrified whisper.

"No, he was just confused," Mrs. Kleyn. "We explained that he had taken a tumble and suggested he move on. Once he understood, the rest was easy. He had loved ones waiting for him, and they helped him cross the veil."

Maggie wiped the tears from her cheeks. "Thank you," she said to Mrs. Kleyn, who nodded.

"So, besides George, there weren't any other spirits in the house?" Sinthia asked.

"None that wanted to talk to us," Mrs. Kleyn said. "I'd love to go up to the lighthouse gallery, but these legs won't let me climb that many stairs; instead, I think I'd like to look at Mrs. Madeira's grave."

"We can do that," Shaun said. "Let me grab a couple of flashlights."

When Shaun returned, he led the small party out to the gravesite of Mrs. Madeira. The group stood silently for so long that Shaun was startled when Mrs. Kleyn said, "There you are. Do you see her, Annie?"

"I don't," Annie admitted.

"It's okay. Her energy is a little weak. Just relax and open yourself up a little more. I'll see if I can give her a little boost."

Shaun's flashlight dimmed, and Shaun found himself blinking his eyes, trying to clear his vision as a faint green mist formed over the grave.

"I see her," Annie said in wonder.

"Good," Mrs. Kleyn said.

Shaun watched as the green mist drifted and flowed into a human shape. He tensed, wondering if this was the same mist that had attacked him the night before. Shaun glanced at Maggie and saw she looked scared. He moved closer to her, uncertain how he could protect her but prepared to try.

"Are you Mrs. Madeira?" Mrs. Kleyn asked.

Shaun thought that Mrs. Kleyn must have received a response because she nodded before continuing. "My name is Mrs. Kleyn, and this is my apprentice Annie Martin. It is good to meet you." Mrs. Kleyn's expressive face told Shaun that she was listening intently to something he couldn't hear.

Shaun gasped in pain, dropping his flashlight as the bulb blew and it became too hot to hold. The mist shot from the monument into the manor, and the lights on the third floor popped on.

"Are you okay?" Maggie asked Shaun, who was clutching his hand to his chest.

"I think so," Shaun said as he cradled his throbbing hand.

"Bridget?" Sinthia asked, and Mrs. Kleyn turned a pale face to her.

"I'm okay," Mrs. Kleyn said. "Annie?"

"I'm good. I just feel a little drained," Annie said.

"Let's go inside, and I'll make us some tea," Shaun offered, and everyone trooped back into the cottage.

"Before we talk about what just happened, I'd like everyone to write about their experience. That will keep us from tainting each other's memories. Are you okay with that?" Shaun asked. Everyone nodded, and Shaun passed out notebooks and pens. Shaun finished writing his recognitions of the evening's events, then rose and headed to the kitchen to make tea.

Shaun put a kettle on the stove and pulled down a large teapot. The sound of a foot scraping across the floor made him turn to see Maggie standing behind him. "All done?" he asked, and Maggie nodded.

"I thought you could use some help," Maggie said as she opened the cupboard to pull out some teacups. Shaun stood and watched Maggie arrange five teacups and a small container of sugar and cream on a tray. "Do you have any cookies?" Maggie asked.

"A few, they're in the pantry," Shaun said, and he watched as Maggie pulled the box out of the pantry and placed a cookie on each of the tea cup's saucers. Shaun waited until she finished before he asked, "What happened at the lighthouse? You looked scared."

"She just looked so angry," Maggie said.

"You saw her?" Shaun asked.

"You didn't?"

"No. I saw a green mist but no features."

"Well, I did, and she was livid." Shaun searched Maggie's face. When she said nothing else, he decided to give her time to process what she had experienced. He poured the boiling water through the teapot's tea strainer before capping it and placing it on the tray Maggie had prepared. He wrapped a towel around the teapot to keep it warm and picked up the tray before addressing Maggie, "Let's go find out what everyone else saw."

Shaun placed the tray on the coffee table and began to pour everyone a cup; then, he settled down and looked at Mrs. Kleyn. "Would you like to begin?"

"Actually, I'd be more interested in hearing what everyone else saw first. Annie?" Mrs. Kleyn said.

"Oh," Annie said, looking surprised, "okay." She paused for a moment gathering her thoughts, and then she began. "At first, there wasn't anything there; then I saw a green mist form. It became solid, and I saw a woman. I assume it was Mrs. Madeira."

"Did you hear her speak?" Mrs. Kleyn asked, and Annie shook her head no.

"I saw her lips moving, but I couldn't hear what she was saying." Annie looked disappointed, and Mrs. Kleyn smiled gently. "It's okay. Her energy was fairly weak. Sinthia, what did you see?"

"Necromancy is not one of my skills, as you know," Sinthia said to Mrs. Kleyn, who nodded that she understood. "I saw kind of a weird distortion, kind of like heat rising off the desert. It did have a green tint, but I didn't see anything beyond that, and I didn't hear anything except you asking questions."

"Shaun?" Mrs. Kleyn asked.

"Pretty much the same, although the mist did get a little thicker as I watched, plus it assumed a vaguely humanoid shape. I also didn't hear anything but you asking questions. Do you think it was the same mist that attacked me the other night?"

"Perhaps," Mrs. Kleyn said. Then she turned to look at Maggie, "And you?"

Maggie blew out a stressed breath before answering. "I saw the mist. It formed into a pretty solid-looking woman, and although I couldn't hear what she was saying, I could tell she was pissed."

"You're right; she did look angry," Annie said. "What did you see, Mrs. Kleyn?"

"My experience mirrors a lot of what you all saw. The energy manifested as a green mist that coalesced into a woman's specter. We spoke, and when I asked her if she was Mrs. Madeira, she looked confused and told me that she was searching for someone."

"Did she say who?" Shaun asked, and Mrs. Kleyn shook her head no.

"No. Her energy was very agitated and scattered. So I tried to boost it."

"Is that what happened with my flashlight?" Shaun asked.

"Sort of. I pulled energy from the earth to channel to her, but it wasn't enough. So she took it upon herself to grab the power from the batteries in your flashlight."

"Did she seem angry to you?" Annie asked.

"As we've spoken about before, you must be careful about assigning motives to the spirits you contact. Projecting our issues onto their actions can taint our interactions with them."

"Is she dangerous?" Sinthia asked.

Mrs. Kleyn took a slow sip of her tea and gazed into the fire. To Shaun, it looked like she was gathering her thoughts. "I'm not sure," she finally said.

"What about what happened to George?" Maggie asked.

"I don't think that Mrs. Madeira is responsible for what happened to George—" Maggie started to interrupt, but Mrs. Kleyn held up her hand. "She may have been a catalyst, but I don't think she pushed him down those stairs."

Maggie thought that Mrs. Kleyn was splitting hairs. If Mrs. Madeira had chased George onto that staircase and he fell, wasn't she responsible for his tumble? Maggie wondered if Mrs. Kleyn was a little too pro-spook.

"I don't want to leave her in this state," Mrs. Kleyn said. "It is my life's work to watch after spirits, and this one is in pain. So I'd like to come back and see if I can contact her when she is in a more receptive frame of mind. How long are you here for Shaun?"

"About a week."

"I shouldn't need more than a couple of days. I want to do some research before we try again. Thank you for the tea, Shaun," Mrs. Kleyn said as she stood up.

"That's it?" Maggie asked, surprised. "What about Shaun? Is he safe staying here?"

Mrs. Kleyn turned to study Shaun's face, and Shaun struggled to not squirm under her scrutiny. She must have been satisfied with what she saw because she nodded. "Shaun's a smart man. I think that he can keep himself out of dangerous situations. No more ghost hunting while you're here," she finished, shaking her finger at Shaun. "You'll just confuse her more. Understood?"

"Understood," Shaun said.

"Good. Come on, Annie. Come on, Sinthia. Let's give Shaun and Maggie a moment," Mrs. Kleyn said as she moved toward the front door. Annie and Sinthia thanked Shaun for the tea and followed Mrs. Kleyn out of the cottage.

Shaun looked at Maggie's worried expression, "Maggie, I have to stay. I'll do my job and keep my head down. No more searching for ghosts. I promise."

Maggie nodded reluctantly. Shaun gathered her into his arms and kissed her.

"I love you, Maggie."

"I love you too."

Chapter Eleven

Bountiful, California – The Madeira Estate

Shaun waved goodbye to Maggie from the steps of the cottage. As her car's tail lights disappeared around the side of the manor, his gaze moved upward to the still-illuminated lights on the manor's third floor. The temptation to investigate was intense, but he had promised Maggie that he would not do anything beyond what his job required. He walked back into the cottage and froze. He had to turn the alarm in the manor on.

He hesitated, torn between his promise to Maggie and leaving the manor unprotected overnight. Then he decided. He'd just open the front door, step into the foyer, enter the code to arm the system, and leave. In. Out. Done.

Shaun retrieved a flashlight and walked to the front of the manor. Feeling a little shaky, he pushed open the manor door and walked to the alarm panel.

After George's death, Shaun had read the manual for the alarm to familiarize himself with the system. The light was yellow, which meant that the alarm was off. He typed in the code and turned to rush out the front door, expecting the light to turn green and a series of beeps to signal that the alarm was activating. Instead, a long beep sounded, and the light remained yellow.

"What the heck?" Shaun said out loud as he looked at the offending buttons. He typed in the code a second time with the same results. Confused, Shaun swung open the panel that covered the keypad and looked at a series of buttons. The buttons were labeled with the names of different rooms, and each had an LED indicator showing its status. One button was unlit, signifying that the alarm was not active in that room. Shaun cringed when he saw it was one of the fourth-floor bedrooms.

Mrs. Kleyn and Annie must have left the door open, Shaun thought. Cringing, Shaun accepted that he had no choice but to go upstairs. If he was lucky, he could get upstairs, close the door and return downstairs without the need to confess his transgression to Maggie. His logical mind argued that he had been entrusted with the alarm code to ensure the manor was kept safe, so this was a part of his job. Thus, he wasn't really breaking his word, but he knew that argument wouldn't fly with Maggie.

Ascending the curving staircase, Shaun crept down the hall to the panel that hid the stairwell to the third and fourth floors. Clicking on his flashlight, Shaun ascended the stairs to the fourth floor.

When he opened the door to the fourth floor, he paused to look down the hallway and froze when he saw the hall illuminate and then dim. When the cycle repeated, he understood and sagged against the door jam in relief. The lighthouse's beam was causing the hallway to illuminate and then dim as it swept past the open bedroom windows. The pulsing of the lighthouse beam made him think of a heartbeat, and the imagery of the lighthouse acting like a beating heart for Madeira Manor appealed to his bardic soul. Shaun smiled as he crept quietly down the hallway to the open door.

The fourth floor had been the domain of the live-in servants of Madeira Manor. It consisted of eight tiny bedrooms that were barely large enough to hold a twin-sized bed and a nightstand. Shaun closed the open door and turned back to the stairwell only to freeze when a floorboard creaked under his foot. In the mortuary-like silence of the empty manor, the quiet creak sounded like a scream of pain. He stared in horror at his offending foot as his senses heightened, searching for any reaction from the ghosts that walked the hall below. The house remained silent.

Sighing in relief, Shaun looked up and startled in surprise. Floating in the doorway to the stairwell was a semi-transparent female form. Shaun could see she was a young woman with carefully coiffed shoulder-length hair and a flowing dress. The dress moved as though caressed by a breeze that Shaun could not feel. The specter's lips moved, and in Shaun's head, he heard a woman's voice, "Have you seen George?" Shaun struggled to make his vocal cords work, but all he could manage was a barely whispered, "No."

The ghost seemed to have heard him just fine because the voice in Shaun's head said, "Will you please find him and ask him to attend me in my study?"

Shaun nodded that he would, and he felt relieved when the specter turned away and stepped down the stairs. *Poor George*, Shaun thought.

"What?" asked the woman's voice in his head as the specter spun around to face him again.

Shaun shook his head and began to back away from the advancing ghost.

"What happened to George?" The voice in his head screamed.

Shaun's hands flew up to clutch his skull in pain. Ice-cold fingers were stabbing into his brain, searching for something. Shaun fell to his knees, still clutching his head, as an agonized woman's scream split the unnatural silence. Shaun watched through squinted eyes as the specter's well-heeled visage transformed into a woman so emaciated that she looked like a walking skeleton dressed in a hospital gown. The carefully coiffed hair had been replaced by a few greasy strands that whipped around the woman's screaming face as though she stood in a raging storm. Her crazed eyes landed on Shaun's kneeling form, and she reached out bony fingers tipped with ragged nails, and the storm that seemed to surround the ghost rushed down the hallway to engulf Shaun's form.

"Here you go, my love," a male voice said as a man's face swam into focus. The man was older with piercing icy-blue eyes and closely cut silver hair. Shaun recognized Mr. Madeira. Although Mr. Madeira was smiling, Shaun felt himself trying to shrink away, but his body refused to move. Mr. Madeira reached out to lift Shaun's head and place a fluffy pillow beneath it. While smiling with his lips but not his eyes, Mr. Madeira continued, "Now you can see your lighthouse better." He stepped aside and gestured grandly to the window directly across from Shaun's bed. Shaun's eyes twitched from the face of Mr. Madeira to look out the window, and he saw the Madeira lighthouse framed by the window. In shock, Shaun realized he was experiencing a moment in Mrs. Madeira's life.

"Sir?" another man's voice called, and Shaun tried to turn to see who had spoken, which was when he realized that the only body part he could move was his eyes.

"In here," Mr. Madeira said, and the man stepped into the room to stand at the foot of Mrs. Madeira's bed. Shaun looked at a much younger version of the man who had died so tragically just days ago, George.

"Ma'am," George said respectfully before turning to address Mr. Madeira. "I'm sorry to bother you, sir, but there is a call for you."

"Thank you, George," Mr. Madeira said dismissively. "I'll be right down."

"Thank you, sir. Ma'am," George said to Mrs. Madeira and then left.

"I have to tend to business, but I'll be back to share dinner with you," Mr. Madeira said as he reached out a hand to grasp Mrs. Madeira's ankle in a bruising grip. Mr. Madeira watched his wife's face closely as his grip tightened and the pain became sharp and world-consuming. Unable to move or defend himself, Shaun felt tears roll down his cheeks in reaction. "You're leaking," Mr. Madeira said in a solicitous tone that denied his responsibility for the pain. Finally, he released Mrs. Madeira's abused ankle, and the pain decreased to a fierce throbbing. "Here," Mr. Madeira said as he pulled a tissue out of the box on the table next to her hospital bed to dab at her tears. Throwing the tissue away, Mr. Madeira leaned over to kiss her forehead, "Enjoy the view." He said before he left the room. Through tear-blurred eyes, Mrs. Madeira stared out her window at the lighthouse, and the statue of the lighthouse keeper stared back.

Shaun awoke to darkness on a hard surface. "Shit," Shaun said as he reached out, trying to figure out where he was, and his hand settled on a metal cylinder, his flashlight. Shaun snatched it up like a life preserver in a dark sea. He clicked the button on, and a dim beam of light illuminated a wall. Shaun swept the beam around, and he remembered that he was on the fourth floor of Madeira Manor. He turned the feeble beam toward the staircase, fearful of what it might expose, but all it showed was the empty staircase. Shaun tried to stand up, but his leg bucked under him when he put weight on his right ankle. Shaun leaned against the wall with a hiss and pulled up his pant leg to see what was wrong with his ankle. His ankle was swollen and ringed by dark red welts. Shaun reached down and matched his fingers to each red blotch as he thought about Mr. Madeira's crushing grip.

Leaning against the wall for support, Shaun limped back to the dark staircase and began his descent. He moved as quietly as possible, praying for safety all the way to the ground floor. He paused in front of the alarm keypad, verified that all the buttons were lit, typed in the alarm code, and limped to the front door as the warning beeps sounded. Outside, he sagged against one of the front door columns and thought about what he had just survived. Mr. Madeira's abuse of his wife was so casual that it felt routine. One didn't achieve that level of indifference to causing another pain unless it was a frequent occurrence. What Shaun had just experienced exposed Mr. Madeira in a different light than the one George had cast of the master of the house as a doting husband.

Shaun straightened up and limped down the porch stairs and back to the cottage, worrying about what he should confess to Maggie.

Chapter Twelve

Between Labor Day and the Autumnal Equinox, the number of tourists in Crescent Bay dwindled. The villagers would breathe a sigh of relief, relishing the short pause before the village's most profitable season, Halloween.

Annie Martin turned on the coffee maker and smiled as she watched her tenant Vince Andreas exit the garden cottage he rented from her. He was walking his cat Raye, a black Scottish Fold with silver stripes on a harness. Vince was a tall man with black hair cut short in a buzz cut and intense green eyes. Annie was admiring his athletic build when Vince spied her and raised his hand in a wave. He and Raye walked out of the garden gate. *He's probably headed to Java Junction,* Annie thought.

"Nice view," a voice said, and Annie's face flushed from being caught watching Vince. Mrs. Kleyn stood in the doorway to Annie's kitchen with a knowing smile.

"It is," Annie said with a grin. "Would you like a cup of coffee?"

"I would," Mrs. Kleyn said as she lowered herself into a seat at the kitchen table. "How are you and Vince getting along?"

Vince wasn't just Annie's tenant; he was also the Fetch for a witchcraft tradition known as Duchas. As the Fetch, his job was to make sure the deeper tradition-specific teachings and the identities of those who belonged to the tradition remained secret.

Annie's grandmother Anastasia had been an elder of the Duchas tradition, and Annie had been her apprentice. Unfortunately, before Annie's training could begin in earnest, Anastasia passed away. As stubborn in death as she had been in life, Anastasia had remained in the house, determined to complete her granddaughter's training. Vince and Sinthia had gone to bat for Annie, insisting that she be allowed to complete her training. Mrs. Kleyn had joined their cause, and the council had approved the unorthodox arrangement. Now Annie received training from her grandmother's spirit with the assistance of Mrs. Kleyn, Sinthia, and Vince. Annie knew that Vince reported her progress back to the council. Still, she understood that his supervision allowed her to continue training with her beloved grandmother.

"Vince and I are doing well," Annie said as she placed a cup of coffee in front of Mrs. Kleyn.

"Good. He and Raye are a hoot," Mrs. Kleyn said as she poured cream into her coffee and stirred. "Raye sure keeps your brownie busy. I caught him sneaking her cat treats yesterday."

The family brownie was another part of Annie's inheritance from her grandmother, and although Annie had never seen the brownie, she had seen him in action. Things would move without visible hands, and sounds filled the air without an obvious source. A brownie was a type of fae that adopted a family and performed acts of service. Annie wasn't sure what services the brownie did for her family, but her grandmother had always admonished her to treat him with respect and offerings of whiskey upon their ancestral altar.

Raye and the brownie were quite fond of each other, and Vince had complained that the brownie had begun to play mischievous tricks on him, such as hiding his keys, jewelry, and tv remotes. Vince's day job as a paranormal reporter paid the bills while he traveled the country as the tradition's Fetch. The brownie seemed to know when Vince was on a tight writing deadline and would throw Raye's ball over Vince's computer's keyboard. Causing Raye to type gibberish as she scrambled across the desk in a mad rush to capture the ball. Vince would yell in frustration, and Raye would give him such a reproachful look that Vince would lose even more valuable time making up for his misplaced frustration. Now, when Vince had a pressing deadline, he would adjourn to Java Junction as the Brownie seemed hesitant to leave Annie's property.

"I'm glad they get along," Annie said. "I can't imagine the chaos if they didn't."

Mrs. Kleyn hooted at the idea of Raye and the Brownie at odds, "That would be truly terrifying."

"Speaking of terrifying, what do you think about Shaun's interaction with the spirit at that lighthouse?" Annie asked.

"I'm not sure. All we have to go on is Shaun's side of the story. I wish the spirits of the manor had been more open to speaking with us. Still, we did help George cross over, so the trip was not entirely wasted."

"True. George seemed like such a sweet soul. I'm glad that he is at peace. Although we didn't see any other spirits, it still felt like someone else was lurking in the background," Annie said.

"Yes. I felt the type of vibration that usually signifies a spirit is present. Particularly on the third floor."

"Agreed," Annie said. "Those rooms on the third floor made my skin crawl. Why do you think the spirit didn't want to talk to us?"

"It could be for various reasons. They may be timid or not have enough energy to interact with us. Plus, sometimes we are aware of them, but they are unaware of us. If Shaun had not had that interaction, I might have believed that the energy we felt was residual instead of active."

"Do you think Grandma might know what is happening with the spirits at Madeira Manor?" Annie asked.

"I doubt it. Spirits don't become omnipresent just because they leave their corporeal bodies."

"Should we ask Grandma to go with us to the manor?" Annie asked.

Mrs. Kleyn paused to mull over Annie's suggestion before shaking her head. "I don't think that would be a good idea. Considering the tone of Maggie and Shaun's interactions, I'd say the spirits are territorial and confused. Adding an unknown entity to the mix might agitate them even more."

"Spirits? Plural?" Annie asked.

"We cannot be certain that Shaun and Maggie interacted with the same spirit. For all we know, multiple spirits reside at Madeira Manor."

"That makes sense," Annie agreed. "What do you think we should do next?"

"We need to do a little more research to figure out how to connect with the spirits. What time do you go into the library?"

"I open today, so 9:00," Annie said.

"Good. I'll walk in with you if that's okay. You can help me with a little of the research."

"Helping patrons with their research is my job," Annie said with a smile.

Shaun peeled his eyes open to look at the clock and groaned. 6:00 am. He calculated that he had managed about three hours of broken sleep. Sitting up, he looked at his foot and winced at the dark purple blotches encircling his ankle. He twisted it to see how tender it was and grimaced at the painful feedback he received. There was no way he would be climbing up and down the lighthouse staircase today. Shaun's mind raced as he tried to figure out how he could continue making progress on the bid with a bum ankle. Finally, he decided to spend the day firming up quotes from vendors, which meant he'd be heading to 1906 Renovation's office in Crescent Bay.

He contemplated making himself a cup of tea but decided he'd rather have a strong cup of coffee from Java Junction.

As Shaun drove down the mountain, he noticed that the farther away he got from the manor, the more his mood improved. He hadn't realized how oppressive the energy at Madeira Manor was.

Shaun parked in front of the 1906 Renovation office, which shared a building with A Peace of the 70s, a gift shop specializing in trinkets and goodies from the hippy era. He smiled at the store's window display which featured oversized smiling daisies and neon-colored banners promoting peace and grooviness. Leaving his briefcase in the trunk, he locked his car and made the short walk to Java Junction.

The smell of good coffee greeted Shaun even before Java Junction came into view. Shaun hoped that the line for coffee wasn't too long this morning, and he was happy to see that the line was short enough to fit inside the building. On some mornings, the line stretched as long as twenty people deep.

When he opened the cafe door, he was met with calls of greeting, which he returned with smiles and nods. Living in a small village where the locals recognized you was pleasant. But, the price for living in such a small village was that everyone knew your private business. For example, in Crescent Bay, gossip was elevated to a cherished tradition known as The Scuttlebutt.

Historically, a scuttlebutt was the freshwater barrel sailors drank from on a ship. The villagers liked to think of the scuttlebutt as the original water cooler around which people gathered to swap news. So, in a nod to the village's nautical history, they had named their gossip chain in its honor. Shaun smiled and let the buzz of conversations drift around him, content with his life. When it was his turn, he stepped forward and smiled at Heather.

"Hi Shaun, I'm surprised to see you here. I thought you were up at the Madeira place," Heather said.

"I was, but I needed to contact some of our vendors for quotes, so I came down to do some work in the office," Shaun said.

"Maggie was in earlier," Heather said, and Shaun looked surprised.

"Really? That's pretty early for her," Shaun said.

"I said the same thing. I guess she had a rough night sleeping last night. So she ordered two large coffees to jump-start her day."

"It must be in the air because I'll do the same. Can I please have two large lattes?" Shaun asked. "Make one of them extra hot so I can drink it later."

"Will do," Heather said as she processed his purchase, labeled his cups, and placed them at the end of the queue of empty cups. Shaun stepped aside and joined the crowd awaiting their coffee orders. Shaun smiled at Heather's assistant Jennifer as she worked the knobs and dials on a large brass coffee maker, which she had named Big Brass Betty. Jennifer was very proud of her coffee maker. She kept it polished and in perfect working order; in fact, she was the one who had named the coffee maker.

"Sounds like you and Maggie are having a hard time sleeping apart," a voice stated, and Shaun turned to see Mrs. Johnson, an older villager who was grinning up at him. "That's nice," she said.

Shaun smiled at Mrs. Johnson, uncertain how to respond.

"My husband Jack and I never slept apart for over 30 years. I still have some rough nights, and he passed away over ten years ago."

"I'm sure Samuel helps you get to sleep," another elderly woman said to Mrs. Johnson with a wink. Mrs. Johnson chortled and blushed before replying, "That's true." Shaun smiled as the two women continued to swap bawdy quips.

One by one, the group shrank until Heather called Shaun's name.

"Thanks, Heather," Shaun said as he retrieved his cups. A chorus of goodbyes sang out as Shaun pushed the doors open and stepped out. He raised one of his coffee cups in a salute and returned to the office with a smile.

A couple of hours later, he was surprised when he lifted his cup and found it empty. Glancing at the office clock, he stood up and stretched. It was too early for lunch, but he needed a break as his brain was swimming with vendor information and repair quotes. Then, a movement drew his eye to the store's front window. Shaun laughed when he spied Mrs. Stanley, the owner of A Peace of the 70s, pulling a scarecrow prop dressed in hippy attire from her van. Halloween was rapidly approaching, and Shaun's adopted town was about to become consumed by the joy of the holiday. That was when he remembered the book he had purchased in Bountiful, *Lighthouses of Horror!* Unfortunately, he'd left the book at Madeira Manor, so he'd have to wait until he returned to see what tales it had to tell. However, that didn't mean he couldn't do some research.

Annie's grandmother Anastasia had worked at the Crescent Bay library for decades. During her tenure, the library had grown from a few shelves of children's books and best sellers located in a spare room at City Hall to a dedicated two-story building with meeting rooms and computers for patrons to use.

The automatic doors swished open, and Shaun felt his shoulders relax as familiar smells rushed to greet him. He had spent many hours of his life happily entrapped in the spells woven into the pages of various texts. With a smile, he approached the front desk where Marie sat. After Anastasia had passed away, Marie was promoted to head librarian.

"Hi Marie," he said.

"Hi, Shaun. What can we do for you today?" Marie asked.

"I need to do a little research on Madeira Manor," he said.

"I heard you were looking into renovating their lighthouse. Pretty strange having a lighthouse up on a mountain," Marie said. "Some say it's haunted too."

Shaun knew that Marie was fishing for something juicy for the Scuttlebutt. Still, he didn't feel that it would be professional to say anything that might seem derogatory about the Madeira property, so he responded neutrally. "It's a beautiful lighthouse; it just needs a little TLC."

"You did such a good job with our lighthouse. I'm sure the Madeira lighthouse will be stunning when you're done."

"Thank you. I'm off to do some research," Shaun said in parting.

"If I can be of assistance, please let me know," Marie said, and with a smile, Shaun turned away to weave his way through the racks to claim a table by placing his briefcase down and spreading out his papers and pens.

"Hi Shaun," a voice said, and Shaun looked up to see Annie striding toward him.

"Good morning," he replied.

"I'm surprised to see you here," Annie said. "I thought you'd still be at the manor."

With a quick look around the room to ensure they were alone, Shaun pulled up his pant leg to show Annie the ring of bruises encircling his ankle.

Annie looked shocked, "Oh my god, what happened?"

"I had another run-in with the ghost."

"After we left last night?" Annie asked, and Shaun nodded. "Hang on," Annie said, and Shaun waited patiently while he wondered what she was doing. Annie returned with Mrs. Kleyn in tow.

"Mrs. Kleyn, good morning," Shaun said.

"Good morning," Mrs. Kleyn answered. "Annie said that you had another encounter with the spirit."

"I did," Shaun said as he raised his pant leg again to show Mrs. Kleyn his bruised ankle. She hissed in sympathy.

"Nasty," Mrs. Kleyn said as Shaun dropped his pant leg, hiding the dark purple blemish. "Annie, have a seat. Shaun, tell us what happened."

In hushed tones, Shaun told Annie and Mrs. Kleyn about his time as Mrs. Madeira and how he had returned from his vision with an injured ankle.

Mrs. Kleyn sat back in her chair with an introspective look on her face, "It sounds like Mrs. Madeira has a story to tell," she said

"Ya think?" Shaun asked with a chuckle, and Mrs. Kleyn sent him an admonishing look. Grinning, Shaun continued, "I'm here to research the manor's history to see if I can understand what's going on."

Mrs. Kleyn smiled in approval and nodded her head. "That's a good idea and one we've already started on. You can help us. Annie, go get the books you brought me, and we'll spread out here with Shaun."

"Do you need some help?" Shaun asked Annie, and she shook her head no.

"I have them on a trolley. Have a seat, and I'll be right back," she said.

Annie returned with a cart filled with library books, magazines, and newspapers. Shaun rose to help her unload and was disappointed to see that *Lighthouses of Horror!* was not a part of the collection. "Do you have a copy of *Lighthouses of Horror!*?" Shaun asked.

"No," Annie said with a look of confusion. "I didn't see that one listed in the book catalog. Do you know the author?"

"I don't. It's a book I picked up at a store in Bountiful, but I left it at the cottage."

"Sorry. It's probably self-published, so we wouldn't have a copy unless someone donated it," Annie said with an apologetic smile.

"That's okay, I'm planning on heading back up tomorrow morning, so I'll read it then. Have you found anything interesting?" Shaun asked.

"Not much," Annie said. "There are a couple of books that include stories about Mr. Madeira and how he built his wealth."

"Do they mention his wife?" Shaun asked.

"Not in depth. They primarily talk about how dedicated Mr. Madeira was to her and how he personally nursed her after her fall until her death. They make him sound like a loving and doting husband, a narrative that isn't supported by the experience you had last night," Mrs. Kleyn said.

"George mentioned that Mr. Madeira had dementia toward the end of his life; do they mention that?" Shaun asked.

"Really? I haven't seen any mention of it," Annie said in surprise.

"Well, he didn't call it that, but from what he said, I just assumed that was what it was," Shaun said.

"What did he say?" Mrs. Kleyn asked.

"He said that after Mrs. Madeira died, he would talk to her, insisting that she was in the room with him. He said that she was tormenting him..." Shaun tapered off as a look of wonder crossed his face. "Do you think Mrs. Madeira was haunting him?"

"It's possible," Mrs. Kleyn said.

"Wow, that must have been so frustrating for him. Imagine you can see a ghost, but no one else believes you and thinks you're losing your mind. Damn," Shaun said.

"Many mediums have ended up in asylums or medicated," Mrs. Kleyn said. "From what you've said and from what we've read, it sounds like there are two histories for Mr. Madeira, a public one and a private one."

"I think we should dig into some of the less than official history sources to piece together the truth," Annie said. "As a wealthy businessman, Mr. Madeira would have hosted a lot of parties. I'll go through the back issues of newspapers and magazines and see what the gossip columnists have to say."

Hours later, Shaun's stomach growled to remind him that the only food he had consumed that day was two cups of coffee. He looked up from the magazine he was reading to offer an apologetic smile to Annie and Mrs. Kleyn. "Sorry, I skipped breakfast this morning."

"And lunch," Mrs. Kleyn said as she glanced at her wristwatch. "Why don't we break for the day? My eyes are tired anyway. Annie and I can do a little more research tomorrow."

"I'll be back at the manor. Call me if you find anything," Shaun said, and Annie nodded.

"We should be ready to come back up in a day or two," Mrs. Kleyn said.

Shaun hesitated as he thought about his injury, "I'm not sure that's a good idea."

"Shaun, for you, spirits are an oddity. Something to dabble in. But as necromancers, it is our soul's calling to see that spirits are respected and helped when possible," Mrs. Kleyn said.

"I'm not sure the ghosts at Madeira Manor can be helped," Shaun said.

"I'm not sure there are ghosts at Madeira Manor," Mrs. Kleyn said, and when Shaun looked confused, she continued. "For us, a ghost is a memory that is locked into a place or item, but a spirit is a sentient soul that is earthbound either by choice or mishap."

Shaun could feel his curiosity gearing up, but his stomach growled, so he tamped it down. "Let me think about it, okay?" Shaun asked.

Mrs. Kleyn shrugged, and Shaun could tell that she wouldn't take no for an answer. Mentally exhausted from all the research, Shaun decided to delay this fight until another day. "I'll be in touch."

Chapter Thirteen

Crescent Bay, California – Foghorn Tavern

Shaun needed time alone to process all that had transpired over the last few days. So instead of walking through the Foghorn Tavern, he climbed the private stairs in the alleyway behind the tavern to the rooms he and Maggie shared.

Excited yips greeted him as Shaun opened the door. "Hi, my little pirates," Shaun said as Anne Bonny and Jack jumped up on him, yipping in greeting. "How about a little walk and then a nap?" Shaun asked as he retrieved their leashes from a hook by the front door and clicked them onto their collars. Shaun let the dogs lead him down the steps and into the tavern's alley. The dogs pulled him from place to place to sniff and pee in various spots. Shaun smiled when he thought of how Maggie referred to this process as responding to their P-Mail.

As the dogs took care of their P-mail, Shaun's mind struggled to organize everything he had read in the library. Sorting through what felt like a flood of useless information from all the articles he had read that morning, searching for anything relevant to the haunting: expensive parties, fancy dresses, society gossip, and kudos for Mr. Madeira from the art world. Articles talked extensively about how Mr. Madeira built a successful real estate empire and became an acclaimed artist later in life. Apparently, after his wife's fall, Mr. Madeira devoted time to tending her with love and devotion. But unfortunately, not much was written about Mrs. Madeira.

Exhausted, Shaun told the dogs that it was snack time and laughed when they reversed course pulling him back toward the stairs yipping with anticipation of doggie treats. Upstairs, Shaun gave them a couple of treats and then stretched out on the couch, closing his eyes as he tried to mesh everything he had read with what he had experienced at the manor. Shaun was sound asleep when the two puppies jumped up on the couch to join him for a quick nap.

When Maggie came upstairs for her supper break, the living room was filled with the gentle shadows of dusk. She pushed open the door and was about to flip on the light switch when a low rumbling made her freeze. She traced the sound to the couch and saw the snoring form of her husband. Anne Bonny and Jack raised their heads to look at Maggie, and she held a finger to her lips. She smiled when the puppies put their heads back down. She was surprised that Shaun hadn't told her he was back in town, but then she shook her head when she realized that, in all likelihood, Shaun had meant to come down and see her but had fallen asleep instead.

He is probably exhausted, Maggie thought. *I doubt he can get a decent night's sleep with all the ghost crap.* She sat her dinner plate on the kitchen table next to Shaun's briefcase and then went back downstairs to get some dinner for Shaun.

The delicious smell of food roused Shaun from his slumber, and he blinked his eyes as he sat up to look around the dimly lit room, trying to orient himself. Then, a click drew his attention, and he turned to see Maggie walking in the front door with a paper bag in her hand.

"Hi, love," he said groggily.

"Good morning," Maggie said as she moved to place the paper bag on the kitchen table and began to unpack Shaun's dinner. "I thought you might be hungry."

"I'm starving!" Shaun said with enthusiasm. "The only thing I've consumed today is two cups of coffee."

"Well, Mario has worked his magic," Maggie said.

Golden breadsticks made of sweet white dough and a hearty dark brown dough swirled together and slathered in butter. Two crocks of hearty beef stew with large chunks of beef, bright orange carrots, and quartered potatoes lovingly simmered in wine gravy. Maggie placed two covered plates in the refrigerator, and when Shaun looked at her quizzically, she said, "Dessert. Mario wanted us to try something new."

"That's exciting. Tell Mario I'll happily be a guinea pig for any of his food experiments."

"Will do. Anne Bonny, Jack, dinner," Maggie said as she set two dog food bowls on the dog's eating mat. Coffee or tea?" Maggie asked Shaun.

"Tea would be nice," Shaun said as he settled at the table. Maggie and Shaun ate in companionable silence until the edge had been taken off their hunger. Then, as their forks slowed, Maggie took a sip of her coffee and smiled at Shaun.

"So, sleeping beauty, what brings you home?" Maggie asked.

Shaun had thought about how to tell Maggie about his latest run-in with the ghosts of Madeira Manor. He had finally decided to treat it like a bandage. Rip it off all at once and deal with the pain in one quick rush. "I had another run-in with the ghost last night."

Maggie froze, and her eyes searched Shaun's face as her heart clenched. *Why hadn't he told her sooner?*

Her question must have shown on her face because Shaun responded, "I should have told you sooner, but it was too early, and then I got swept up in research, and then I passed out on the couch." Shaun paused for Maggie to respond, but she stayed mute. "I don't have any excuse."

"Oh, you have excuses; you just listed them. What you don't have is a valid reason," Maggie said, and Shaun recoiled as though slapped.

"Ouch," Shaun said, but Maggie just raised her eyebrow in reaction and stood up to begin clearing the table. Uncertain about what to say, Shaun decided the best thing to do was to stay quiet. So he sat in miserable silence as he watched Maggie throw away their trash and rinse their silverware.

"Dessert?" she asked, and Shaun shook his head no. His stomach was in knots.

"More tea?" she asked, and Shaun shook his head again.

"Okay, I have to help open the restaurant for the dinner rush. Will you be here when I get back or are you headed back to the manor tonight?" Maggie asked.

"Maggie," Shaun pleaded, and Maggie stared at him coldly, saying nothing. "Please, can we talk about this?"

"Oh, you want to talk now. Sure, but make it fast. I don't want to leave the staff shorthanded." Maggie leaned against the countertop, crossed her arms, and motioned for Shaun to continue.

Not knowing how to fix his mistake, Shaun decided to tell Maggie what had happened the night before. When Shaun reached down to pull up his pant leg and expose the dark bruises, Maggie hissed in reaction.

"I don't think you should go back," Maggie said.

"I have to," Shaun insisted. "It's my job."

"This is not in your job description," Maggie said as she pointed at Shaun's injured ankle. "What did Daniel say?"

"I haven't told Daniel," Shaun said. "But I think I should be safe if I stay out of the manor after dark."

"And the lighthouse," Maggie added.

"And the lighthouse," Shaun agreed. "I think I'll be okay as long as I stay in the cottage after dark; at least, that's the impression I got from Mrs. Kleyn."

"You spoke to Mrs. Kleyn?" Maggie asked, and Shaun flinched internally.

"She was at the library with Annie when I went in to do some research."

Maggie decided to ignore the fact that he had told both Annie and Mrs. Kleyn about his injury before he told her. "I'm not sure that Mrs. Kleyn is on our side," Maggie said.

"What? Why?" Shaun asked in surprise.

"From what she has said, I'm sure that she feels like the ghosts' needs trump that of us mere fleshies," Maggie said.

"Fleshies?" Shaun said with a laugh, and Maggie smiled in return.

"Well, I'm not sure what else you'd call those of us who are still walking around in a body."

"I love you," Shaun said as he gathered Maggie into his arms. "You always make me laugh."

Maggie allowed Shaun to kiss her, and she felt the balance of her annoyance with him fade away. She had known who Shaun was before she had married him, and she mostly found his myopic focus endearing.

"So, are you staying the night?" Maggie asked. Shaun thought about driving the dark winding roads up the mountain to the empty manor. The day crew would be long gone, and he'd be the only corporeal person on the property, alone with the ghosts.

"Yes. I'll drive back up in the morning," Shaun said.

"Good," Maggie said with an approving peck on the lips. "Dessert?"

"Yes," Shaun said with a smile.

Maggie retrieved the two plates from the refrigerator and placed one in front of Shaun. With great anticipation, Shaun removed the cover. He saw a rectangular piece of cake, covered in a silvery grey-blue icing which reminded Shaun of moonlight. In the middle of the cake sat a ripe orange pumpkin made of ice cream, topped with a chocolate stem and green fondant leaves. Behind the pumpkin, a thin disk of white chocolate had been sunk into the frosting resembling a rising full moon. "Wow," Shaun said. "What's it called?" Shaun asked.

"Mario is torn between Autumn Night and The Pumpkin King."

"It's so cool. I almost don't want to eat it," Shaun said.

Smiling, Maggie cut through the icing to reveal a dark chocolate cake beneath the frosting. "Chocolate," she said lustfully and took a bite before moaning in appreciation.

Shaun cut through the cake with a fork and then laughed when he saw that the dark chocolate cake included miniature vanilla truffles in the shape of bones. The truffles melted on Shaun's tongue before he could chew them, making the cake taste even more decadent. Shaun included some pumpkin ice cream with his next scoop of cake. He closed his eyes as the pumpkin-flavored ice cream blended with the chocolate cake, causing him to echo Maggie's earlier moan.

"I think we have a winner," Maggie said, and Shaun nodded in agreement.

"It's amazing," Shaun said. They savored each bite until their plates were empty, and then they sat back and looked at each other in wonder.

"I guess that's enough sugar to keep me going for the night," Maggie said with a laugh.

"I think I'm going into a sugar coma. If it's okay with you, I think I'll stay up here and crash tonight. I'm still pretty tired," Shaun said.

"Of course," Maggie said. "I don't think we're going to be too busy tonight. Probably just locals looking for a little companionship."

"Thanks, Maggie," Shaun said.

Chapter Fourteen

Crescent Bay, California – Foghorn Tavern

Maggie was correct. Most of her customers that night were locals coming in for a nice dinner or a few drinks with friends.

When Maggie checked in to see how the kitchen staff was doing, Mario raised an eyebrow in question, and Maggie gave him a big smile. "You smashed it! Shaun and I think your new dessert is phenomenal."

"Thank you," Mario said.

"If you're satisfied, we can put it on the seasonal menu for October and November," Maggie said, and Mario nodded in agreement. "Now, you need to tell me what to call it."

"Antonio had an idea about that," Mario said. Antonio was Mario's number two in the kitchen. "What do you think about running a contest to name the new dessert?" Mario asked.

"Oh, I like that. We could offer the winner a $25 gift certificate," Maggie said. Then, Maggie addressed Antonio, "Would you and Mario work on a description of the dessert for a flier we can put in the menus promoting the contest?"

"Will do," Antonio said.

"Terrific," Maggie said. "I'm going to go mingle with the customers."

Maggie stopped by the various tables to see how her customers were doing and swapped some Scuttlebutt. Maggie smiled when she pushed through the swinging doors into the back room where the larger booths were located. She saw Sinthia, Annie, and Mrs. Kleyn sitting in one of the booths.

"Hi ladies, how was your dinner?" Maggie asked as she approached.

"Wonderful. We were just discussing if we had room for dessert," Sinthia said.

"How about a dessert on the house? We have a new creation from Mario, and I'd be interested in your input," Maggie asked.

"Sure!" Sinthia said.

Maggie gathered their empty plates before returning to the kitchen to retrieve their desserts. She returned with three pieces of cake and a carafe of coffee to top off everyone's drink.

"Will you join us?" Sinthia asked, and Maggie nodded.

Annie wiggled around on the booth bench to make room, and Maggie settled down to watch the reaction of everyone as they tried Mario's new creation. From the sounds of appreciation and expressions of pleasure, Maggie could tell they were enjoying their desserts.

"I think I'm going to explode," Annie said as she pushed her empty plate away and picked up her coffee cup with a sigh. "That was amazing! What do you call it?"

"No name yet. We're going to be running a contest, to name it," Maggie said.

"Smart," Mrs. Kleyn said. "You'll sell a ton of cake." Maggie smiled her thanks for the compliment.

"We were talking about Shaun's latest interaction with the ghosts of Madeira Manor," Sinthia said.

"Yes, he and I discussed that over dinner before I came down. I told him I wasn't comfortable with him going back, but he insists," Maggie said.

"If he stays inside the cottage at night, I think he'll be safe," Mrs. Kleyn said.

"What about during the day?" Maggie asked.

"I think he's pretty safe during the day. The type of spirit interactions taking place at the manor require a lot of energy. I believe the spirit leeches energy from the workers during the day and then discharges it at night."

"That doesn't sound good for the workers," Maggie said.

"They may feel a little tired, but I doubt they notice," Mrs. Kleyn said. Mrs. Kleyn's casual attitude about a spirit stealing energy from the living added to Maggie's concern that Mrs. Kleyn was not rooting for the fleshies.

"If you're worried, I can help you create a protective talisman for Shaun," Sinthia said.

"What exactly does that mean?" Maggie asked.

"In this case, I think we'd fill a small bag with some stones and herbs that he could carry in his pocket," Sinthia said.

Maggie hesitated. Growing up in the Gnome household, Maggie had been exposed to many of Mrs. Gnome's new-age beliefs. She had even adopted a few of them herself, but she wasn't completely sold on magic being the answer to all of life's problems. She felt torn between her skepticism and not wanting to insult Sinthia by turning down her offer.

Sinthia watched emotions flit across Maggie's expressive face, and before Maggie could formulate a response, she continued. "Swing by my house tomorrow afternoon between your lunch and dinner rush, and we'll whip up a talisman."

"Thanks," Maggie said in surrender. If nothing else, she would enjoy a little time with Sinthia.

In the morning, Maggie kissed Shaun goodbye and admonished him to not do anything dangerous.

"I'll text you tonight from the cottage so you know I'm okay," he said.

"Thank you. By the way, Sinthia and I will be putting together a little something to protect you from the ghosts," Maggie said.

Shaun's eyes lit up, and he grinned. "When?"

"This afternoon."

"Damn, I would have loved to watch," Shaun said, and Maggie smiled at his inquisitive nature.

"I'll tell you all about it," Maggie said.

Shaun grinned in response, "Protected by Witches. Cool."

"Witch," Maggie said. "I'm just a dabbler."

"You know what makes a person a Witch is hotly debated in the metaphysical community. Some believe one is born a witch through familial lineage or past life experience. While others insist that a person can only be initiated to be a Witch by someone who has previously received training and initiation themselves. Still, others feel that none of that is necessary."

"Well, as far as I know, none of that applies to me, so there will only be one Witch working on your talisman," Maggie said.

"Oh, it's going to be a talisman? What type?"

Maggie laughed, pulled Shaun's coat off the coat rack, and held it out. "Enough. We both have to get going."

Shaun took the coat from Maggie but made no move to put it on. Instead, he watched Maggie's face as questions raced through his agile mind. "Okay, just tell me what type of talisman you're creating."

"Sinthia said it was a bag with herbs and stones," Maggie said as she took Shaun's coat back and held it out, indicating that he should put it on. Shaun slid into his coat and then turned to curl his arms around Maggie in a hug.

"Well, as far as I am concerned, you are a beautiful and powerful Witch who has bewitched my heart," Shaun said, and Maggie groaned.

"You are such a goof."

"But I'm your goof," Shaun said with a silly grin.

"You are," Maggie said with one last kiss. Then she grabbed Shaun's hand and led him out the door, locking it behind them.

"Stay safe," Maggie said sternly.

"I will," Shaun promised.

Shaun pulled up to the gates of Madeira Manor and felt his stomach sink when he saw a police car blocking the way.

Shaun rolled down his window as the patrolman approached.

"May I help you?" the policeman asked, and Shaun nodded.

"Yes, sir, my name is Shaun Morrow, and I've been hired to work on the Madeira Manor lighthouse."

"May I see some ID?" the policeman asked, and Shaun handed him his driver's license with a weird sense of Déjà vu. The policeman looked it over and said, "One moment, please."

There was a beeping sound as the policeman keyed a microphone clipped to his shoulder. "Sir, I have a Shaun Morrow at the gate. He says he has been hired to work on the lighthouse." A tinny voice replied, "Yes. Send him through, but tell him we need to interview him before he can assume his duties."

"Will do," the policeman said. "You heard?" the policeman asked Shaun, who nodded. "Okay, you can go on up to the manor. Officer Serger will speak to you there."

"What happened?" Shaun asked.

"I'm sure he'll fill you in," the policeman said as he got into his car to move it out of Shaun's way, then he motioned for Shaun to proceed.

When Shaun pulled up to the front of the manor, an eerie silence lay over the house. Shaun realized that none of the usual construction staff or vehicles were in evidence. Instead, another police car was sitting in front of the porch. An older policeman leaned against the back bumper, arms crossed, obviously waiting for him.

Shaun parked his car and approached the waiting policeman with an extended hand. "Hello, I'm Shaun Morrow."

"Hello, Mr. Morrow. I'm Officer Serger," the officer said as he shook Shaun's hand. "I just have a few questions; then you can go about your normal duties."

"Okay," Shaun said apprehensively as the patrolman pulled a small spiral notepad and pen from his pocket.

"According to the foreman, you left the premises yesterday morning early, and he said when his crew knocked off for the day, you had not yet returned. So where did you spend yesterday and last night?"

"I spent the day working in Crescent Bay. It got late, so I spent the night in town with my wife."

The officer nodded his head and made a few notes on the notepad.

"Can you tell me what happened?" Shaun asked.

The officer gave him an assessing look and then nodded his head. "Sometime last night, someone broke into the manor and vandalized the property."

"Oh no," Shaun said in concern. "Wait, didn't they trip the alarm?"

"We're waiting for a full report from the alarm company, but they say they did not receive any alerts last night. The foreman insists that he armed the alarm before he went home last night, which means someone who knew the alarm code turned off the alarm, did the damage, and then turned the alarm back on."

"Why would anyone do that?" Shaun asked in confusion.

"Maybe someone had a grudge against the Madeiras or even the State. Perhaps some locals aren't happy with the manor becoming a tourist attraction. Who knows why anyone does anything."

"Still, vandalizing such a beautiful place," Shaun said. "Is anything missing?"

"We don't know yet. The State is sending a conservator with an inventory list. They should be here shortly. In the meantime, I'd appreciate it if you stayed out of the manor."

"No problem," Shaun said.

"I wanted to let you know that we entered the cottage you're staying in to see if there had been any vandalism, but the space seems untouched. If you find anything missing, please contact me." The officer said as he handed Shaun a business card.

"Of course," Shaun said as he fished one of his business cards out of his wallet and handed it to the officer. "Here is my contact information if you have any additional questions."

"Thank you, Mr. Morrow."

Shaun returned to his car and drove around the manor to the cottage. It felt weird unlocking the door and wandering through the rooms, knowing that strangers had done the same thing only hours before. He dug through his limited personal belongings, but everything seemed undisturbed. Shaun felt lucky to have been in Crescent Bay when the vandals had broken into the manor. Shaun knew that sometimes the most dangerous entity at a location was another human being. He cringed at the thought of telling Maggie about the break-in. This would be yet another reason for her to be worried about him. Shaun took a moment to send Maggie a quick text telling her he had reached the manor and would call to chat during her dinner break. He hoped the text's tone was light enough that he wouldn't worry her. In an attempt to shrug off the weirdness of the day, he gathered his tools and went to do more work on the lighthouse.

Maggie pushed open the gate to the Gnome residence and walked up the front porch steps to ring the doorbell. Heavy footfalls sounded inside the house, and Maggie smiled when the door opened to show Mr. Gnome's stern face. His expression softened when he saw who had rung the bell. "Maggie. Sin said you were coming by to do some woo-woo stuff today. Come on in."

"Thanks," Maggie said as she stepped past him to enter the house.

"I think I'll go get a cup of coffee," Mr. Gnome said to Maggie as he stepped out the front door and shut it quietly behind him. Maggie turned to walk into the Gnome's kitchen, knowing that was where she would find Sinthia.

"Tom gone on patrol?" Sinthia asked, and Maggie nodded as they shared an understanding smile. Although Tom tolerated Sinthia's woo-woo stuff, as he called it, it still made him uncomfortable. Maggie thought about how different his reaction to the paranormal was from Shaun's. Both men had very logical and analytical minds. Still, something in Mr. Gnome's makeup wouldn't allow him to step beyond hard and fast facts into the unknown.

"Coffee?" Sinthia asked, and Maggie nodded. "I've been thinking about what we should use for Shaun's talisman, and I think what he needs is a shield. A cloak of unimportance, if you will. Something that will make him less interesting to the spirit. What do you think?"

"Sounds like a good idea," Maggie said.

"Good. I gathered a few spell components, herbs, and stones, to aid us. We will call on their natural energies and blend them into a united focus."

"Okay," Maggie said a little hesitantly. "And how do we do that?"

"We're going to hold each component in our hands while we envision what we are asking the component to do. For example, this is a piece of Hematite," Sinthia said as she plucked a black stone with a silver sheen measuring about the size of a quarter out of one of the porcelain bowls sitting in the center of the kitchen table. "Hematite's natural energies include protection and reflection of negativity. So, you can understand why those two attributes benefit the magic we're creating. We build a picture in our minds of the stone, creating a protective barrier around Shaun, deflecting any negative energy sent his way, and grounding it."

"Grounding?" Maggie asked.

"Yes. You don't want that energy to bounce around looking for a victim, so instead, you see it absorbed into the ground and neutralized. Like you did when we cleansed Shaun's aura," Sinthia said.

"I have a question about that. How does the ground feel about being used that way?" Maggie asked with a small smile.

"Fortunately for us, the earth doesn't perceive energy as negative or positive; it's just energy to be absorbed."

"Nice," Maggie said, and Sinthia nodded in agreement. "What else do we have?"

Sinthia held up each herb and explained why she had chosen it. The last thing she held up was a small beige canvas bag with a drawstring across the top. "We place all the charged components into this bag, and then Shaun can keep it in his pocket or under his pillow at night when he sleeps."

"Such a plain package for such a powerful spell," Maggie said. "It feels like we should put a symbol on the outside."

Surprised, Sinthia nodded, agreeing, "I had thought about doing that. But I couldn't settle on any particular sigil."

"Do you have a pad of paper and pen?" Maggie asked, and Sinthia pulled a pen and a spiral pad out of her oversized bag. She passed them to Maggie and then watched as Maggie began to draw a series of lines and curves into a sigil that sent shivers through Sinthia's body.

"Where did you see that?" Sinthia asked in a hushed tone.

"I saw it in a dream last night. It felt important," Maggie said distractedly as she added one last stroke to her drawing. Then, glancing up, she froze when she saw the look on Sinthia's face. "What's the matter?"

Sinthia stared down at the drawing of one of her tradition's most secret sigils, one that no one outside of the Duchas tradition should have known. She raised her shocked face to Maggie's worried one. "Maggie, you have to be honest about this. Please, tell me where you saw this sigil."

"I wouldn't lie to you; I saw it in a dream. But I don't understand. Is it evil or something?"

Sinthia's mind raced with the ramifications of what that simple drawing might mean. In the Duchas tradition, an apprentice was chosen by the God and Goddess. They were revealed to their mentor in various ways. Could Maggie be her apprentice?

For Sinthia, her introduction to the Duchas tradition happened while she was in high school. Sinthia's parents had been required to travel out of town for a couple of weeks. They had felt that Sinthia was too wild to stay home alone, so her grandmother had been tasked with watching over her while they were gone.

One evening Sinthia had been sitting in her room chanting rhythmically as she had knotted together a macramé hanging. It had been the 60s, and Sinthia had a lucrative business selling her macramé creations to the other students at her high school.

Her grandmother had been walking by her door but had frozen in place when she heard Sinthia chanting. "Where did you learn that?" Her grandmother had asked, and Sinthia had looked up from her work to shrug in response.

"It's not hard," Sinthia had replied. Then she began to explain the different knots in the macramé piece.

"Not the knots, the chant."

"Oh," Sinthia said, a little embarrassed that her grandmother had caught her singing to herself. "I guess it's just a way to keep myself entertained. It doesn't mean anything. As Mom says, it's just gibberish."

But Sinthia's mother was wrong. It wasn't gibberish but a powerful chant of making. Without realizing what she was doing, Sinthia was weaving magic into every knot of her macramé. That interaction led to her grandmother initiating her into the Duchas tradition.

Sinthia had always hoped her daughter Sarah would be revealed as her apprentice. But as the years went by, she despaired of having an apprentice to pass on her legacy. Now she sat across from a daughter of her heart. A daughter who had dreamed of a sigil reserved for advanced initiates of the Duchas tradition.

"Sinthia?" Maggie asked in concern.

Sinthia needed time to understand the full ramifications of what Maggie had drawn. She didn't want to lie to Maggie, but Sinthia had sworn an oath of secrecy that she was unwilling to break. When a witch in the Duchas tradition was found to be an oath breaker, the Fetch was dispatched to retrieve artifacts of the tradition from the offending witch's home. At the same time, the elders bound the witch's power making it impossible for the oathbreaker to access the power of their training. A bound witch could still practice the spirituality of their faith, like communing with the God and Goddess, but they could never channel the power of the tradition again.

"It feels powerful," Sinthia said to delay. "Do you know what it means?" Sinthia asked, and Maggie shook her head. "Then it's probably best to leave it off. I'll do some research and see what I can find."

Maggie nodded as Sinthia closed the notebook and put it back into her purse. "Now, let's work on the visualization we'll use to charge the spell components."

After Maggie left, Sinthia called Mrs. Kleyn.

Maggie was enjoying a delicious dinner cooked by Mario when her phone rang. She smiled when she saw that it was Shaun.

"Hi, handsome," Maggie said as she answered her phone.

"Hello, beautiful. How was your day?" Shaun asked.

"Good," Maggie said as she picked up the talisman from her tabletop and dangled it before her eyes. "We made a gift for you."

"The talisman? Cool! Tell me all about it!"

Maggie shared the story of the talisman's creation, including Sinthia's reaction to the sigil she had drawn.

"You must have seen it somewhere," Shaun said.

"I guess," Maggie said hesitantly. "How are things at the manor?"

"A little weird," Shaun said and told her about the vandalism.

"But your cottage was fine?" Maggie asked.

"Yep."

"Do you think it was the ghost?" Maggie asked.

"The fact that this didn't happen until a night when no one else was on the property could indicate someone with a little patience, and inside information broke in. But..."

"But?" Maggie asked.

"But, this afternoon, I talked to the foreman. The security company told him the alarm had been turned on at 5 pm and wasn't turned off again until he arrived this morning. Plus, they didn't receive any alerts overnight."

"Shaun, I'm worried."

"I know, Maggie, but I'm sitting in the cottage, and it's locked uptight. I'll spend the evening watching bad TV and then crash. I promise."

"Okay. Now I have to figure out how to get this talisman to you."

"Daniel is coming up tomorrow. Why don't you give it to him?"

"Perfect," Maggie said.

Chapter Fifteen

Crescent Bay, California – Annie Martin's home

Sinthia stood on the front porch of Annie's home and rang the bell, nervous about where this conversation with Mrs. Kleyn might lead.

Annie was all smiles when she answered the door, "Hi Sinthia, come on in. Mrs. Kleyn is in the kitchen. Would you like some coffee?"

"No, but water would be nice." Sinthia wasn't sure if her tense stomach could handle yet another cup of coffee.

"No problem," Annie said as she led Sinthia through the house to the kitchen. Mrs. Kleyn sat at Annie's kitchen table, sipping a cup of coffee.

"Hi, Bridget," Sinthia said in greeting. "I appreciate you letting me interrupt your day."

"Don't be silly. Have a seat and tell me what has you so concerned," Mrs. Kleyn said.

"It's that obvious?" Sinthia said with a small smile.

"Yes. Did something go wrong with the talisman?"

"Actually, something may have gone extremely right," Sinthia said as Annie placed a glass of water in front of her. "Annie, I'm sorry to ask this, but could you give us a few minutes alone? We have some elder business to discuss."

"Oh," Annie said in surprise, "of course. I'll just step out back. Let me know if you need anything." Annie walked out the back door to her yard, and Sinthia turned back to Mrs. Kleyn.

"It feels weird kicking her out of her own home. I used to hate it when my grandmother would do that to me so that she could talk to the other elders," Sinthia said as she watched the door close.

"But you understand now," Mrs. Kleyn said, and Sinthia nodded in agreement.

"I'll make sure she understands, too," Mrs. Kleyn said. "Our tradition's secrets must be slowly revealed to be absorbed correctly. Elders are the gatekeepers that teach and protect their apprentices. Besides, it's good to give new apprentices a little humility."

"Apprentices," Sinthia said with a small smile. "That's what I'm here to talk to you about," Sinthia told Mrs. Kleyn about her session with Maggie and her surprise about the sigil.

"Which sigil was it?" Mrs. Kleyn asked.

"Cosain," Sinthia said as she pulled the notebook out of her purse and flipped to the page where Maggie had drawn the sigil. She placed the open notebook in front of Mrs. Kleyn.

"The sigil of spiritual protection. Well, I would say that congratulations are in order," Mrs. Kleyn said. "It looks like you have an apprentice."

"Potential apprentice," Sinthia said. In the Duchas tradition, after an apprentice had been identified, they had until the next full moon to decide whether or not to accept initiation into the tradition. The offer was only made once. If the individual declined, that door was closed for the rest of their life.

"Luckily for you, the full moon was just a couple of days ago. So the two of you have most of this cycle to come to a decision," Mrs. Kleyn said.

"True. I'm just not sure how to approach Maggie," Sinthia said.

"That can be tough. But she was open to performing magic with you, so this shouldn't be too much of a shock. Is she already affiliated with a religious organization?"

"No. I think Maggie is too much of a free spirit to be constrained in one of the mainstream religions."

"We witches tend to be rebels," Mrs. Kleyn said with a smile. "You know her better than I do, but she strikes me as a very direct person. So I think I'd start there."

"I never thought about Maggie being my apprentice. I had always hoped that Sarah would be revealed as my apprentice," Sinthia said.

"It's painful watching your children grow to adulthood while you hold such a vital part of your life secret. I raised four children, and none of them became my apprentice," Mrs. Kleyn said.

"I'm sorry," Sinthia said as she reached across the table to lay her hand on top of Mrs. Kleyn's.

"Ah well, helping Anastasia with Annie's training has been an unexpected blessing."

"Yes. Thank you for agreeing to help Annie and Anastasia," Sinthia said.

"Annie has shown terrific potential, and so few of us are chosen to be Necromancers. It would have been a big loss to the tradition to refuse to train her."

"Still, you went to bat for her with the Elder Council. Vince and I won't forget that."

"It was fun shaking up the Elder Council. But, unfortunately, a few members are getting too hide-bound for my taste. In fact, I was talking to Vince about causing a little more trouble. People get elected to the council, and unless they do something extreme, they get re-elected repeatedly until they choose to retire or die. That would be fine, but I think they get a little too comfortable. Fresh blood is good for a system like ours."

"What were you thinking about doing?" Sinthia asked.

"I'm toying with the idea of term limits," Mrs. Kleyn said.

"What?" Sinthia said in surprise. She and Mrs. Kleyn spent over an hour discussing the politics of the Elder Council and how it might be updated without losing the integrity of the tradition. A tap on the back-door window broke into their conversation, and they looked up to see Annie standing on the other side.

"Come in," Sinthia called.

"Sorry," Annie said with an apologetic smile. "I have to run to the bathroom. Too much coffee."

"No, problem. We were pretty much done here," Sinthia said. "Thank you, Annie, for letting me invade your home. Bridget, thank you for your sage advice."

"My pleasure. Congratulations."

"Thank you," Sinthia said as she gathered her purse, gave Annie a quick hug, and headed out.

Chapter Sixteen

Crescent Bay, California – The Foghorn Tavern

Sinthia timed her visit to the Foghorn Tavern so that she arrived during the break between the lunch and dinner rushes. She smiled at Suzy, who looked up from an open reservation book. "Hi, Sinthia. Are you meeting someone for a late lunch, or do you need a table for one?"

"Actually, I was wondering if I could speak to Maggie," Sinthia said

"Oh, sure. She just went upstairs for a break. Do you want me to give her a call?"

"Please."

With a nod, Suzy picked up the desk phone, tapped in some numbers, and spoke to Maggie. "Hi Maggie, it's Suzy. No, everything is fine. Sinthia is here and was wondering if she could speak to you." Suzy paused to listen, and then she continued, "Sounds good. I'll send her up." Suzy hung up the phone and spoke to Sinthia. "She said you should go on up."

"Thanks," Sinthia said as she walked through the swinging doors that separated the dining area from the bar.

"Hi, Sinthia," Max, the bartender, said as she walked up. "What can I get for you?"

"I'm headed upstairs to talk to Maggie," Sinthia said.

"Ah, enjoy," Max said, and Sinthia smiled her thanks as she ascended the stairs to Maggie's second-floor apartment.

Sinthia paused at Maggie's door, trying to settle the butterflies in her stomach. She was so nervous that it felt like she would jump out of her skin. Then, with a deep breath, she knocked on Maggie's door.

"Hi, Sinthia. Come on in," Maggie said when she answered the door. "I was just having lunch. If you'd like to join me, I can call down for something from the kitchen." Maggie said as she led the way to her dining room, where her lunch was waiting.

"I'm good, but I could use some water," Sinthia said.

"Coming right up," Maggie said. "Have a seat."

Sinthia greeted the two dogs with a couple of pats and then sat down at the table where Maggie's interrupted meal was set up and tried to collect her thoughts.

"Here you go," Maggie said as she placed a glass of water in front of Sinthia before sitting back down. "What's up?" she asked.

"I have something very important to talk to you about, but first, I must swear you to secrecy."

"Secrecy?" Maggie asked. "What's this about Sinthia?"

"You trust me, don't you?" Sinthia asked.

"Of course."

"Then I need your word that what we're about to speak about stays between us. You can't even tell Shaun."

"Okay, now you have me worried," Maggie said.

"There's nothing to worry about," Sinthia insisted.

Maggie examined Sinthia's face trying to glean what this was about. Then she shook her head, "I'm not comfortable lying to Shaun."

"I'm not asking you to lie to Shaun; just keep what I'm about to tell you between us."

Maggie's eyebrow shot up in a satirical reaction. "You're asking me to keep something from Shaun. Technically, that may not be lying, but it still doesn't feel like I'm being honest with him. What if someone asked you to do that to Tom?"

Sinthia looked away from Maggie, feeling guilty because that was precisely what she had done to Tom for their entire relationship.

Sinthia had waited until she had turned eighteen before hitting the road and hitchhiking up the coast, landing in Crescent Bay, where she met Tom. He had been a young patrolman who had offered her a place to stay instead of taking her vagrant butt into custody. From that simple act of kindness, their relationship had grown. Keeping the inner secrets of the Duchas tradition from Tom had been hard. Still, she knew that

Tom's attitudes about marriage were old-fashioned, and he would not have understood her need to keep pieces of her life secret. She thought back over the years to all the times she had needed to hide important moments in her life because they were wrapped up in the secrecy of her training. She searched Maggie's anxious face and decided she couldn't do that to Maggie and Shaun.

"I've made a mistake," Sinthia said as she pushed away from the table and stood up.

"What?" Maggie said in shock as she watched Sinthia turn and head for the front door. "No, wait. I'm sorry, Sinthia."

"No, I'm sorry. Please forgive me," Sinthia ran out the door and rushed from the tavern as she dashed tears from her eyes.

What the hell was that about? Maggie wondered, but since she didn't want to add fodder to the Scuttlebutt, she refrained from rushing after Sinthia. She sat for a moment in shocked silence, then she picked up her phone and called Sinthia. "Dammit, Sinthia," she said when the call was forwarded to voice mail. She hung up without leaving a message.

No longer hungry, Maggie piled up her lunch dishes and pushed away from the table to begin pacing in her living room. *What could Sinthia have wanted to tell her? Who had Sinthia wanted to keep in the dark? Sinthia had mentioned Shaun. Was Shaun in danger?* As her anxiety peaked, Maggie's mind ran in circles, and she tried Sinthia's phone again. When the call went through to voice mail, she left a message, "Sinthia, I don't know what's going on, but if Shaun's in danger, you have to let me know. Please. Please. Call me back. I'm freaking out."

Sinthia rushed out of the tavern and automatically turned toward the beach. She needed to give herself some peace to think about her next steps. The universe had given her an apprentice, which should have been a joyful event, but all she felt was anxiety. How could she expect Maggie to keep her training a secret from Shaun? Plus, Sinthia wasn't sure that Maggie could keep such an enormous secret from her inquisitive husband. Sinthia understood that the reason she had successfully kept Tom in the dark was because the occult stuff made him uncomfortable. People don't pursue topics that make them uneasy.

Sinthia walked toward the shore and paused to take her sandals off before walking ankle-deep into the low lapping waves. As the chilly water covered her bare toes, she envisioned the salt in the saltwater, pulling the tension and anxiety from her body and allowing her a quiet space to think. She thought of a younger Maggie running wild in and out of their home with Sarah by her side. She thought about Maggie's curiosity about Sinthia's faith and the magic that wove through it.

Sinthia had given Maggie her first tarot deck, and she smiled, remembering the tentative readings Maggie had done for her. Initially, the card interpretations had come from the deck's instruction book. But, once Maggie had felt confident enough to trust her insights, her tarot readings had showcased her intuitive skills. She remembered the wonder on Maggie's face during those times when her intuition had tapped into a piece of unknown information. Sinthia's faith had given her many such moments of wonder and joy. Could she deny Maggie those moments? But, in the bigger picture, was it really Sinthia's choice? It seemed like that decision should be Maggie's, but how could Maggie decide without all the facts?

Sinthia's toes began to ache from the cold water that continued to ebb and flow around her feet. Her anxiety had been pulled out to sea, leaving a more solid feeling in its wake. Sighing, Sinthia turned away from the sea, preparing to trudge through the sand to the sea wall where she could have a seat and brush the sand off her feet before putting her sandals back on. She froze when she saw Vince sitting on the sea wall watching her. He raised a hand in hello, and she waved back.

As she approached, Vince studied Sinthia's face, thinking she looked troubled. She sat down next to him and began brushing sand off her feet.

"I suppose Bridget told you," Sinthia said, and Vince looked confused.

"Told me what?" he asked.

"About Maggie."

Vince shook his head no, "Is there something wrong with Maggie? Is that why you're troubled," Vince asked.

Sinthia searched Vince's face as she considered whether to confide in him. Vince was her tradition's Fetch, which meant he was both the protector of the tradition and a defender of tradition's practitioners. She and Vince had become close during their campaign to have Annie's unconventional apprenticeship approved by the Elder Council.

"I'm torn and could use some Council From The Fetch," Sinthia said.

Vince straightened. The phrase *Council From The Fetch* was a formal request for his input as the tradition's Fetch. "How may I serve?" he responded in the traditional way.

Sinthia shared the revelation of Maggie's potential apprenticeship and Sinthia's concerns about Shaun. When she completed her tale, Vince nodded in understanding.

"The need for protecting our tradition's deepest secrets is a difficult but necessary burden. I don't know Shaun very well, but he seems like a man with an open mind," Vince said.

"He is," Sinthia agreed. "Perhaps too open," she said with a smile. "He collects information like a magpie collects shiny bobbles. I doubt that Maggie could hide her apprenticeship from him."

"Do you think that he is incapable of keeping a secret?" Vince asked.

"No. I'm sure Shaun can be trusted to keep a secret; I'm just not sure he could resist prying into places he shouldn't."

"Ah," Vince said in understanding. "That's tough. What did Maggie say?"

"I didn't tell her."

"Wait. You didn't tell her about the apprenticeship?" Vince asked in confusion.

Sinthia shook her head no as she stared out toward the water, "I told her that I needed to swear her to secrecy and when I added Shaun to that vow, she balked."

"She just flat-out refused?" Vince asked.

"Not exactly," Sinthia hedged. "She turned the tables on me and asked me how I would feel if someone had asked me to do the same thing to Tom and all I could think about was all the times I betrayed Tom in the past."

"Betrayed?" Vince asked in shock. "How exactly have you betrayed Tom?"

Sinthia shrugged and continued to stare out into the turbulent waves feeling depressed.

The Duchas tradition had arrived on America's shores via Irish immigrants, but its practitioners kept it a closely guarded secret. That secrecy had been vital as people who refused to conform to the Christian church's teachings were given the label of heretic and either driven from their homes or killed as a warning to others.

During the Victorian era, spiritualism had gained general acceptance, and slowly America had begun to move away from the rigid beliefs of its Puritan roots. The new age movement of the 60s had brought many of the Duchas's outer court teachings into mainstream America. Teachings such as divination, astrology, numerology, and herbalism. One of the benefits of a more enlightened America was that Witches with spouses who were not a part of the Duchas tradition could be more open about their general practices. How much they shared varied depending on the spouse.

"Are you saying you betrayed Tom by upholding your oaths?" Vince asked. Sinthia didn't answer; she just wiped a stray tear from her cheek and continued to stare gloomily toward the horizon. Vince decided to try a different tactic, "Tom seems like a man of honor."

"He is," Sinthia agreed miserably

"Then he would never ask you to break your oaths." Sinthia turned her gaze away from the sea to watch Vince's face as he continued. "When you became an apprentice, you took an oath to hold our deepest teachings secret from the uninitiated. You may have made those oaths before you exchanged your marriage vows with Tom, but your marriage vows did not negate your previous oaths."

"Hm," Sinthia said as she considered Vince's words.

"Alright," Vince said. "In order to betray someone, you must actively cause them harm. So how has your adherence to your oaths injured Tom?" Sinthia drew in a breath to reply, but Vince stopped her by raising a finger. "Give me solid examples, not vague impressions colored by societal guilt," he admonished her.

"Societal guilt?" Sinthia asked.

"Yes. The guilt that society uses to force us to conform to its expectations."

"Ouch," Sinthia said, but Vince could see the edges of her mouth tilt into a sad smile. "I fell into that trap, didn't I? A good wife wouldn't keep anything from her husband."

"Societal guilt is a hard trap to avoid. The society we are born into teaches us what is acceptable and punishes anyone who deviates from those norms. They teach us to feel guilty when we refuse to limit ourselves within their restrictive parameters."

"I know that, but I guess I'd forgotten my hippie roots. There was a time when I would have gladly done the opposite of what was expected of me, just to watch people squirm. I guess I've become domesticated."

"Never, my friend. You just need to dust off your rebel heart and remember who you are."

Sinthia finished brushing off her feet and putting her sandals back on as she and Vince sat in companionable silence.

Tom knew she practiced an earth-based spirituality, and she shared with him only as much as she felt he could accept. While dating, Tom had begun referring to Sinthia's religious practices as woo-woo. Having her beliefs discounted with such a frivolous term had felt belittling, and Sinthia had sought out her grandmother for counseling. Her grandmother had helped her understand that Tom's nickname for her faith was his way of distancing himself from that which made him uneasy. As she reflected on those conversations with her grandmother, she realized she hadn't betrayed Tom by keeping her secrets. If she had forced her beliefs upon him, she would have been harming him to make herself feel better, which would have been a betrayal. Sinthia felt like a great weight had been lifted off of her shoulders.

"Alright, so I have some shadow work to do," Sinthia said, and Vince nodded in agreement. Shadow work was the name the Duchas tradition assigned to the act of proactive self-reflection, and it was a life-long process.

"The gift of an apprentice often signals the next step in a Witch's personal journey," Vince said.

"I appreciate the council of the Fetch," Sinthia said, using the formal words that signaled an end to Sinthia's conversation with the Fetch.

"It is an honor to serve," Vince answered with the customary response.

"So, may I speak to you as your friend?" Vince asked, and Sinthia nodded. "I think you need to trust the God and Goddess. They would not have revealed Maggie as your apprentice if it wasn't meant to be."

"True," Sinthia agreed. "But what about Shaun?"

"I think Shaun is a reasonable man. He and Maggie seem to have a relationship of equals. As such, Shaun may be one of those fortunate spouses that can be told of the outer teachings and yet respect the need for the secrecy of the inner teachings," Vince said.

"I'm glad the Goddess put you in my path today," Sinthia said. "I was about to do something foolish."

"She knows us better than we know ourselves. It sounds like you have made up your mind."

"I have. I'm going to talk to Maggie."

"I think that's the right decision. You know where to find me if you need any backup," Vince said.

"Indeed, I do," Sinthia agreed.

The cell phone reception at the beach was notoriously poor, and as soon as Sinthia's phone was back in range, it began to vibrate. As she pulled it out of her oversized purse, it continued to shake as multiple text messages were delivered. Maggie had left her ten text messages that had steadily become more frantic. In the middle of reading yet another text, Sinthia's phone rang, and when she looked at the ID, she saw it was her daughter Sarah.

Sinthia tapped the button to answer, "Hello, Honey," Sinthia said.

"Mom, are you okay?" Sarah asked in a worried tone.

"Of course, what's wrong?"

"Maggie came by the house looking for you. She said that you and she had some sort of disagreement, and you had rushed out of her apartment. What happened?"

Crap, Sinthia thought. "It was just a misunderstanding."

"Well, she has everyone up in arms. Dad is looking for you," Sarah said.

"Ah, fuck," Sinthia said under her breath.

"What?" Sarah asked.

"Nothing. I'm fine. I was down at the beach, which is why I didn't get any phone messages."

"Sin?" A male voice called, and Sinthia flinched.

"Your dad has found me," Sinthia whispered into the phone, making Sarah laugh.

"Then I best hang up. I'll let Maggie know that Dad has you," Sarah said.

"Yeah, thanks," Sinthia said as she hung up on her daughter's laughter. She waved to her husband, who was striding down the street toward her.

"Hi, Honey," Sinthia said with a big smile, hopeful that Tom hadn't been too worried.

"Maggie's looking for you," he said as he approached. "Where were you?"

"Can we talk about this away from The Scuttlebutt?" Sinthia said as she glanced around to see who was watching their exchange. Tom mirrored her actions and then nodded his head.

"Hungry?" he asked, and Sinthia smiled up at him.

"Starving."

"How about a pizza?"

"Sounds good. Let me text Maggie, so she knows I'm okay." Tom waited patiently as Sinthia tapped her phone's screen and sent Maggie a text. "Let's go get some pizza."

Tom asked about Sinthia's riff with Maggie during dinner, but when Sinthia told him that it had to do with some woo-woo stuff, Tom shut the conversation down.

Sinthia's text to Maggie had included an apology, clarification that, as far as Sinthia knew, Shaun was safe, and a request for a meeting. Sinthia received a terse response stating that Maggie was busy and that she'd text her tomorrow to schedule a time.

Tom watched Sinthia's face while she read Maggie's reply, "Is she okay?" he asked.

"She's pissed, but I can't blame her. I didn't handle that conversation well."

"I'm sure you'll work it out," Tom said, and Sinthia hoped he was right.

Chapter Seventeen

Bountiful, California – The Madeira Estate – Artist Cottage

Shaun's eyes opened, and he stretched, enjoying the feeling of the soft bed and warm blankets. He rolled onto his side, thinking about going back to sleep and starting his day later than usual. His hand slid under his pillow and his fingers curled around a cloth bag. He pulled the bag out and pressed it to his nose to breathe in the smell of the enclosed herbs.

Daniel had brought the talisman to Madeira Manor the day before with instructions from Maggie on what Shaun should do with it. Once Daniel had left, Shaun had untied the cord and peeked inside the little bag to see what items it contained. He wasn't sure if he should have, but he couldn't help himself. He hadn't been able to identify all of the herbs, but he knew that the stone was hematite, and with a little Googling, he had been able to figure out why it had been included. Shaun had enjoyed a calm day and peaceful night, carrying the talisman with him and sleeping with it under his pillow as Maggie had directed. Shaun reached for his phone with a smile, checked the time, and decided it was too early to call Maggie. Instead, he texted her that he'd had a quiet night's sleep and thanked her for the talisman; then, he got up to shower and begin his day.

After his shower, Shaun was surprised to see that Maggie had tried to call him. Before returning Maggie's call, he finished getting dressed and went downstairs to make himself a cup of tea.

"Good morning," Maggie said when she picked up her phone.

"Good morning. I'm surprised you're already up. My text didn't wake you up, did it?" Shaun asked.

"No. Unlike you, I had a hard time sleeping last night."

"Really?" Shaun asked, concerned. "What happened?"

"I had a weird exchange with Sinthia," Maggie said.

"Tell me," Shaun said, and so Maggie did.

"And you have no clue what she wanted to talk to you about?" Shaun asked.

"No, but how could she expect me to keep something a secret from you?"

"I don't know, but Sinthia has always been pretty straightforward with me."

"Me too," Maggie agreed.

"So, if she feels that something needs to be kept a secret, it must be pretty serious."

"Are you saying I should keep what she tells me a secret from you?" Maggie said in surprise. "Isn't that going to drive you crazy? Not knowing, I mean."

"Perhaps," Shaun said. "But I trust you."

"Hm," Maggie said.

"She loves you, Maggie. I doubt she would do anything to harm you, and by extension, me."

Maggie thought back over her history with Sinthia and the Gnome family. Maggie knew that Sinthia called her the daughter of her heart, and she loved Sinthia like a mother.

She weighed all those thoughts against Sinthia's request and realized that Shaun was right. Sinthia wouldn't ask her to do anything that would harm her.

"You're right. I'll talk to her today."

"And then you can tell me all about it," Shaun said teasingly, but he backpedaled when Maggie didn't reply. "I'm joking, Maggie."

"Are you sure?"

"Certain. A little mystery is good in a relationship."

Maggie texted Sinthia and asked if she could come over for coffee. She smiled at how quickly Sinthia replied yes. She was nervous about whatever Sinthia wanted to talk to her about, but she knew that patching up this disagreement would be a relief for both of them.

She strolled through the village smiling and waving to her neighbors, who returned the gestures. The signs of summer were being replaced by those of autumn. A hay bale here, a stock of dried corn there, even the weather was hinting that autumn was on its way. The morning sea air was crisp and cold as it breathed down the streets.

When Tom answered the door, he studied Maggie's face before saying, "Are you okay?" Maggie nodded, but Tom noticed her eyes sparkled with unshed tears triggered by his concern. Tom smiled reassuringly and reached out to squeeze Maggie's arm gently. "You'll work it out. She's in the kitchen. I'm going to go out so you can have some privacy." Maggie smiled her thanks.

Sinthia sat at the kitchen table with a steaming cup of coffee. She smiled tentatively as Maggie entered, "Good morning," she said.

"Good morning."

"Would you like a cup of coffee?" Sinthia asked, and Maggie shook her head no.

"Have a seat," Sinthia said as she gestured to an empty chair. "First, I'm sorry that I gave you a scare. After leaving the tavern, I went down to the beach and missed your texts. I have something very important to share with you, but I'm bound by an oath of secrecy I've honored for decades."

Maggie looked surprised, an oath of secrecy that Sinthia had taken decades before? What the heck was Sinthia talking about?

Sinthia watched Maggie's face and nodded, agreeing, "Yeah, it's heavy, and I'm torn. I have an opportunity to offer you that will be life-changing, but I can't break that oath."

"I spoke to Shaun about our conversation," Maggie said.

"And," Sinthia said as her tension rose.

"He said that you wouldn't do anything to harm me or us, and he encouraged me to talk to you."

"You told him I asked you to keep something a secret from him?" Sinthia asked, and Maggie nodded her head yes. "And he was okay with that?"

"He said he was. He felt you wouldn't ask me to do something like that if it wasn't important."

"He's right. So, let me ask you again. Will you keep what I'm about to tell you a secret from everyone, including Shaun?" Sinthia's heartbeat sped up as she watched Maggie consider her response. Maggie might be her only chance to pass on the unbroken lineage of her ancestors.

Maggie studied Sinthia's concerned face and then took a leap of faith, "Yes." She watched as the stress drained from Sinthia's tensed muscles, and a gentle smile graced her face.

"Thank you," Sinthia said gently. "Okay, where to start." Over the years, Sinthia had fantasized about the conversation she would have with her future apprentice. After her daughter had been born, the person starring in those daydreams had always been Sarah. Now she looked at Maggie as she struggled to find the right words.

"I have a proposition for you. I don't need a response today. You have about three weeks to decide, but what I am about to offer you will only be offered once, and if you turn it down, it will never be offered again." *Perhaps to either of us,* Sinthia thought to herself. But she didn't say that out loud as she didn't want the fact that Maggie might be the only apprentice Sinthia would ever have to impact Maggie's decision.

Maggie's decision had to be focused on what was best for her. "So, please take the time you need to consider it seriously."

Feeling uncomfortable, Maggie tried to lighten the mood, "This had better not be a multi-level marketing thing."

"It's not," Sinthia said with a smile. "Okay. You know that I'm a witch."

"Sure," Maggie said with a shrug.

"What do you think that entails?" Sinthia asked.

"I know you believe in a God and a Goddess and working with nature and the seasons. The moon is also important. Plus, you believe in stuff like astrology, the tarot, and such."

"True. What if I told you everything you just said was window dressing for a deeper spiritual path?"

"Okay," Maggie said hesitantly, uncertain where Sinthia was going.

"A spiritual path with deep secret teachings that are centuries old. A path that demands a lot from its followers while offering great rewards."

Maggie felt a rush of energy through her body. What was Sinthia trying to tell her?

"I am an elder in the Duchas tradition. The Duchas tradition is an ancient Witchcraft tradition that can trace its arrival in our country back to the 1600s. Our tradition is secret due to the world's history of religious bigotry. Plus, not everyone can integrate our inner teachings. Our tradition can only be passed from a mentor to an apprentice who has been chosen by the God and Goddess."

"By the God and Goddess," Maggie said in disbelief. "How do they do that?"

"It varies," Sinthia said. "In my case, my grandmother caught me singing a chant of making specific to the tradition."

"You hadn't heard it before?" Maggie asked.

"No. It just popped into my head fully formed," Sinthia said as she pulled a spiral notebook out of her bag, flipped to the page where

Maggie had drawn the sigil, and placed it in front of Maggie. "In your case, the God and Goddess gave you one of our most powerful sigils of protection."

In disbelief, Maggie stared down at the sigil she had drawn for Shaun's talisman. "Are you saying that this drawing means something?"

"I am," Sinthia said as she unwrapped a silk cloth from around a large leather-bound book. The book looked very old and tattered from frequent handling. Sinthia turned to a specific page and spun the book so that Maggie could read the text. At the top of the page was a duplicate of the sigil that Maggie had drawn. The handwritten text on the page identified the sigil as Cosain, the sigil of spiritual protection. Maggie read the short paragraph under the sigil and looked up at Sinthia in wonder.

"Are you saying that I'm your apprentice?" Maggie said in a voice filled with disbelief.

"I am," Sinthia said as she searched Maggie's face to understand how Maggie was feeling.

"Wow," Maggie said as she pushed her chair back from the table as though she needed to distance herself from the conversation.

Sinthia sat quietly, watching Maggie, trying to give her time to process what she had just learned.

"Wow," Maggie repeated as she stood up and moved over to the sink to stare out the back window into Sinthia's garden.

"Wait, does Tom know? Is that why he always calls this your woo-woo stuff? Is he trying to help you keep it a secret?" Maggie asked.

"Tom knows that I practice Witchcraft, but he doesn't know any of the deeper stuff which we call the inner secrets. He thinks what I practice is more new age than ancient."

"Wow," Maggie said again, and then she laughed at herself. "I keep saying that, but this is a lot to absorb. Hey, what about Sarah? Is she your apprentice too?"

"No," Sinthia said. "I always expected her to be, but the God and Goddess had other plans." Sinthia looked away as her eyes pricked with unshed tears.

Maggie looked stricken, "Oh, Sinthia, I'm so sorry. You've had to keep this a secret from both her and Tom?" Sinthia kept her face turned away, but she nodded her head. "I'm so sorry," Maggie said as she came up behind Sinthia's chair to wrap her arms around her.

Sinthia accepted the comfort, and when Maggie stepped away, she retrieved a tissue from a box on the table to dry her eyes.

Maggie walked back to her seat and looked at Sinthia's tear-streaked face.

"Alright, so I need a little more info. What would being your apprentice entail?" Maggie asked.

"We start with a year and a day of training. Your training regimen would include both homework and participating with me in rituals. You would have to keep all the inner teachings a secret from everyone except the tradition's elders and apprentices," Sinthia said.

"Are there other elders and apprentices in Crescent Bay?" Maggie asked in surprise.

"I can't answer that until after you take your oath to the tradition. Keeping the identities of other witches a secret is a part of the oaths I took," Sinthia said.

"Don't you think that's a little extreme? I mean, most people are okay with the whole witchcraft thing."

"Unfortunately, even in our more enlightened times, people are still discriminated against when they fall outside the norm. I have a friend who was fired because she was exposed as a Witch."

"Oh, come on, fired? Wouldn't the company have been sued for religious discrimination or something?" Maggie asked.

"Sure, if that reason had been listed on her termination paperwork, but the listed reason was downsizing."

"What makes you think that it wasn't downsizing?"

"She was the top salesperson in the company, but she trusted the wrong person with her beliefs, and they spread gossip about her. After her boss heard the rumors, it was announced that her department was too large and needed to lay off someone. But instead of laying off the least productive employee, which might have made sense, they laid her off."

"Hm," Maggie said, unconvinced.

"Okay, how about this? A woman lost custody of her children during a divorce because her soon-to-be-ex equated Witchcraft with child abuse. He convinced the judge that giving him sole custody was in the children's best interest."

"Seriously?"

"Seriously," Sinthia affirmed. "If you don't believe me, you can Google it."

"Damn," Maggie said, and Sinthia nodded.

"So, you can see why secrecy is so important."

"I guess so," Maggie said. "But how can I keep this from Shaun?"

"You can tell Shaun that you are studying Witchcraft with me, but you cannot tell him about the tradition or our inner teachings."

"Sort of an open secret," Maggie said.

"Those are often the easiest ones to keep," Sinthia said.

"Okay, so what exactly is an inner teaching?" Maggie asked.

"The inner teachings are the practices, methods, and rituals we use to deepen our connection with divinity. They are specific to our tradition and cannot be found anywhere else. As you go through your training, I'll let you know which of our teachings are considered inner teachings and thus a secret."

"That isn't a lot to go on; what happens if I say yes and then change my mind after I've begun my apprenticeship?"

"You forfeit your book of shadows," Sinthia said as she closed the large leather-bound book she had used to show Maggie the protection sigil. "Along with your tools and ritual implements. Then I would have to bind your magical abilities."

"But what would keep me from blathering about the tradition to everyone I know."

"Your honor," Sinthia said.

"You're telling me that no one has exposed the tradition to the uninitiated over the centuries?"

"Unfortunately, I cannot say that," Sinthia said.

"Really, what happened?"

"The few times that has happened, the outcome wasn't pretty. The oaths we take are not just to our mentors but also to our ancestors and the God and Goddess. When mortal measures aren't enough to convince a person to live up to their oaths, the Lords of Lugh step in and deliver justice."

"That sounds ominous," Maggie said.

"It is. You don't want to draw the attention of the Lords of Lugh. They cannot be reasoned with as they do not see things in shades of grey, only black and white. To them, something is either right or wrong, and breaking your oaths is wrong."

"So, they're like cosmic cops," Maggie said, making Sinthia smile and nod. "Like I said, this is a lot to absorb."

"It is, but in the Duchas tradition, a potential apprentice has until the next full moon to decide. That means you have about three weeks to make up your mind."

"Okay," Maggie said as she pushed back from the table and stood up. "I have to go get ready for the tavern to open. I'm going to have a lot more questions."

"I'll answer the ones that I can."

Chapter Eighteen

"Shaun?" A male voice called.

Shaun poked his head over the edge of the spiral staircase and saw Mr. Heard, the construction foreman standing on the ground floor.

"What's up?" he called down.

"The guy from the alarm company is here, and he wants to ask you a couple of questions."

"Oh. I'll be right down," Shaun said.

"We'll be in the manor's kitchen," Mr. Heard called back as Shaun finished jotting down some of his findings before he began his descent.

Shaun entered the manor through the servant's entrance and felt a slight pang in his heart when he walked past the empty cafe table where he and George had shared their tea. The foreman leaned against the kitchen counter, chatting with a young man in his 20s.

"Ah, Shaun, good. This is Mr. Steymer from the alarm company. Mr. Steymer, this is Shaun Morrow from 1906 Renovation," Mr. Heard said.

"Mr. Steymer," Shaun said as he extended his hand to shake.

"Mr. Morrow. It's good to meet you."

"I need to check in with the crew. If you need anything else, let me know," Mr. Heard said as he turned to leave.

"Thanks," Mr. Steymer said as he turned back to Shaun. He pulled out a shiny key and a scrap of paper and handed both of them to Shaun. "The State thought it was best to re-key the manor; this is your copy. And here is the new alarm code. When you finish your work here, you can turn them in to Mr. Heard."

Shaun took the paper and key with a distracted look on his face.

"Is everything okay?" Mr. Steymer asked.

"Yes. I'm sorry, but your name sounds so familiar. Have we met before?"

"No. But my mother was the head housekeeper here at the manor for most of her life. Perhaps George mentioned her," Mr. Steymer said.

"That's it. I knew your name sounded familiar," Shaun said with a smile. "So, your mother worked here," Shaun said, and Mr. Steymer nodded.

"Yep. She worked here right up until Mr. Madeira passed away."

"You must have spent a lot of time here, too," Shaun said.

"When I was younger, I did, but the manor was less welcoming once Mr. Madeira became ill."

"Was Mr. Madeira's illness a long one?" Shaun asked.

"Yes. I think the signs of his dementia were ignored for a long time because people relied on their jobs at Madeira Manor to stay afloat."

"That must have been tough," Shaun said sympathetically.

"It was, but it was also difficult watching such a strong man degenerate into a paranoid shadow of the person he had once been."

Paranoid? Shaun wondered. He hadn't spoken to George about how Mr. Madeira had died because the loss of Mr. Madeira had been so fresh, and George had still been in pain.

"I once heard Mom talking to Dad about one of Mr. Madeira's spells. Those spells frightened her," Mr. Steymer said.

"What would he do?" Shaun asked.

"He'd have long conversations with Mrs. Madeira, who had been dead for over a decade at that point, and insist that she was tormenting him. That was especially traumatizing for the staff who had loved them both. I remember Mom talking about the pain of watching Mr. Madeira's illness, stealing the loving memories of his wife, and leaving behind nothing but torment. It was rough. A lot of the staff quit, and replacing them became a challenge."

"Really? Why?" Shaun asked.

"As the staff left, rumors of the manor being haunted grew."

"Haunted?" Shaun asked, trying to sound neutral, and Mr. Steymer studied his face before nodding. "Do you think the manor is haunted?" Shaun asked.

Mr. Steymer puffed out a breath and looked away from Shaun to glance around the empty kitchen. "If we're quiet, if we listen, we can hear houses breath," he said distractedly.

"What?" Shaun asked, and Mr. Steymer shook himself out of his trance and looked embarrassed.

"Sorry, it's a line from Rose Red, a story by Stephen King about a haunted house. That line has always reminded me of this house. Maybe it's the history of the place, but it has always seemed alive to me."

Shaun stayed quiet, hoping Mr. Steymer would elaborate on why he felt that way about the manor. He was rewarded for his patience when Mr. Steymer continued.

"When I was a little boy, I loved exploring the manor. During the summers, I'd beg my mom to take me with her to work so that I could play in the woods and explore the property. I'd slip away from my mom and search for the manor's secrets. I was sure that if I pushed on all the molding and fancy wall ornaments, I'd eventually find a hidden passage. I loved exploring the manor, but the third floor gave me the willies. I never knew Mrs. Madeira. She passed away before I began to visit the manor, but even so many years later, the third floor was like a shrine to her memory.

"The maids kept the third floor dusted and clean as if Mrs. Madeira had just stepped away and could be back at any moment. I mean, you've seen it. All her stuff is still there, including the hospital bed she died in." Shaun nodded his head and bit his tongue to keep quiet. "The last time I was here as a child, I screwed up my courage and snuck up to the third floor. I had already searched all the other floors repeatedly, so I was certain that the secret passages must originate on the third floor. I crept into Mrs. Madeira's bedroom and began my search. I was pushing and trying to twist all that intricate artwork around the fireplace, gently knocking on walls and listening for a hollow echo that could indicate a void in the space beyond. I worked my way around the room until I reached the window that faced toward the lighthouse. I was studying that creepy faceless statue when freezing cold hands came to rest on my shoulders. I wanted to scream and run, but I couldn't move. Then came the sound of congested breathing from right behind me. The hands on my shoulders increased their pressure until my shoulder bones were screaming in agony. I began to shake because the heat was being sucked out of my body, and I was freezing. The raspy breathing grew louder, and I realized that the hair by my right ear was moving in rhythm with the breathing as though someone was pressing against me from behind, breathing in my ear. Then a voice hissed, 'Lies.' "

Shaun watched Mr. Steymer's face as he waited for him to continue. But Mr. Steymer had retreated to an inner landscape where a frightened young boy was experiencing a terrifying encounter.

Unable to stand it for another moment, Shaun attempted to reengage Mr. Steymer, "Did you run?"

"No. I fainted. My mother's shift ended, and the staff helped her search for me. George found me curled up on the floor beneath the window."

"That must have been embarrassing," Shaun said as he tried to empathize with the frightened little boy.

"It was, especially since I had wet myself." Shaun cringed in sympathy, and Mr. Steymer shrugged in response. "I tried to tell George what had happened, but he wouldn't listen. He was angry that I had intruded on Mrs. Madeira's rooms and thought I was telling a story so I wouldn't get in trouble."

"Did your mom believe you?" Shaun asked.

"I think she did, but she didn't have a lot of options. My family needed her job, so she punished me by grounding me for a month and banning me from coming to work with her again. Although, after that experience, I never wanted to come back here. I didn't cross the manor's threshold again until I was an adult working for the alarm company. I'm still not comfortable here," Mr. Steymer confessed.

"I can understand that," Shaun nodded as he thought about the spirit that prowled the manor's empty halls.

Chapter Nineteen

Crescent Bay, California – The Foghorn Tavern

As she moved through her day, Maggie struggled. She smiled at her patrons and helped her employees, but her mind was obsessed with Sinthia's offer.

By the time the lunch rush was over, Maggie had a raging headache. She arranged to cover her shifts and took the afternoon and evening off. Collapsing on the bed in her apartment, she pulled the pillow over her face and drifted off into an exhausted sleep.

She was sitting on a couch in a large loft that was brightly lit by a full moon shining down through the domed glass roof. The loft had been divided into sections by arranging pieces of furniture into functional spaces. The area she sat in appeared to be a study area with floor-to-ceiling bookcases crammed full of texts.

"Would you like tea or coffee?" A voice asked, and Maggie turned to the woman sitting across from her. The woman was in her 60s, with long silver hair, dressed in a flowing blue tie-dyed caftan covered in glittering silver stars. She recognized Anastasia Pallas, Annie Martin's grandmother.

"Coffee, please," Maggie said, and she smiled when she accepted the mug. "Where are we?" she asked as she glanced around the space.

"We're in my Tearmann."

"Ah," Maggie said as if she understood what a Tearmann was, although she had no clue.

Anastasia smiled a small smile as she poured herself a cup of coffee and took a sip. Then with a contented sigh, she pushed herself back into her overstuffed hunter-green wing chair and studied Maggie's face. "I have been sent to answer any questions you have about the Duchas tradition and Sinthia's offer."

"Wait. How do you know about what Sinthia and I spoke about?" Maggie asked.

"Is that the question you truly want to ask me?" Anastasia responded. Maggie paused and then shook her head.

"I'm afraid," Maggie blurted out.

"Fear of the unknown is nothing to be ashamed of; it means that you're an intelligent person. I'll try to give you enough knowledge to lessen your fear."

"Thank you, but why?"

"I owe Sinthia an unpayable debt. She put a lot on the line to see that my lineage would continue. So I would like to return the favor."

"Annie?" Maggie asked, but Anastasia refused to answer, and Maggie realized that she was probably bound by the same oaths as Sinthia not to expose other practitioners of the Duchas tradition.

That was when Maggie remembered, "Wait, you're dead."

"And you're asleep. So what's your point?" Anastasia asked.

Maggie shook her head in confusion, but Anastasia was getting annoyed. "Look, I had to pull a lot of strings to get this time with you; let's not waste it. Please ask me your most pressing questions before I have to leave."

Maggie's brain was swamped with questions, many of which had nothing to do with Sinthia's offer, such as what it was like to be dead and what came after, but she sensed that Anastasia would not answer those questions.

"What if this is all a mistake? What if I'm not Sinthia's apprentice?"

"Impossible. As Christians like to say, God, or in our case the God and Goddess, don't make mistakes. Mistakes occur when we humans make poor choices."

"And you think it would be a poor choice for me to turn Sinthia down?" Maggie asked.

"No, I didn't say that."

"But if I say no, Sinthia said I will never be offered this opportunity again," Maggie pressed.

"That's true, but this decision is not binary, good or bad. It is more nuanced than that. You stand at a crossroad, and if you say yes, your life will fork off in one direction. If you say no, your life will fork off in the other direction. Neither one is preferable to the other, merely different."

"But how do I know which fork is the right one to take?" Maggie asked. "How did you decide?"

"My mother was not chosen to be an apprentice, but she had a magical soul. She filled my days with the joy of nature and folklore tales of fairies, dragons, and other mystical creatures. So, when my grandmother offered to mentor me, I jumped at the chance."

"But, did you ever regret your choice?"

"The path of Witchcraft is not always an easy one. The God and the Goddess expect their children to work on evolving their souls through self-examination and growth."

"Self-examination? That doesn't sound so bad."

"We can admire the beauty of a rose, but do we really think about the process of growing a bud? The petals expanding and growing in that tight womb until they can no longer stay bound up and are forced to burst forth to uncurl and bloom? That is what happens to a witch. The end product is a beautiful thing to behold, but the process can be arduous and painful."

"Painful? That's not much of an incentive," Maggie stated.

"Our souls were placed on this earth to grow, and growth is always painful, but we can grow by intention or by accident. Growing with intention is less painful."

Maggie nodded her head in agreement. What Anastasia was saying rang true. The times she had chosen to improve her life had always been easier than when she had been forced to grow due to circumstances beyond her control.

"Sinthia mentioned we'd start with a year and a day. What exactly does that mean?"

"It is a traditional period of time where the two of you can see if this path is for you before you take any binding oaths to the God and Goddess. You and Sinthia will share oaths to each other, and if at the end of that time you both want to continue, you will move from being a dedicate to being an initiate of the Duchas tradition."

"And if either of us doesn't want to continue?" Maggie asked.

Anastasia shrugged, "Then a ritual of parting is performed, and you both go on your way. No harm, no foul."

"Plus, the Lords of Lugh will keep me in line."

"Ah, Sinthia told you about them. Yes. The Lords of Lugh hold us to our oaths."

A sweet-sounding chime rang three times, and Anastasia sighed. "That's the Brownie letting me know that our time is about up."

"Brownie?" Maggie asked, confused as she looked around the room.

"Don't concern yourself with him right now. We have time for one more question."

Maggie blew out a breath as she tried to decide which of the myriad of questions that were swimming through her brain to ask. Maggie felt like she had heard many warnings and reasons not to become Sinthia's apprentice; surely, there must be positives too. That thought helped her form her last question.

"Most of what we've talked about is negative; what would you like to tell me about the positives of this path?"

"I'm sorry if my warnings have been a little heavy-handed, but this is a very serious decision, as you know. To be a witch is to be open to the magic in the world around us. To see the divine in the first daffodil that pushes through the snow and know that same spark of divinity lives within us all. It is about dancing with the powers that ebb and flow with the seasons and the lunar cycle. It is work, but it is also joy."

The chime sounded again, and Maggie's eyes popped open as the sound echoed off her bedroom walls. Maggie looked around in confusion, but the room was dark. When the chime rang again, she realized that her cell phone had woken her up. Throwing her pillow across the room, she slapped her hand across the nightstand, searching for her phone. Then, without looking at the ID, she hit the answer button.

"Hello," she croaked.

"Maggie?" a voice replied.

"Shaun?" Maggie asked.

"Yeah, are you okay? You sound weird."

"I'm okay, just waking up. Give me a second." Maggie struggled to focus. Her consciousness felt out of sync with her physical body.

"Waking up?" Shaun said as he checked the time and saw that it was 5:00 in the evening.

"I had a headache, so I took a nap. Hang on a minute. Let me get some water."

"Okay," Shaun said as he listened to the sound of Maggie moving around in their apartment, opening a cabinet, and filling a glass with water.

"Better," Maggie said, sounding more solid.

"I'm sorry you weren't feeling good," Shaun said.

"Thanks. I don't think I've been sleeping well."

"Me neither. I miss having you in bed beside me," Shaun said, and Maggie smiled as her heart gave a happy tug.

"I miss you too," she said.

"I called to see if you spoke with Sinthia."

"I did," Maggie said as she settled into a chair at her kitchen table.

"And?" Shaun prompted.

"And, she wants to teach me to be a witch."

"Wow," Shaun said. "That's cool."

Maggie smiled at Shaun's enthusiasm, "I guess it is."

"Did you say yes?" Shaun asked.

"Not yet."

"Why not?"

"Well, apparently, it's a big commitment."

"I would imagine so," Shaun said gravely. "Did she say what tradition you'd be learning? I did a lot of reading after the cleansing at the lighthouse, and there are quite a few. Some require multiple years of dedicated study..."

Maggie let Shaun babble on as an indulgent smile spread across her face. Shaun's enthusiasm for odd factoids was one of the things she found so endearing about him. She tuned back in as he tapered off.

"So, when do you think you'll make up your mind?"

"She gave me about three weeks."

"Three weeks? Why three weeks?" Shaun asked.

Maggie hesitated. Sinthia hadn't said she couldn't share why with Shaun, but she wasn't sure what might be considered an inner secret of the tradition.

"Maggie?" Shaun asked when she didn't answer. Then he understood, "Ah, you can't tell me."

"I'm not sure if I can or not," Maggie said.

Shaun swallowed his disappointment, "That's okay. If you're not sure, it's probably best not to."

Maggie understood how difficult not knowing would be for Shaun, and she appreciated his effort to squash his curiosity for her sake, "Thanks," she said. "I'll tell you what I can, but I appreciate your understanding when I can't. So, how will you feel being married to a witch if I say yes?"

"Witches are pretty sexy," Shaun said, making Maggie laugh. "But seriously, I want whatever makes you happy."

"Thanks," Maggie said.

"If I can be a sounding board for you, let me know. I have some books you can check out too."

"That's a good idea," Maggie said.

"They're stacked next to my bedside," Shaun said.

"I'll give them a look. So, how was your day?" Maggie asked.

Shaun filled Maggie in on his day, including his time with Mr. Steymer.

"So, he had a run-in with the ghost even before Mr. Madeira died," Maggie said.

"He did, and from what he said about Mr. Madeira's dementia, it makes me wonder if Mrs. Madeira was haunting him."

"Nasty," Maggie said. "So Mr. Madeira didn't have dementia?"

"I'm not sure. I think he was ill. But as far as I can tell, he didn't speak to Mrs. Madeira until after he was in decline."

"Are you saying his mental illness made him vulnerable to being haunted?"

"I think it's possible."

"That's horrible," Maggie said.

"I'm sure it was. I think we should give Mrs. Kleyn another chance with the ghost. What do you think?"

"I think it would be a good idea. Do you want me to give her a call?"

"I'd appreciate it. Let Mrs. Kleyn know she'll need to do it soon. I only have a couple more days here."

"Understood. I'll do that as soon as I hang up. I'll let you know what she says," Maggie said as she stood up and walked into the bedroom and over to Shaun's side of the bed, where multiple piles of books were stacked. "Which pile of books should I be looking at?" Maggie asked.

"I think that pile is a little further back toward the wall since it's been a while since I was researching witchcraft."

"We need to get you another bookcase or two," Maggie said with a smile.

"I should go through what's already on my shelf and figure out which texts need to be donated to the library. I just have a tough time letting go of a book once it's in my possession. You never know when you'll need the wisdom it holds."

"You could go digital," Maggie said.

"I could, and I have for my fiction reading, but I still like holding a research book in my hand to highlight and write notes in the margins," Shaun said.

"Writing in a book? Sacrilegious," Maggie said in a teasing voice.

"I know, I know. A lot of folks treat books like untouchable treasures, but for me, it's the content that is the treasure, not the paper it's written on. I'd rather see someone reading a book with a creased spine and ruffled pages than a pristine book taking up space on someone's shelf. The first is a beloved companion; the second is a status symbol."

Maggie picked up a book entitled, *Witchcraft for the Sole Practitioner*. "I think I found the pile."

"Good. If you have any questions, give me a call."

"Will do."

"Sounds good. I love you, Maggie."

"I love you too."

Maggie hung up the phone and leaned down to pick up the pile of Witchcraft books. She carried them over to the kitchen table, refilled her water glass, and called Annie.

"Hello, Maggie," Annie said.

"Hi Annie," Maggie said. "I just got off the phone with Shaun, and he was wondering if you and Mrs. Kleyn were still interested in returning to the manor."

"We were just talking about that. I called the tavern earlier to see if you had time to chat but was told that you weren't feeling well. Are you feeling better?"

"I am. I had a headache, so I gave myself the night off."

"I'm glad you're feeling better. Since we thought you were out for the night, I arranged for everyone to meet here for some pizza and a chat. You can join us if you want."

"I'd like that. I'll bring the wine," Maggie said.

"Terrific. Folks are swinging by around 7:00."

"Sounds good. I'll see you then."

Maggie followed Annie into her kitchen and was surprised by who she saw gathered around the kitchen table. She had expected Mrs. Kleyn and Sinthia, but Annie's boarder Vince Andreas was also sitting at the table.

"Hello," Maggie said to those assembled as she held up two bottles of wine.

"Nice," Annie said as she took the bottles from Maggie and uncorked one to let the wine breathe as she reached up into the cabinet to pull down wine glasses.

Once everyone was settled with a glass of wine and a slice of pizza Mrs. Kleyn called the gathering to order. "I'm glad you could join us, Maggie. We wanted to discuss our options and what we discovered since visiting the manor."

"That sounds good, but before you start, let me share some info that Shaun discovered. He spoke with a man whose mom was the housekeeper at the manor. When he was a boy, he had an encounter with the ghost." Maggie retold the story that Shaun had shared with her.

"How terrifying," Annie said in sympathy. "Poor little guy."

Maggie nodded in agreement, "Plus, this guy told Shaun that as Mr. Madeira's illness progressed, he began to complain that his wife was tormenting him. The staff thought it was just his dementia, but I wonder if it was more."

"It could have been. As cognitive abilities decline, many people begin to receive glimpses of the afterworld," Mrs. Kleyn said.

"I think Shaun agrees. Have you had any luck researching the history of the manor?" Maggie said.

"We didn't find anything beyond the public face of the Madeiras. He was a successful real estate mogul and devoted husband to a much younger woman from a poor family. He took care of her after an accidental fall left her completely paralyzed. No breath of scandal or hidden histories," Annie said.

"If we want the truth, we'll need to speak with the spirits," Mrs. Kleyn said.

"Shaun said he's open to you trying again, but it needs to be soon," Maggie said.

"The moon is waning; we might have an easier time communicating with the spirits than we did on the full moon," Mrs. Kleyn said.

"Why is that?" Maggie asked.

"Full moon energy is more about abundance and growing things. The waning moon phase is a time of inner workings and crone energy. The Crone is the cutter of the thread of life, and she deals with the dead," Mrs. Kleyn said.

Maggie noticed that Vince was nodding his head in agreement, and she wondered what role he played in this strange gathering. But then, something bumped against Maggie's leg, and when she looked down, she saw a very concerned-looking black and grey striped cat staring up at her.

"Well, hello there," Maggie said.

"Mert," the cat said as it leaped up to sit in Maggie's lap.

"Raye, she didn't invite you up," Vince said in admonishment.

The cat's attention swiveled away from Maggie's face to Vince's as it repeated, "Mert."

"Oh, she's okay," Maggie said as she stroked the cat's soft fur. "How could anyone deny such a concerned little kitty?" Raye was a Scottish-fold, and her perpetually folded ears gave her a worried expression. "I'm just surprised as I probably smell like Jack and Anne Bonny, our puppies."

"Raye gets along with most dogs," Vince said with an affectionate smile.

"I bet she does," Maggie said as she began to scratch the cat under her chin, eliciting a loud purr from Raye. Maggie smiled as the cat circled three times in her lap and then settled in for a nap.

"She likes you," Vince observed, and Maggie thought his simple statement carried a lot of weight. His cat's approval had elevated her in his estimation.

"I'd like a day to prepare for our return," Mrs. Kleyn said. "Would you ask Shaun if we could come up to the manor tomorrow night?"

"Of course. What are you going to prepare?" Maggie asked.

"I think it would be good for Annie and me to fast before we attempt another communication with the spirit. Plus, I want to blend a couple of oils and some incense to assist our communication."

"Fast?" Maggie asked.

"Fasting is often used to elevate your awareness beyond your material body into the spiritual realm. It may make it easier to connect with the spirits. Vince, would you be willing to come with us? We could use a protector."

"Wait, I'm not sure Shaun wants another person up there," Maggie said, concerned that their handful of participants was growing into an entourage. "You didn't need a protector last time. If you think you need protection, perhaps we shouldn't go. Wait. Is Shaun in danger?" Maggie asked, feeling concerned that Shaun was up at the manor alone.

Sinthia reached across the table and laid a hand on top of Maggie's, "I'm sure Shaun is safe. He's keeping the talisman we made with him at all times, right?" Sinthia asked, and Maggie nodded her head yes. "Then he should be safe."

"But why would Mrs. Kleyn and Annie need a protector?" Maggie pressed.

"During a trance, I would protect their physical body. That way, they can relax and focus on connecting with the spirit world," Vince said.

Maggie examined Vince's face and wondered how he was connected to Mrs. Kleyn and Annie. He obviously had an inside understanding of what they were discussing.

Sinthia watched the questions race across Maggie's face, and she jumped in before Maggie could formulate an answer. "Sounds like we have an agreement. Let's gather back here tomorrow afternoon, say around four." Everyone agreed, and Sinthia stood up. "Maggie, could I speak with you for a minute?"

"Sure," Maggie said, smiling down at the fur ball in her lap. "Sorry, sweetie, I need to get up." Raye stretched and then stood on her hind legs to give Maggie's chin a gentle head butt before jumping out of her lap. "See you all tomorrow," Maggie said as she stood up and followed Sinthia out of the room.

Sinthia walked Maggie out the front door and onto the porch, "Did you have a chance to speak with Shaun about our discussion?"

"I did," Maggie said.

"And?" Sinthia prompted.

"He was supportive. In fact, he recommended a couple of books," Maggie said with a smile, and Sinthia chuckled.

"I bet he did. Which ones?" Sinthia asked.

"I don't know. He has a pile of them. I guess he wanted to do some research after your cleansing of the lighthouse. One was something about a solitary practitioner, and another said it was a bible."

Sinthia smiled, "Trust Shaun to study across a wide spectrum on a subject. The sole practitioner book is closer to what we would call the outer court teachings. The Bible is probably The Witches Bible Complete. That one is closer to our inner court teachings. Neither one contains secrets from the Duchas tradition, but they will give you a good overview of the full spectrum of what someone may mean when they call themselves a Witch. If you have any questions or want some other book recommendations, give me a call."

"Will do," Maggie said as she pulled on a chunky black cardigan sweater. "It's getting chilly at night. Autumn is on its way."

"It is," Sinthia said with a grin. "I can't wait to begin decorating."

Chapter Twenty

Bountiful, California – Madeira Estate – The Artist Cottage

Shaun was curled up on his bed in the cottage at Madeira Manor, preparing to read about the Madeira lighthouse in *Lighthouses of Horror!* when his cell phone chimed. He grinned as the new ringtone he had chosen for Maggie played, Witchy Woman by the Eagles.

"Hello, beautiful," Shaun said when he answered his phone.

"Hi, handsome," Maggie replied. "I just got home from a pow-wow with Sinthia, Annie, Mrs. Kleyn, and Vince."

"Vince?" Shaun asked.

"Yeah. I'm not sure why he was there, but Mrs. Kleyn seemed to think she needs him to be a part of this."

"Alright," Shaun said hesitantly. "What did you all decide?"

"They'd like to come up to the manor tomorrow night. They're mixing together some magical stuff to bring with them."

"Really? Like what?" Shaun asked, intrigued.

"I'm not sure. They mentioned oils and incense."

Shaun fished beneath his pillow for the talisman Sinthia, and Maggie had made for him. He pressed the bag to his nose to smell the fragrant herbs. "I wonder if they're using the same herbs you used in my talisman."

"I'm not sure," Maggie said. "Are you keeping it with you?"

"It's tucked under my pillow," Shaun said as he put the talisman back under his pillow.

"Are you in bed?" Maggie asked in a saucy tone.

"I am. I was about to begin a new book."

"Another book?" Maggie asked teasingly.

"I had to buy it. It's a local self-published work entitled, *Lighthouses of Horror!*"

"Oh god," Maggie groaned. "You're going to give yourself nightmares. I assume it has a chapter on the Madeira Lighthouse."

"It does," Shaun affirmed. "It also has a chapter on our lighthouse in Crescent Bay."

"Of course it does," Maggie said dryly. "They have no idea what the true story is, but I guess that's okay."

"So, what's the plan for tomorrow night?" Shaun asked. Maggie filled him in on the details.

"I'm pretty exhausted. I think I'll call it a night," Maggie said.

"Sounds good," Shaun said. "Sweet dreams, I'm looking forward to kissing you tomorrow night."

Maggie smiled, "I look forward to kissing you too. Please stay safe and have sweet dreams."

"They'll be of you," Shaun said.

Shaun hung up, put his cell phone down, and decided he'd run to the bathroom before he settled in to read. He walked over to the blackout curtains planning to draw them closed when he spied a figure slipping around the far side of the gallery of the lighthouse.

"Hey!" he yelled as he tapped on the window to get the person's attention. He shielded his eyes against the rotating beam of the lighthouse as he tried to peer through the window to see if the door at the base of the lighthouse was open. "Shit!" he said when he saw the door was wide open. Shaun quickly pulled his clothes back on and sprinted down the cottage's staircase to the first floor and out the door. He stood at the lighthouse's base and watched as a figure stood on the gallery far above next to the statue of the lighthouse keeper.

"Hey!" he yelled again as he waved his arms to get the person's attention. Shaun slapped his pockets, looking for his cell phone. He'd need to call the police. Someone who was willing to break into a lighthouse and climb to the top might be dangerous or suicidal. If nothing else, they could arrest them for breaking and entering as well as trespassing. Then he remembered that his cell phone was on the bedside table. "Shit!" Shaun said in frustration. Now he was torn between going back to get his phone or climbing the lighthouse to confront the trespasser. But something about the figure made him uneasy.

He watched the figure standing on the lighthouse gallery. Then, as the beam from the lighthouse swept across it, the figure faded out, only to fade back in after the beam had swept past. *That doesn't make sense,* Shaun thought as he struggled to understand what he was seeing.

As Shaun's mind struggled to give a rational reason for what was happening above him, he was unaware that his body had begun to inch back toward the cottage. His foot caught on something on the ground, and he tumbled to the earth, banging his elbow into a hard surface. Shaking his head to clear it, he realized he had tripped over Mrs. Madeira's grave. That was when he realized who was walking on the gallery in the lighthouse. Shaun frantically searched his pockets, looking for his talisman, only to remember that he had left it tucked under his pillow.

"Shit, shit, shit," Shaun chanted as he began to crab walk back away from the tombstone until he could scramble up to his feet and lurch toward the open door of the cottage. A woman's scream split the air, and Shaun risked a glance over his shoulder to see the screaming woman on the gallery dive off the lighthouse to speed toward the ground.

Still cursing, Shaun turned back around and ran full tilt for the cottage, certain that he would feel Mrs. Madeira's icy fingers encircling his throat and choking him. Shaun sprinted through the cottage door and pounded up the steps to the second floor, where he dove onto the bed and jammed his hand under his pillow to clutch the protection talisman. The screaming continued as Shaun pushed himself back against the headboard, clutching the talisman to his chest. He could feel his heart beating frantically. In his mind, a chant of *please, please, please* looped repeatedly as he prayed for his safety.

The scream grew louder, and Shaun used it to track the ghost's progress. *She's through the cottage's front door. She's on the staircase. She's here!* He thought as the scream became so loud that he had to clasp his hands over his ears.

The scream stopped abruptly, and the silence was so profound that Shaun's ears rang with the emptiness. Shaun stayed still, feeling like a rabbit hiding in its burrow as a hungry wolf paused outside, sniffing and searching for its next meal.

As he watched the empty door to his room, a mist formed, and as it became more solid, he recognized the ghost of Mrs. Madeira. Her clothes were torn and muddy, and her hair was tangled into dirty black coils that wiped around her head like she was standing in a storm.

Her face searched the room, and her eyes passed over his huddled form multiple times without acknowledging his presence. A look of frustration creased her face, and her jaw dropped open unnaturally wide as she began to scream again. The wind surrounding her body expanded and began to whip through the bedroom. At first, it made the drapes and papers flutter, but it grew stronger until the paintings on the walls rattled and threatened to be pulled off their hooks. Shaun stayed as still as he could as he was pummeled by pieces of clothing, books, and papers.

Lighthouses of Horror! flew off his nightstand and slapped up against the side of Shaun's head. As Shaun reached up to bat it away from his face, his hand popped open, and the talisman was ripped from his grasp. Shaun dove for the talisman, but it whipped away from him to fly around the vortex of wind that was tearing the room apart.

Shaun's terrified eyes locked with the ghost's as he was revealed, and the ghost's scream became even more piercing as she focused on him. Her arm came up, and she pointed at Shaun with a finger capped with a ragged nail that looked like a claw. She took a step toward Shaun, telegraphing his demise with every movement.

A flutter of white caught Shaun's attention, and he saw the talisman headed his way. He made a desperate lunge trying to grab it, but he missed. Instead of grasping the cloth bag, he batted it toward the ghost. As the bag passed through the ghost, a loud popping sound exploded into the room, and the ghost disappeared. The wind stopped abruptly, sending all the detritus picked up by the vortex to the ground.

Shaun scrambled off the bed to retrieve the talisman, only to drop it again as he hissed in pain. The talisman was freezing cold. He carefully grasped one of the strings that tied the bag closed and used it to carry the talisman over to the bed, where he sat down to catch his breath. He looked at the mess left behind by the spirit's outburst as he pulled a comforter over his shaking body. Then, he realized it didn't matter what Mrs. Kleyn wanted; Mrs. Madeira would have to be exorcised from the property because she was too dangerous.

Slowly Shaun's shaking stopped, and he touched a tentative finger to the talisman to discover that it had returned to a normal temperature. He was too wired to get to sleep now, so he decided to burn off some of his nervous energy by cleaning the bedroom. He dropped the talisman in his pants pocket and began his chore, hoping it would ground him.

Once the bedroom had been set back to rights, Shaun felt that a cup of cocoa was in order. He picked up *Lighthouses of Horror!* from where he had placed it on top of his pile of books and made his way back down to the first floor. He cringed when he saw that the cottage's front door was wide open. He reached into his pocket and wrapped his hand around the talisman as he approached the open door, listening for any sounds. The night remained still, so Shaun took a chance and looked out the door toward the lighthouse. He cursed when he saw that the lighthouse door was still open. Should he risk closing the lighthouse door? Would it trigger the ghost to attack again? Finally, he decided it would to too dangerous to leave the door open overnight. He stepped across the cottage threshold and began walking toward the lighthouse quickly and quietly. Even though he was careful, the lighthouse door made a solid metallic clanking sound when he closed it. Shaun stood still and listened to the night. He relaxed when the gentle rhythm of nocturnal insects returned.

"Chocolate," he said as he turned back to the cottage.

Shaun decided it was time to break out the big guns, so he dug out his canister of drinking chocolate. Sarah Gnome had introduced him to the richly decadent drink. It was too intense to be consumed regularly, but he felt he deserved it tonight. He smiled as he stirred the dark powder into the warmed milk, thinking about chocolate being the remedy for a brush with Dementors in the Harry Potter mythology. *J.K. Rowling was right*, he thought as he brought the mug to his nose for a long sniff, followed by a sip. "Nice," he said as he took his mug over to the kitchen table where his book sat. He was still feeling vulnerable and unconsciously chose to sit in the chair that put his back to the wall.

He took another sip of the chocolate and examined the now creased cover of *Lighthouses of Horror!* He shook his head in disgust at the horrible font chosen for the title. It was a gothic font in a dark red with drops simulating blood leaking from the bottom of each letter. The gruesome title was embossed over a black and white photo of the Madeira Lighthouse, photographed from the servant's entrance. Shaun looked closely at the picture and realized that Mrs. Madeira's gravesite was missing. So, the photo must have been taken before her death.

Flipping the book over, he looked at the author's photograph. The picture was in color and showed an older man with a long white beard, wearing a red-plaid flannel shirt, a dark brown cowboy hat, and worn cowboy boots, standing next to the chained doorway of the lighthouse at Crescent Bay. The paint on the lighthouse was peeling, and long dry weeds choked the ground around its base. Which told Shaun that the picture had been taken before the Crescent Bay lighthouse renovation began. The author's biography said that the author, Peter Beyer, was a native of Bountiful who had a lifelong interest in ghosts and the paranormal.

The book description made Shaun smile and shake his head at the sensationalism. It read,

> *"Lighthouses are silent sentinels that have faithfully stood on our rocky shores guiding sailors away from the dangers of the shallows. While these monuments to man's nautical achievements may have protected sailors as they traveled by sea, those that manned the lighthouses did not have as peaceful a journey. The life of a lighthouse keeper could be a lonely and monotonous one that often led to insanity and volatile actions. Walk with Peter Beyer as he hunts for ghosts in Lighthouses of Horror!"*

Shaun flipped to the chapter on the Crescent Bay lighthouse and read another version of the tale he was familiar with. It wasn't the entire truth, but then only a handful of people knew the full story of what had happened to cause the Crescent Bay lighthouse to be haunted. The writing wasn't poor, but it was sensationalized. Talking about unrequited love and suicide.

Shaun turned to the chapter on the Madeira Manor lighthouse and settled in for a read.

Author's note

I have tried to tell the tale of the haunted Madeira Manor lighthouse for years. Still, it wasn't until after the death of Mark Madeira that any of the parties with inside knowledge were willing to speak with me. I believe they feared retribution from the powerful and wealthy man.

The following is a narrative I've pieced together from interviews with past employees and family members of Mark's wife, Teresa.

The tale of the Madeira Manor lighthouse is a cautionary tale warning against dedicating one's life to obtaining wealth while neglecting one's soul. Money may buy material things, but it can never buy the enduring love of others, and in the end, love is the only thing of actual value.

Mark Madeira was born in 1957 into a traditional middle-class family in America. Mark's father worked in an architectural firm as a draftsman while his mother took care of the household duties. Mark's Catholic parents had wanted to have a large family, but Mark's difficult delivery left his mother barren. So, Mark's parents' hopes and dreams for their large family fell onto Mark's shoulders. His parent's undivided attention was both a blessing and a curse. He wanted for nothing, but he was also under a lot of stress from his parents to perform at an extremely high level.

Mark grew up during the socially turbulent '60s, with his worldview being shaped by his religiously conservative parents. Mark's parents were concerned about the country's direction with the loose morals and drug use of hippies, plus the unpatriotic individuals who protested the war in Vietnam. His parents worked to instill their rigid moral beliefs into their son and enrolled him in Catholic schools to help keep him on the straight and narrow. They forbade him to date as they said a relationship would distract from his studies.

Mark wanted to follow in his father's footsteps, but his father wanted him to be more than a draftsman. So instead, he encouraged Mark to become an architect. Mark had a natural aptitude for form and design. He completed his Master of Architecture degree just as the real estate boom of the '80s began. It was the decade that created the catchphrase "Greed Is Good," and Mark focused all his time and efforts on chasing the mighty dollar. His designs were innovative and futuristic, and soon he became a much sought-after architect. His laser-focused dedication to his career brought him a lot of financial success. As a result, he was able to open up his own architectural firm, where he employed his father to be in charge of general operations.

Mark discovered there was more to creating a successful architectural business than producing beautiful buildings. He was expected to wine and dine with the rich and powerful, but familiarity bred contempt. The lifestyles of his wealthy customers included casual sex and rampant drug use, two activities that Mark's strict upbringing expressly forbade. For the next decade, Mark struggled to smile and schmooze people he felt were morally deficient while fighting the temptation to join them in their depravity.

As the 80s passed into the 90s Mark faltered. On New Year's Eve his company sponsored a party for their top customers. As the clock struck midnight Mark found himself embracing a beautiful woman and as the party continued on Mark took her to bed. When he confessed his transgression to his father, his father suggested that he wouldn't be as tempted to sin if he had a wife and family. Taking his father's recommendation to heart, Mark began to look for a suitable wife. Unfortunately, most of the women Mark dated were women his wealthy clients set him up with. Mark soon decided that none of them would suit as they were morally bankrupt. Then his eye fell on Teresa

Smithfield, a young secretary who worked at his firm. Her manner was respectful, and although her clothing was cheaply made, it was modest in its cut. Mark was hesitant as he was 20 years older than Teresa, but the more he interacted with her, the more he felt that she would be the one to help keep him from temptation.

The first time he approached her about going out on a date, she had politely turned him down. Instead of deterring Mark's attention, it reinforced his belief that Teresa was the one. Mark began a long campaign of flowers, candy, and cards to convince Teresa to date him, and finally, he wore her down.

Teresa's childhood had been the polar opposite of Mark's. Teresa had been raised in a large family of five by one of those hippies that Mark's parents had villainized. Teresa's mother wasn't particularly concerned with the stability of her bedmates, and Teresa's father abandoned her mother before Teresa was born. Teresa's oldest sister, Anna, tried to keep her younger siblings in line, but they ran wild through the neighborhood.

In high school, Teresa's typing teacher, Mrs. Houston, took Teresa under her wing and hired her as a receptionist. It wasn't a lot of money, but it was enough for Teresa to buy a little better clothing to wear instead of her sister's hand-me-downs. However, when Teresa's mother found out about Teresa's job, she insisted that she turn over the majority of her paycheck. When Teresa refused, her mother threatened to throw Teresa out of her home. Finally, Teresa relented, but she squirreled away the meager balance, planning for her escape.

After her senior year of high school, Mrs. Houston helped Teresa enroll in the local community college. Teresa applied *herself to her studies and completed her office specialist certification. Her first job was at Mark Madeira's architectural firm.*

Now she was being courted by the owner of the company, a world-renowned architect. The parade of men who had danced in and out of her mother's bed had turned Teresa off of dating, so Teresa's experience with men was minimal. Which meant that she was unprepared for Mark's aggressive pursuit. Mark took her to expensive restaurants, gave her lavish gifts, and showered her with his undivided attention. Teresa was swept up in the romance and found herself married and settled into Mark's enormous mansion, almost before realizing what had happened.

Once Mark had succeeded in winning Teresa's hand in marriage, his attention moved away from Teresa and refocused on building his empire. Teresa was ill-equipped for life as the wife of a wealthy businessman, and she struggled to find her footing. Mark brought in fashion designers and etiquette coaches to fill in the voids in Teresa's education, but all the instruction did was reinforce how out of place Teresa felt.

Mark and Teresa had been married less than two years when Mark's parents were killed in a plane crash. Teresa tried to comfort her husband, but he refused to let her see him mourn. Instead, he began to spend even more time at his office.

One day during a surprise visit to her husband's work, Teresa discovered that he was expanding his office to include a suite with a full bedroom and bath. When Teresa voiced her disapproval, Mark shut her down. He insisted that an occasional night spent sleeping at the office would help his productivity as commuting from the office to their home in the mountains consumed valuable time. But for Teresa, the expansion was another sign that she and her husband were drifting apart, and she blamed herself.

Mark and Teresa had been trying to conceive a child since their wedding night. Still, almost three years into their marriage, Teresa remained barren. Although Mark never voiced his opinion, Teresa believed Mark blamed her for their childless state. Teresa saw Mark's desire to sleep alone at his office as yet another sign that she had failed him as a wife.

As Mark grew more distant, Teresa spent days alone rambling through the large manor with no one but the staff to keep her company. The couple's interactions became limited to social gatherings where Teresa was expected to smile, be polite, and act the role of a happy wife. No whisper of impropriety or scandal was allowed to tarnish the public persona that Mark was building. Mark wanted the world to see him as a successful businessman with a beautiful and happy wife who was enjoying every luxury that money could buy. To guard that fiction, Mark hired Davis. Davis was Mark's fixer who did whatever was necessary to keep his boss' reputation untarnished.

Davis was a very tall and muscular man surrounded by an energy of barely suppressed violence. Teresa was scared of Davis and did her best to avoid him whenever possible.

Mrs. Madeira's sister Anna told me that Davis had always made Teresa uncomfortable. But when Teresa had approached her husband about her concerns, he had poo-pooed her. Saying that although Davis had a rough history, she had nothing to fear because Davis was paid well to protect everything that belonged to Mark. Teresa had felt a rush of warmth at the idea of belonging to Mark. But she'd learn that belonging to Mark had less to do with love and more to do with possession.

One fateful day Teresa was adrift without anything to fill her day, and she decided to visit Crescent Bay. She spent the afternoon wandering around Crescent Bay's abandoned lighthouse and speaking to the villagers about their rich history. It was then that she decided to work toward preserving America's lighthouses and the history attached to them.

Mark encouraged Teresa to set up a charity, perhaps hoping it would fill her time and reduce her dependence on him. Or he might have seen it as a way to add to his prestige.

A decade passed as Teresa struggled to give her life value by focusing on her charity. She worked with the different officials and held fundraisers to raise money for her cause. Her successes gave her confidence and a sense of fulfillment.

During this time, Mark's business became the premier architectural firm and was in high demand. His business's success allowed him the freedom to pursue a life-long passion that he had been unable to indulge in, creating art.

He built an artist cottage behind Madeira Manor and began to paint and sculpt full-time. His innate instinct for shape and form, which had served him well in creating buildings, translated to his art. His creations gained critical acclaim, and the ownership of a Mark Madeira creation was seen as a status symbol.

Mark and Teresa enjoyed their parallel lives; Teresa enjoyed interacting with different city leaders and traveling to fundraise for her charity. While Mark enjoyed holing up in his artist studio creating art. In private, when their two lives intersected, the pair were polite with each other, but the couple was living more like roommates than a married couple. Although this wasn't how Teresa had envisioned married life, she was content.

Teresa's charity had successfully saved four lighthouses before Teresa experienced her first failure. The lighthouse at Sand Dollar Cove.

The Sand Dollar Cove lighthouse was a smaller lighthouse perched at the outer point of a cove in the small town of Chelsey on the east coast. A prominent developer was interested in the land the lighthouse stood on but had no interest in preserving the lighthouse. A group of concerned citizens contacted Teresa's charity asking for assistance. When Teresa flew to Sand Dollar Cove, she fell in love with the beautiful old lighthouse and its history. Thus, began the battle between Teresa's charity and the developers. In the end, the town decided to sell the land and the lighthouse to the developer. This was the first time Teresa had failed, and the inevitable destruction of the lighthouse plunged her into a deep depression.

Mark couldn't stand to see his wife moping around the manor. So he purchased the lighthouse from the developer and paid to have it moved and rebuilt on their property at Madeira Manor. He even created a sculpture of a lighthouse keeper to honor all the hardworking men who had served as lighthouse keepers through the years. He had hoped to lift his wife's spirits by saving the lighthouse for her, but instead, the lighthouse became a daily reminder of her failure.

Mark was frustrated by his wife's continued depression. My interviews with the staff revealed that the couple began to fight loudly and violently. One day Teresa climbed to the top of the lighthouse and either slipped or jumped from the gallery walkway. Teresa hit the sloped wall of the lighthouse and crushed her spine, which led to her being fully paralyzed. Mark brought in a team of experts, but no one could repair the damage to Teresa's body.

In her bedroom, Teresa was confined to a hospital bed where Mark paid for round-the-clock care. The staff told tales of his undying devotion to his bedridden wife. Stories about the hours he sat by her bedside to read her the society pieces from the newspaper and keep her company. Teresa's health declined despite the best care the Madeira money could buy. Then, one evening, she passed away in her sleep.

Teresa had languished in her hospital bed for almost a decade, and now that his beloved wife had died, Mr. Madeira was inconsolable. He locked himself away in his cottage for months creating art to help him grieve. The art he made during his mourning period is considered by many to be his most spectacular work. His creations included the memorial he installed over his wife's final resting place at the base of her beloved lighthouse.

That spring, Mr. Madeira decided that he needed to shake off his grief and try to reenter society. Mark hired an event planner to organize a charity auction of his art hosted at Madeira Manor. The event was limited to business associates and art patrons. People were curious about Madeira Manor and its unique landlocked lighthouse, so the event was well attended. Mark ordered the door to the lighthouse padlocked to keep curious visitors from climbing the tower and getting hurt. But that didn't keep people from sneaking outside to see if they could find a way in. After yet another guest had to be escorted back to the manor by the groundskeeper, Mark decided to post Davis at the lighthouse's base to discourage nosy guests.

The auction was in full swing when a woman's scream split the air. Those assembled stood frozen for a moment as they searched each other's faces looking for confirmation that they had indeed heard a woman scream. When the scream repeated, people sprinted toward the sound, which seemed to be emanating from behind the manor. The tableau that the guests saw was shocking. A woman in a beautiful sequined dress was standing over a man's body which lay crumpled at the lighthouse's base. The woman drew a breath to scream again as her husband rushed over to wrap his arms around her and move her away from the scene.

Mark walked over to stare at the man on the ground and saw that it was Davis. One of the guests knelt by Davis's body and checked for a pulse, then he looked up at Mark and shook his head no. Mark had already assumed that Davis was dead from the awkward angle of his neck. He glanced up to the lighthouse's gallery and jerked back in surprise. A woman in a billowing white dress stood on the gallery watching the scene below.

"Who is that?" A man asked.

The woman on the gallery moved to sit on the gallery's railing. Then she leaned forward and let herself fall.

The assembled group screamed in unison as the figure plunged downward, but instead of hitting the ground, the figure faded away.

The horrified screams dissolved into confused silence as Mark's guests turned to look at him for an explanation. "Is this a sick joke?" a distressed woman asked, and Mark shook his head in denial. "Ghost," a voice said behind Mark, but everyone avoided his eyes when he spun around to see who had spoken.

"Out!" he screamed. "Everyone out!" But before anyone could move, another man stepped forward, "I'm sorry, Mr. Madeira, but this is an active crime scene. No one can leave." Mark looked at the man and saw that it was Leif Jonston, the chief of police for Napa Valley. "Everyone, please move back into the manor while I make some calls. We'll try to make this as quick as possible." Chief Jonston herded everyone back into the manor and then used the phone in the kitchen nook to call for reinforcements.

After their investigation, the police ruled Davis's death an accident. The report didn't mention the apparition that many guests had watched jump from the lighthouse.

The court of public opinion was divided. Some believed they had seen a ghost, and some searched for other explanations.

It has been this author's experience that some people will twist themselves into incredibly complex knots to deny the reality that ghosts walk among us. So, I'm not surprised that some of

Mr. Madeira's guests refused to accept what they had seen with their own eyes.

The doubters believed that Mr. Madeira's months of isolation and grief had led him to create a gruesome performance art piece in homage to his wife's accident. Further, they speculated that Davis had fallen from the lighthouse while setting up the illusion and died.

That horrifying night was the beginning of the end for Mr. Madeira's successful rise in both business and the art world. His company began to lose contracts and hemorrhage money. Finally, the stockholders voted to remove Mr. Madeira as the company's President and gave him a large settlement.

Mr. Madeira, now in his 70s, was at loose ends with nothing to keep him occupied. He had lost his business, and his artwork had become tainted by the horrid retelling of the events of that fateful evening. He spent hours wandering aimlessly through the halls of his manor, muttering to himself and having conversations with Teresa. His insane ramblings scared away most of the staff. The ones I've spoken to said that the manor had already taken on a haunted air long before Mr. Madeira began to manifest symptoms of his oncoming dementia.

I had difficulty finding servants of the Madeiras who would agree to be interviewed for this book. The few I did convince to speak to me anonymously shared frightening tales of Mr. Madeira's final years.

At first, the servants found Mr. Madeira's extended conversations with his dead wife endearing. But still, as the years progressed, the mumbled conversations became screaming rants filled with accusations of unfaithfulness and threats of physical retribution. As a result, the staff would tiptoe through their tasks during his rages to avoid interacting with Mr. Madeira.

One maid told a tale of getting fresh bedding from a linen closet and hearing Mr. Madeira scream Teresa's name. She froze in fear as she tried to figure out exactly where he was, and when Mr. Madeira yelled again, she realized he was getting closer. Feeling trapped, she crammed herself into the linen closet, closing the door. She stood in the dark closet, shaking in fear as she listened to Mr. Madeira approach and pause outside the linen closet door. I asked her what Mr. Madeira was yelling about, and she told me that he was berating his dead wife about how ungrateful she was. The maid said the most unsettling part of the exchange was that she thought she could hear a woman answering his accusations in a thin whispery voice. That was the day she decided to quit. She was convinced that Mr. Madeira's crazy was rubbing off on her.

Beyond the insane ramblings of Mr. Madeira, servants spoke about cold spots, apports, and a general sensation of being watched when alone in a room. The haunting seemed to focus on the third floor where Mrs. Madeira died, her burial plot, and the lighthouse.

You may ask if I think Madeira Manor and its landlocked lighthouse are haunted, and I have to say I'm not sure. I prefer to do my own investigations, but unlike the other lighthouses included in this book, the Madeira Manor lighthouse is not accessible to the public. So, all I have to go on are the reports of the handful of people I interviewed. I'd say yes if I answered your question based on those interviews alone. Madeira Manor and its landlocked lighthouse are haunted.

Shaun closed the book and picked up his cup of cocoa to take one last sip as he thought about what he had just read. He wondered why he hadn't heard about the death of Mr. Madeira's man, Davis before this. Had the death been covered up? The book didn't say if the coroner had deemed Davis's death an accident. Shaun was torn between trying to get a couple of hours of sleep or diving into some research. His brain was racing, but his body was exhausted. Deciding to compromise, he got up to wash his cup and headed to bed, where his laptop was.

Getting into bed, he piled up the pillows behind him and spread the comforter over his legs. He put his computer in his lap and turned it on. He smiled when his computer's laptop screen showed its desktop image. It was one of his favorite shots of Maggie, taken during their honeymoon in Ireland. Maggie was laughing at Jack Rackham as he frantically gave her doggie kisses. Shaun's heart swelled with love, and he reached out to gently stroke Maggie's face. He thought about Sinthia's offer to train Maggie as a Witch and felt slightly envious. How cool would it be to learn magic and stuff from a real Witch?

Shaun believed that Maggie possessed a mystical quality. He had seen her make choices based on nothing more than a feeling, and those decisions had usually turned out for the best. While dating, she had given him a couple of tarot readings. The readings exposed more of his inner nature than he wanted. It was as though the tarot cards were acting like x-rays that allowed her to peer into his soul. His Maggie definitely had some psychic skills that Sinthia might help her nurture.

Shaun hoped that Maggie would accept Sinthia's offer, but Shaun resolved to support her either way.

Opening his browser, Shaun typed in the names Mr. Madeira and Davis and settled in to do some research.

Chapter Twenty-One

Maggie's car had one more passenger than the last time she had pulled up to the gates of Madeira Manor. Mrs. Kleyn rode in the front seat while Sinthia, Vince, and Annie rode in the back. Maggie parked the car and pulled her phone out of her pocket to call Shaun.

"We're here," she said when he answered.

"I'll be right down," Shaun said before hanging up.

"He's on his way," Maggie told her passengers.

"Good," Mrs. Kleyn replied. "I'm looking forward to speaking to Mrs. Madeira."

"What if she won't talk to you? This may be your last chance to make contact and cross her over," Maggie asked.

"As a necromancer, it is my calling to contact earthbound spirits and ensure they are not in distress. But not all spirits want to cross over. As the Kybalion states, as above, so below," Mrs. Kleyn said.

Maggie shook her head in confusion, "The Kybal-what?"

"The Kybalion. It is a book of Hermetic Principles," Mrs. Kleyn said as if that clarified Maggie's confusion, which it didn't.

"Okay," Maggie said, slowly trying to be patient. "And that other stuff about above and below?"

"As above, so below. As within, so without. As the universe so the soul," Mrs. Kleyn said. To Maggie, it felt as if the energy in the car had shifted and expanded. "That phrase is called the Principle of Correspondence. In my example, I was using it to explain that a disembodied soul is no different from an embodied one. Have you ever heard that you can't save everyone, only those who want to be saved?" Maggie nodded her head. "It's the same with souls. We can only help those who want to be helped. Thus, as above, so below."

"Ah," Maggie said as if she understood Mrs. Kleyn's point, but she decided that she'd have to put it aside and do a little research. Maggie smiled when she saw a car's headlights approaching on the other side of the gate. "That will be Shaun," Maggie said as she opened her door and walked to meet her husband.

Maggie and Shaun shared a smile as he walked from his parked car and the electronic gate rolled open.

"Hi, love," Shaun said as the gate opened enough for him to step through and gather Maggie into his arms for a kiss.

"Hi, sweetheart," Maggie said when they broke apart. "I've got a full car tonight."

"I can see that," Shaun said with a slight wave toward Maggie's car. "Follow me," Shaun said as he stole one more kiss and then trotted back to his car. Shaun and Maggie drove past the manor and into the parking area in front of the cottage.

Shaun opened the cottage door and gestured for everyone to go inside. "Have a seat," Shaun said.

As everyone settled in, Vince approached Shaun and put out his hand, "Good to see you again."

"You too, Vince. What's your role here tonight?"

"Annie told me a little about what's happening, and I asked if I could tag along as protection."

"Interesting," Shaun said slowly as his mind raced with questions.

He was about to ask one, but Mrs. Kleyn spoke, "Since our time is limited, I'd like to head over to the manor with Annie to see how the energy feels tonight."

"Do you want me to come with you?" Vince asked.

"Not yet. There seems to be a pattern of the spirit becoming agitated by the presence of men."

Boy, I'll say, Shaun thought, but before he could voice his opinion, Mrs. Kleyn continued.

"I'd like to keep the spirit as calm as possible to start. Annie, are you ready?" Mrs. Kleyn asked, and Annie nodded. "Good. We should be back shortly."

"Shaun, do you need to disarm the alarm?" Maggie asked.

"No. The construction foreman couldn't turn the alarm on before he left." Shaun said. "They're sending out a repairman to look at it tomorrow."

"Do you think that's Teresa's doing?" Annie asked Mrs. Kleyn.

"I wouldn't be surprised. Her presence in the manor is probably causing all sorts of unexplained problems with the electronics," Mrs. Kleyn replied. "Let's go see if we can bring her some peace."

They watched Annie and Mrs. Kleyn leave the cottage, and when the door shut behind them, Shaun turned to his guests. "Would you like something to drink? Coffee, tea?"

"Just water," Sinthia said. "we need to keep our energy clear of stimulants until this is over."

"I'll have the same," Vince said.

"Maggie?" Shaun asked, and Maggie's gaze shot over to Sinthia's face.

"I'll have water too. Do you want some help?" Maggie asked Shaun.

"Nope, I've got it. Water all around. Why don't you have a seat, and I'll be right back," Shaun said.

After Shaun returned with four glasses of water on a tea tray, everyone settled into the armchairs in front of the fireplace. Shaun was uncertain how to tell Maggie about his interaction with the ghost of Mrs. Madeira the night before. Still, he felt it was important to tell her about his experience and what he had read about the Madeiras' marriage. He took a deep breath and then jumped in with both feet.

"I had an experience last night—" he began, then stopped to look at Vince. "If I share what I experienced with you, will it impact any messages you might receive tonight?"

"No," Vince replied. "I'm not a medium. Like I said, I'm just here to protect."

"But why you?" Shaun asked.

"Right place, right time?" Vince said with a shrug, and when Shaun sent him a skeptical look, Vince continued. "You know I write about the paranormal." Shaun nodded. "My travels have exposed me to a lot of interesting and odd things. That exposure has allowed me to pick up some skills over the years. One of those skills is protecting people from ghoulies and ghosties and long-leggedy beasties. And things that go bump in the night."

Shaun smiled at the reference to an old Cornish litany.

"Shaun, what happened last night?" Maggie urged.

"Right, sorry," Shaun said, and then he told them about his interaction with Mrs. Madeira the night before. When he finished, everyone sat in shocked silence. Maggie was staring at her lap, and Shaun tensed up, waiting for Maggie's justified anger to rein down on him. When her gaze lifted, he saw she was pissed.

"What is wrong with that bitch?" Maggie asked. Shaun froze, confused by Maggie's statement, then he realized that she wasn't pissed at him but at the spirit. "But, you're okay?" she asked, and Shaun nodded.

"You're lucky that Sinthia and Maggie made that talisman for you. Can I see it?" Vince asked. Shaun dug it out of his pants pocket and dropped it into Vince's hand.

Vince held his palm flat as he examined the bag with more than his five senses. "So, this is designed to act as an invisibility shield against spirits," Vince said for clarification, and Sinthia nodded her head. Vince shut his eyes as his hand closed the bag. "It feels solid," he said in a distant voice. Then he opened his eyes and looked at Sinthia. "You do good work."

"Thanks," Sinthia said with a smile.

Vince handed the bag back to Shaun with his thanks. Vince's actions piqued Shaun's curiosity. Did Vince have some sort of training? Shaun wanted to ask Vince a hundred questions, but there would be time for that later. Instead, he needed to focus on what was happening tonight.

"Do you think I should tell Mrs. Kleyn about my experience when she returns?" Shaun asked, and Sinthia shook her head.

"She's pretty firm about not wanting to know anything before she does a session," Sinthia said. "You can fill her in after if you want."

A loud squeak announced the opening of the front door and the return of Mrs. Kleyn and Annie.

"Any luck?" Vince asked.

"No," Annie said.

"I think we'll have to do a séance," Mrs. Kleyn said.

"That's my cue," Vince said as he stood up. "Do you want to take a moment or head back right now?"

"Wait," Maggie said, "how is Vince going to be able to watch over you and not trigger the ghost?"

"I was thinking about that," Vince said. "Shaun, would you let me borrow your talisman?"

"What talisman?" Annie asked, and Shaun pulled the talisman out of his pocket.

"This one. Sinthia and Maggie made it to hide me from the ghost," Shaun said.

"Spirit," Mrs. Kleyn corrected Shaun and then extended her hand for the talisman.

"What's the difference between a ghost and a spirit?" Shaun asked as he dropped the talisman into Mrs. Kleyn's hand.

Mrs. Kleyn took her time examining the talisman before she answered. "It's semantics, but I was taught that a ghost is an energetic memory of a living person lodged into a material item or place. Whereas a spirit is sentient."

"So, in your training, a ghost is what paranormal researchers refer to as a residual haunt, meaning it's like a recording. While a spirit is a sentient entity."

"Sounds about right," Mrs. Kleyn said distractedly as she continued to examine the talisman, then she smiled up at Sinthia. "Nicely done."

"Thank you," Sinthia said as she returned her smile.

"Shaun, if you're willing to loan Vince your talisman, I think it will be effective," Mrs. Kleyn said.

"I guess so," Shaun said, and Mrs. Kleyn handed the talisman to Vince.

"You said you wanted to do a séance. What exactly would that entail?" Shaun asked.

"A séance can take many forms. The most frequent type uses a spirit board or a glass with letters on a tabletop. I have used those methods in the past, but for this, I brought my black mirror," Mrs. Kleyn said as she gently patted her oversized tote bag.

A black mirror? Neat. Shaun thought. He couldn't help himself; he had to ask. "Can I see it?"

"No. My mirror is consecrated and must never be touched by anyone but me or exposed to anything but candlelight," Mrs. Kleyn said.

"Cool," Shaun whispered, and Mrs. Kleyn smiled.

"I think I'd like to try and make contact on the grand staircase," Mrs. Kleyn said.

"Why not in Mrs. Madeira's bedroom?" Shaun asked.

"Staircases are 'tween spaces, and as such, the veil between our world and the next will be thinner there, making contact easier," Mrs. Kleyn said.

"Tween?" Maggie asked.

"It's short for between," Shaun said. "They are spaces and times with no precise position, which exist as a bridge between one thing and another. Many metaphysical schools of thought believe tween spaces are magical because of their fluid nature. In our physical world, a tween space might be a staircase, hallway, basement, or attic. An example of a tween time would be midnight or dawn."

"Exactly," Mrs. Kleyn affirmed. "When we walked the house, I felt an energy fluctuation on the staircase, which is a 'tween space. I think we'll have good luck there, and if not, we can move to Mrs. Madeira's bedroom."

"Sounds like a plan," Vince said. "Let's go."

Vince closed the cottage door behind him and looked at the manor. Even though the windows were dark, the manor felt alive to Vince. His body reacted with an involuntary shiver, and he put his hand in his pocket to ensure that Shaun's talisman was still there. His body relaxed when his fingers brushed against the talisman's fabric. He looked up at the waning moon as he said a silent prayer to the Goddess. *Please watch over us and keep us safe as we go forth to help this tortured soul.* Then he hurried to catch up to Annie and Mrs. Kleyn, who were almost to the manor's door.

The group paused on the threshold to the servant's entrance, and Mrs. Kleyn closed her eyes to see if she could sense any change in the house. Annie mirrored her actions while Vince waited patiently. When Mrs. Kleyn opened her eyes, she looked at Vince and shook her head.

Annie opened her eyes and looked at Mrs. Kleyn, "It doesn't feel any different."

"Agreed," Mrs. Kleyn said. "Let's head to the staircase."

Vince jumped when the overhead light in the kitchen snapped on, and a protective spell flew to his lips. Annie's giggle kept him from casting the spell.

"Sorry," Annie said with a chuckle, "but you looked so startled. The rooms have motion sensors that trigger the lights."

"You could have told me that," Vince said with a self-deprecating grin, and Annie shrugged in apology, but the curl of her lips belied her sincerity.

"Let's go," Mrs. Kleyn said, and she led the way through the kitchen, past the library, and into the front foyer.

"Wow," Vince said as he looked up at the sweeping double staircase. "That's not creepy at all." Annie nodded her head in agreement.

"Let me take a moment to sense which staircase we should set up on," Mrs. Kleyn said. Then she grasped the mahogany railing of the right staircase and climbed up to about the halfway point, where she paused and closed her eyes. Annie and Vince stood in silence as they waited for her to decide. Vince studied the carvings on the staircase and wondered how carvings of cherubs and small forest creatures could appear so menacing.

Mrs. Kleyn climbed down from the right staircase and repeated her motions on the left staircase. "I think we'll set up here," she said. "Please bring up my tote, be careful, and only carry it by the handles; my mirror is inside."

Annie lifted Mrs. Kleyn's tote and carried it carefully up the steps to where Mrs. Kleyn stood.

"Thank you," Mrs. Kleyn said as she took her tote from Annie. "Annie, why don't you sit on the right side of this tread? I'll sit on the left to use the wall for support." The staircase was wide enough for Annie and Mrs. Kleyn to sit on the same tread. "Vince, do you have a flashlight?"

"On my phone," Vince answered.

"That will do. I can't unwrap my mirror until these lights are off. Shaun said the lights would stay off if we turned them off at the switch. Would you find the light switches for this room?"

"Will do," Vince said.

While Vince searched for the light switches, Annie and Mrs. Kleyn settled onto the step and began to breathe slowly in sync with each other, preparing for the seance.

"Found them," Vince called from a panel near the front door. Then, with a click, the front parlor was plunged into darkness. "Crap, one second," Vince said, and then his face was illuminated by his cell phone. With a couple of swipes, Vince turned on his cell phone's flashlight and walked over to Mrs. Kleyn and Annie.

"Thanks, Vince. Let me light my candle, and then you can turn that off." Mrs. Kleyn reached into her tote and pulled out a large purple pillar candle and a lighter. After the candle was lit, Mrs. Kleyn placed it on the tread above where she sat with Annie and turned back to Vince. "Okay, you can turn that off."

Vince tapped a button on his cell phone and then put it back into his pocket, "What do you want me to do?" he asked Mrs. Kleyn.

"You can stand guard below."

Vince nodded and placed himself at the bottom of the staircase below the two necromancers.

Mrs. Kleyn waited until Vince had settled in, and then she reached into her tote and pulled out a bulky package. Vince and Annie watched as Mrs. Kleyn unwrapped layer after layer of black silk from around her black mirror. Vince craned his neck, trying to get a better look at the mirror, and he could tell that it was about eight inches in diameter, concave, and completely black. Although Vince had never owned a black mirror, as his skills didn't lean toward seership, he understood how to make one. The process involved astrological timing, a sacred flame, and a lot of focused meditation.

A movement drew Vince's eyes away from Mrs. Kleyn, and he searched the foyer to see what had drawn his attention. He saw that the flickering candlelight had turned the playful smiles of the round cherub faces into evil leers. He was staring closely at one cherub that looked like it had fangs when Mrs. Kleyn's commanding voice echoed through the empty house, making Vince jump.

"I call to the one who straddles the veil between this world and the next. I call to she, who is the cutter of the thread of life. I call to she, who has been known by many names, Cerridwen, Annis, Hekate, and Macha. Wise woman of the ages. Come forward and help your priestess contact the spirits who wish to communicate with those gathered here this night."

Mrs. Kleyn opened her eyes and stared unblinking into the mirror she held in her lap. Annie focused on the mirror and tried to channel helpful energy to Mrs. Kleyn in case she could use a boost. Vince stood still on the floor below the two necromancers, with all of his senses alerted to potential danger.

The silence stretched on as the three witches waited for a spirit to make contact. Then, finally, Mrs. Kleyn took a deep breath and looked up from the mirror in her lap. "No luck," she said in obvious disappointment. "Let me wrap my mirror up, and we'll give it a try in Mrs. Madeira's bedroom."

Vince and Annie watched as Mrs. Kleyn put her wrapped mirror back into her tote, and after a nod from Mrs. Madeira, Vince moved over to turn on the lights. Mrs. Kleyn blew out the candle and handed it to Annie after admonishing her to be careful not to spill any melted wax. The trio walked up the stairs and down the hallway to the hidden stairwell leading up to the third floor.

Mrs. Kleyn opened the hidden panel exposing the stairwell to the floors above, and Vince grinned. "Cool," he said, and Annie nodded in agreement.

On the third floor, Mrs. Kleyn led the way to Mrs. Madeira's bedroom. When Vince saw the hospital bed, his smile faded. "That's pretty morbid," he said. "Why would they keep that?"

"I don't know," Annie said.

"Sometimes, people who have lost a loved one find themselves unable to release any of the deceased belongings. It's as if they can't face their loss, and if they dispose of their beloved's material goods, they'll be forced to admit they're gone," Mrs. Kleyn said.

"That's sad," Annie said.

"Death is hard for those we leave behind," Mrs. Kleyn said sagely. "I think we'll set up in the sitting area," Mrs. Kleyn said as she gestured toward a pair of wing-backed chairs and coffee table arranged in front of a fireplace in the left wall of the bedroom. Mrs. Kleyn walked to one of the chairs, sat down, took the pillar candle from Annie, and lit it. Then she looked at Vince, "Please extinguish all the lights on this floor."

"Will do," Vince said, and then he moved from room to room, clicking off the light switches. Returning to the room where Annie and Mrs. Kleyn sat, he noticed that the lighthouse light was still sporadically illuminating the room. Vince walked to the window across from the hospital bed to look at the lighthouse. Adrenaline rushed through his body when he spied a man standing on the gallery of the lighthouse, staring back at him. "Woah," Vince said, and then he smiled in relief when he realized it was a statue. A small chuckle caught his attention, and he turned to see Annie's smiling face.

"Got ya," she said teasingly, and Vince nodded.

"It did," he said as he leaned forward to look at the statue. "This place is creepy."

Annie joined him at the window to stare at the statue. "I guess Mr. Madeira created it as a tribute to lighthouse keepers."

"It's still creepy," Vince said, and Annie nodded in agreement.

Returning her smile, he pulled the heavy drapes over the window and nodded to Mrs. Kleyn that his task had been accomplished.

Mrs. Kleyn pulled the wrapped mirror out of her tote bag, unwrapped it, placed it on an easel behind the lit candle, and addressed Annie.

"Annie, if you'd join me," Mrs. Kleyn said. "I'd appreciate it if you would stand behind me, rest your hands on my shoulders, and channel some energy to me," Mrs. Kleyn said.

"Of course," Annie said as she moved to do Mrs. Kleyn's bidding.

Mrs. Kleyn reached forward and arranged the pillar candle so the flickering flame reflected in the mirror's center. "Okay, I think we're ready to give this another shot," Mrs. Kleyn said. She took a couple of deep breaths, preparing to enter a trance. Annie synchronized her breathing to match Mrs. Kleyn's. As she did, she could feel her awareness contracting until the world consisted of nothing but the flame flickering darkly in the black depths of the mirror.

Mrs. Kleyn repeated her evocation to the Crone Goddesses beseeching them to help her make contact with the spirits of Madeira Manor.

When Annie saw the mirror's surface filling with a light gray mist, she thought her eyes were playing tricks. She blinked her eyes rapidly, trying to clear them, but the mist remained. The mist swirled and churned, obscuring the surface of the mirror.

"Yes," Mrs. Kleyn said in a voice as quiet as a whisper. "Teresa, come through. You are among friends. Tell us how we can help you."

From his vantage point by the window, Vince watched Annie's face as she dropped into her trance and stared intently into the mirror. The energy in the room shifted, and Vince looked away from Annie to try and figure out what had changed. Everything looked the same as it had a moment before, but now it felt as though the room was crackling with static electricity. Vince looked back at Annie, and he could tell that she was seeing something in the mirror, and he felt a momentary twinge of envy. His skills leaned toward battle magic, which was part of why he was the Fetch.

As Annie stared into the mirror, the mist cleared, and she could see a miniature copy of the bedroom they were sitting in. But the bedroom in the mirror was colored in shades of grey and flickering candlelight. The image shifted and zoomed in until the hospital bed filled the mirror. But, instead of being empty, this bed was occupied by a still figure covered in a thin sheet and propped up by large pillows. Annie recognized the woman in the bed as Mrs. Madeira. But she looked so frail compared to the pictures of the smiling woman Annie had seen during their research in the library. As Annie watched, Mrs. Madeira's eyes darted to her left, and Annie thought she looked frightened.

Mr. Madeira walked into view, stood next to the bed, and pressed a kiss to Mrs. Madeira's cheek. "Good morning, my love." Annie felt confused because the voice didn't come from the mirror but from within the room. Looking up, Annie was startled to see that the scene from the mirror was happening in the room before her.

"You can go," Mr. Madeira said to a woman dressed in a classic white nurse's uniform. "I'll take care of her."

"Yes, sir," the nurse said, watching as Mr. Madeira began to run his hands over Mrs. Madeira's hair. The nurse smiled sadly at his devotion to his injured wife and carefully closed the door behind her as she left.

Mr. Madeira continued to stroke and play with Mrs. Madeira's hair, although, to Annie, it looked more like a man petting a dog than a man trying to comfort his wife.

Mr. Madeira leaned down to whisper in his wife's ear, and although his face was masked in a look of loving concern, his voice was sharp and spiteful.

"I gave you everything a woman could want; a beautiful home, money, travel. So why would you want to kill yourself?"

Mrs. Madeira's eyes widened slightly in surprise, and Mr. Madeira snickered. "Yes, I know that your fall wasn't an accident. I watched the whole thing from this very window." Mr. Madeira said as he gestured to the window across from the hospital bed. "I came up here to ask you a question and saw you walking on the lighthouse gallery. I watched you climb the railing and pause to consider your next step. I thought about calling out for you to stop, but I didn't think you had the guts to take that last step. I was wrong. Your leap was a thing of beauty. A perfect swan dive, unfortunately, what waited below was not the warm and welcoming waters of a pool but the cold, unyielding cement of the tower. It was a brave act that you probably thought would bring you freedom, but once again, the universe affirmed that you cannot leave me so easily."

When Mr. Madeira said the words *once again*, Teresa's eyes flashed over to examine his expression. Mr. Madeira nodded his head, and an evil grin twisted his lips. "Yes, I said again. I knew all about your affair with that lighthouse keeper. A little fucking didn't bother me, but I knew I would need to step in when you decided to leave me. I protect what is mine, and you, sweet Teresa, are mine. Davis took care of him for me," Mark said as he continued to stroke her hair in a mockery of tenderness.

"Davis snatched your lover from his home and took him to a mortuary owned by some of his old mob buddies. I hear that death by fire is excruciating, but that seemed like the right punishment for trying to steal what belongs to me. Oh, you're leaking," Mark said with barely suppressed joy as tears began to roll down Teresa's cheeks. Mark pulled a tissue from a box on the nightstand and started dabbing at Teresa's tears playing the caring husband. "Don't cry; it's not like your lover is gone. He will live on forever as a piece of art. It was very satisfying pounding and grinding his bones into the sand to be added to the cement."

Teresa looked out the window at the statue of the lighthouse keeper with horror. Stunned by her husband's depravity, was he telling her the truth or just trying to torment her? She thought back to the day her husband had presented the statue to his adoring public; it had been one of the most challenging days she had ever endured. She was forced to play the role of an adoring wife while her heart was breaking from the abandonment of her lover. She remembered Mark smiling, drinking, and accepting compliments on his new sculpture. How could he have been so relaxed if what he said was true?

"You don't believe me," Mark said. "I guess I can understand that. Did you know that your lover had a hip replacement?" Teresa would have nodded yes if she could have moved. An accident had destroyed her lover's hip and forced him to retire from the Navy. Mark fished a metallic ball from his pocket and held it up for her to see. "A crematorium's fire is good for destroying flesh and making bones brittle, but it doesn't destroy metal. I've carried this in my pocket since I fished it from his ashes. It makes a nice worry stone." The last shred of Teresa's sanity snapped, and deep in her mind, she began to scream over and over in horror.

Mark faded from Annie's vision, but Teresa's body didn't move. Annie watched as subtle changes took place. First, Teresa's hair grayed, then her skin took on the appearance of crepe paper as it began to sag away from a form that had become emaciated and skeletal. Throughout the transition, Teresa's eyes stayed locked on her lover's burial place. Then the body on the bed began to fade, and the sheet drifted down flat on the bed. Finally, footsteps echoed through the room, and Mark walked up to stand beside the bed.

"You're finally gone," he said to the empty bed. "I'm going to bury your body under a beautiful memorial I'm creating for you. I will put it where your body fell. So for all eternity, you will lay at the lighthouse's base, and that will be as close to your lover as you'll ever be."

As Annie watched, a flicker of energy behind Mark evolved into the transparent spirit of Teresa. She was dressed in what many necromancers described as her death state. Spirits could modify their appearance, but most spirits first appeared in the form they died in. Teresa was wearing a hospital gown that hung limply on her skeletal form. Her gray hair was dirty, tangled, and oily on her shoulders. The nails on her fingers were ragged and torn. The quality of care that Mrs. Madeira had received had waned during the final years of her convalescence. As Mark talked, the blank look on Teresa's face became a snarl of rage, and then Teresa threw back her head and screamed. The scream filled the room. When Mark didn't react, Teresa began to claw her face in frustrated anger. Long streaks of blood flowed down Teresa's cheeks as she focused her frustration on herself.

Mark continued to talk to the empty bed, oblivious to the angry spirit standing behind him. "You see, even in death, you will not leave me. Like I told you all those years ago, you belong to me."

Still screaming, Teresa swiped at Mark's face with her blood-covered nails. Mark gasped, and his hand slapped the side of his face in surprise.

Startled, Teresa stopped screaming and studied Mark's expression. "Bugs," Mark said as he rubbed his hand against his cheek as though he was trying to soothe a bite. A horrifying grin spread across Teresa's face, and she took another swipe at Mark, but this time Mark didn't react. Teresa cocked her head as if trying to understand why he had felt the first scratch but not the second. She took a third swing, but Mark didn't react. Annie watched as Teresa's spirit began to fade as she took repeated ineffectual swings at Mark. Finally, Teresa's image became an odd distortion that looked more like heat rising off a hot road than a human figure.

If Annie could have spoken to Teresa, she would have explained that she was depleting her energy by attempting to make repeated physical contact with Mark. But this was a residual memory, not a sentient spirit, so speaking to her would have no more impact than talking to a television screen.

"Well, I think we're done here," Mark said as he looked away from the bed to survey the room. "I don't think I'll be coming back up here. It's a little depressing now that my favorite plaything is gone." Mark patted the mattress and then walked from the room. Annie could hear Teresa weeping, and she tracked the sound across the room to the window.

Vince was watching Annie's face, and as her gaze turned from the bed to the window, a cold draft wrapped around him, making him shiver in reaction. A tear fell from Annie's eye and flowed down her cheek as he watched.

"Oh, Annie," Vince whispered, and then he jumped when a woman's enraged scream split the air. "What the fuck?" he said in reaction, and then a whirlwind of ice-cold air surrounded him. The air plucked and pulled at his clothes and hair, battering his face until he had to clench his eyes shut.

The curtains on the window behind him whipped forward and wrapped around his throat, tightening to choke off his air. Vince spun around to face the window, thinking that he needed to pull down the curtains, and as he reached out to wrench the curtains off the curtain rod, his fist struck the window creating a long crack. He pulled the curtains away from his throat and yelled, "Stop!" But instead of stopping the whirlwind, his yell seemed to agitate it.

The curtains were torn away from his hands to fly around the whirlwind, reminding Vince of the classic sheeted ghost before they spiraled back to wind around his legs. Vince felt himself falling toward the window. With a desperate twist of his body, he managed to hit the window sill with his torso instead of falling through the window. Vince grunted when his elbow hit the glass, causing it to shatter. Glass rained down onto the ground below. Vince said a silent prayer of gratitude that it wasn't him plummeting to the ground. He pulled his elbow in toward his body and grimaced when he saw that he was bleeding.

Annie gasped when Vince yelled, breaking her trance. She clutched a hand to her heart as her focus was jammed back into her body and the current time. The sensation was uncomfortable like she was trying to squeeze her soul back into a body two sizes too small. A gentle touch on her hand drew her attention to Mrs. Kleyn's soft voice, repeating, "It's okay. Just breathe nice and slow. Nice and slow." Annie focused on following Mrs. Kleyn's directions, and soon it felt like her soul had integrated with her body.

"Better?" Mrs. Kleyn asked, and Annie nodded. "Good," Mrs. Kleyn said as she focused on Vince, who was still yelling and struggling with the whirlwind.

"Vince," Mrs. Kleyn called in a calm but authoritative voice. "You need to be silent and slowly move over to us."

Vince did as Mrs. Kleyn directed. He stopped yelling and took a step toward the fireplace. Each step he took moved him further away from the angry whirlwind, which stayed stationary in front of the window. Vince looked at Mrs. Kleyn with a quizzical look on his face.

"I think the talisman's shields are designed to camouflage the wearer's energy and image but not sound," Mrs. Kleyn said. A look of understanding crossed Vince's face.

"You're hurt!" Annie said when she spied the blood on Vince's arm. Annie grabbed Vince's arm to examine the shallow scratches.

"Teresa," Mrs. Kleyn said gently. "Teresa, can you hear me?"

As Annie watched, the cyclone seemed to expand and contract, and Mrs. Kleyn nodded as though the change was an answer to her question. "Good. Teresa, you no longer need to stay here. You are free to cross over to the other side of the veil."

Instead of calming the cyclone, Mrs. Kleyn's statements agitated it. The cyclone expanded, and the hospital bed's loose sheets began flapping in the wind.

"Teresa," Mrs. Kleyn said in a firmer tone, "the only thing tying you to this plane is you. You are your own jailer. You are free to go."

"Mark," a voice said in a hard-spiteful tone.

"He's crossed over," Mrs. Kleyn said, and hell broke loose.

The room was filled with a shrill woman's scream of rage as the whirlwind expanded to fill the entire space. Then the lights began to flash on and off.

"My mirror!" Mrs. Kleyn cried in anguish as she dove to cover her black mirror.

Chapter Twenty-Two

Bountiful, California – The Madeira Estate – Artist Cottage

The energy inside the cottage was tense. Maggie and Sinthia sat quietly by the fireplace, trying to relax but failing. After Annie, Mrs. Kleyn, and Vince had left the cottage, Shaun had begun to pace the room in agitation. When lights came on within the manor, Shaun stopped walking to watch the ever-changing illumination, trying to figure out what the witches were doing. Shaun gasped when the lights on the third floor turned on.

"What?" Maggie asked anxiously.

"I think they're on the third floor," Shaun said, and Maggie rose to come and stand next to him. They stared upward at the lit windows, and Maggie clasped Shaun's hand, seeking comfort. When the lights clicked off, Shaun and Maggie continued to stare anxiously at the dark manor.

Teresa's bedroom window shook as though from an impact. "What the hell?" Shaun asked as he turned to Maggie. "You saw that, right?" he asked, and Maggie nodded.

"What?" Sinthia asked anxiously as she stood up from her chair to join them by the window.

"I'm not sure," Shaun said as he dropped Maggie's hand and walked out the front door of the cottage in an attempt to see what had caused the commotion. The night was dark, which seemed wrong to Shaun, and then he realized that the lighthouse was dark. He stared at the dark silhouette of the lighthouse and its forever lighthouse keeper standing watch on the gallery.

A thumping sound drew Shaun's attention back to the manor. As Shaun watched, the bedroom window shook again and then shattered. Glass rained down from the broken window. Shaun took a step toward the manor with the intent of helping, but a hand on his arm stopped him. He looked down into the worried face of his wife.

"No, Shaun, you don't know what they're doing in there. You might make it worse," Maggie said.

Before Shaun could reply, a woman's shrill scream split the quiet mountain air making Maggie and Shaun jump. Their eyes searched the dark woods and manor, looking for the source, but the scream came from every direction.

A shaft of light burst from the broken window in Teresa's bedroom and cut through the darkness like a killing blade. The light began to flash rapidly as the screaming continued.

A stream of mist poured out of the broken window and slithered down the wall. The mist pooled at the base of the manor, covering a pile of freshly raked leaves.

Shaun could hear raised voices coming from Teresa's bedroom. He couldn't determine what they were saying, only that they were in distress. Shaun couldn't stand out here if they needed help. So, he gently removed Maggie's hand from his arm, gave her a reassuring smile, and moved toward the manor.

Shaun cautiously approached the servant's entrance while keeping an eye on the odd mist.

"Be careful," Maggie called.

"I will," Shaun called back, and the pool of mist began to swirl into a whirlwind.

"Shaun," Maggie said with concern.

"It's okay," Shaun assured her just before the whirlwind pounced. Shaun was suddenly surrounded by a freezing wind that whipped around him, carrying leaves and shards of glass from the ground.

"Shaun!" Maggie screamed, but Shaun couldn't respond as he was focused on protecting his eyes from the flying glass. Sharp edges sliced through his hands and exposed flesh as Shaun curled up on the ground, trying to cover as much of his body as possible.

Maggie stopped screaming and sprinted to where Shaun was lying curled up under the deadly whirlwind. She covered her eyes as she plunged through the whirlwind and hissed as a piece of glass sliced across the back of her right hand. Maggie curled her body over Shaun's, uncertain what else she could do to protect him as the wound on her hand dripped blood onto the earth. Maggie didn't know it, but she was chanting under her breath. Praying to anyone who would listen, "Please, please, please, please," she repeated.

Maggie felt her awareness shift, and she experienced an odd expansion of her awareness as a feeling of calm permeated her body. She could sense Sinthia standing on the steps of the cottage and knew that she was struggling as she tried to figure out what she should do. Maggie was aware that Annie, Vince, and Mrs. Kleyn were rushing down the stairs inside the manor. In her mind, she saw a beautiful woman with flowing red hair wearing a golden-yellow robe, surrounded by fire. The woman smiled at Maggie and reached out a hand toward her. A feeling of love and strength radiated from the woman, and Maggie felt comforted by her presence. In Maggie's mind, the woman said, "I can help if you allow me."

"Please," Maggie begged, and the woman nodded in response. An odd feeling of detachment filled Maggie, and she watched from a distance as her body moved without conscious thought. Maggie saw herself turn Shaun so she could reach his forehead, and then she began to stroke her finger across his brow. She was surprised to see that her finger left a red trail in its wake, and then she realized that she was drawing on his forehead with blood from her sliced hand. Her hand continued to move, and when her hand fell away, she recognized the symbol on Shaun's forehead as the sigil of spiritual protection she had drawn for Sinthia.

The sigil seemed to agitate the whirlwind, and it began to move erratically as though searching for something. Then, it swirled away toward the lighthouse as the servant's entrance banged open. Vince, Annie, and Mrs. Kleyn spilled out of the manor.

"Teresa," Mrs. Kleyn's voice called as she followed the whirlwind.

Sinthia rushed over to Maggie and Shaun. "Oh, my goddess, are you okay?" Then she froze when she saw the bloody sigil on Shaun's forehead. "Maggie, what have you done?" she asked.

In confusion, Maggie looked up at Sinthia, "It wasn't me."

Sinthia searched Maggie's face trying to understand what she was seeing, "Then who was it?"

"I don't know," Maggie said as she struggled to explain what had just happened. "I think it was a goddess. She had beautiful red hair and was surrounded by fire."

Shaun's hand reached up toward his forehead, but Sinthia caught his wrist and stopped him. "Leave it," she said. "It's the most powerful protection you'll ever have. A sigil drawn by a goddess using your loved one's freely offered blood."

"Blood? Maggie!" Shaun said in shock as he struggled to his knees and began to inspect Maggie for wounds.

"I'm okay. My hand got sliced by some glass, that's all," Maggie assured him as she showed him the shallow slice on the back of her hand.

"Wow," Annie said when she saw the sigil drawn on Shaun's forehead. Vince scribbled something on a pad of paper and handed it to Shaun.

The pad of paper had the company logo of the State's hired contractor at the top, and Shaun figured that Vince must have found it inside the manor. The note read, *Sorry you got hurt.* Shaun looked at the note in confusion, wondering why Vince wasn't speaking to him.

Annie stepped in to explain. "We think the talisman doesn't shield against sound. When Vince spoke upstairs, Teresa attacked him."

"Damn," Sinthia said softly. "We made the talisman too specific. Sorry about that, Vince."

Vince shrugged and gave Sinthia an understanding smile.

"But why isn't Teresa attacking us? We're speaking," Maggie asked.

"Mrs. Kleyn believes that Teresa only attacks men. That sigil on Shaun's forehead is protecting him," Annie said.

"She attacked me," Maggie said.

"Did she attack you, or were you hurt because you stepped into the whirlwind around Shaun?" Sinthia asked.

Maggie thought about it and then nodded. "You're right. So, she only attacks men. There's a story there."

Annie nodded, "Yes, there is, and I'll share it with you after this is over."

Mrs. Kleyn walked back to where the group was standing. "I'm having trouble getting through to her—," she began. But she stopped speaking when she spied the sigil on Shane's forehead and Maggie's blood-smeared hand. "Brid?" she asked Sinthia, who replied, "I think so. She joined with Maggie to protect Shaun."

"Then you are truly blessed," Mrs. Kleyn said. "I could use some help from the Goddess."

"Is Teresa being stubborn?" Sinthia asked.

"Her hatred has bound her to this space; she has to release it before she can move on," Mrs. Kleyn said.

"Hatred?" Sinthia asked.

"Yes, she was horribly abused by her husband, and after she passed, her hatred remained. She learned how to pull energy from those around her and focus that energy to punish her tormentor. But now he's gone, and she has no one to expend that energy on. That was okay while the manor stayed mostly empty, but the arrival of the construction crews gave her an energy boost. She's still charged up from the energy she leeched from the construction workers today. Until that well of energy is tapped, I don't think I can get her to listen to me."

The group stood and watched in frustrated angst as the whirlwind spun like a destructive top upon the place where Teresa's body was buried.

Vince took the pad of paper back from Shaun, scribbled something, and handed a note to Annie. The note read, "Don't worry. Trust me."

"What are you going to do?" Annie asked with concern, but Vince just smiled.

As the group watched, Vince moved to stand in front of the lighthouse. He pulled Shaun's talisman out of his pocket and dropped it as he began to speak in a commanding voice, "I walk with the Goddess Morrigan. I am her warrior and a protector of her children. Morrigan, your warrior, asks that you shield me from harm as I walk into battle in your sacred name."

Annie gasped as the whirlwind began to move across the lawn toward Vince but when she tried to rush to his aid Sinthia held her back. "Trust him. He is our Fetch, and he walks with the Goddess."

Shaun stored that bit of information for later. *What the heck was a Fetch?* he wondered. But, he had a feeling that he was getting a forbidden peek into the secret workings of the tradition that Sinthia wanted Maggie to join, so he kept his mouth shut.

The whirlwind moved toward Vince, and as it approached, a red-tinged fog rose from the earth to surround Vince's form. The whirlwind pushed against the fog, causing vivid red lightning bolts to spark across its surface.

A frustrated woman's scream split the air as Teresa's energy beat against the Goddess's shield, trying to reach Vince. Slowly, the attack's ferocity waned as Teresa's energy was depleted. The whirlwind disappeared, and the night became quiet. A white mist lay in a pool just beyond the red fog, and Mrs. Kleyn walked over to stand beside it.

"Teresa," she said in a gentle voice. "Can you hear me?"

The mist took on an opaque shape of a woman's form, which lay crumpled on the ground shaking with sobs.

"Oh, Teresa," Annie said in sympathy as she walked over to stand by Mrs. Kleyn's side. Teresa lifted her tear-stained face to look at Annie, reaching out a hand. Annie extended her hand, and although Teresa's hand was not solid, Annie could feel their energies mingle.

"Speak from your heart," Mrs. Kleyn said quietly to Annie.

"I'm sorry you suffered so in life. No one deserves the type of treatment you received," Annie said as tears of sympathy slid down her cheeks. "But the man who did this to you is dead; he no longer has a hold over you. You're free." Teresa shook her head in disbelief, but Annie refused to give up. "Look at the manor," she said as she motioned to the dark building. "It is empty. No servants and no Mark. Can't you feel how empty it is? I promise you, Mark is dead. He has crossed over into whatever afterlife he earned. You no longer have to walk these dark halls."

Teresa paused and stared intently at the manor; then, she turned her face to Annie with a hopeful and beseeching look. A faint whisper filled the air, "Swear?"

"I swear on all that I hold dear. Mark is dead, and you are free."

Suddenly the yard was illuminated as the lighthouse light clicked on. The beam of light was stationary, creating a shining bridge between the lighthouse and Teresa's bedroom.

The corners of Teresa's lips slowly turned upward into a beautiful smile as her face filled with joy. "Thank you," the voice whispered as Teresa began to float upward toward the beam of light.

Shaun struggled to watch Teresa's ascent, but the bright light from the lighthouse made it challenging. Through squinted eyes, he watched Teresa rise to join with the light. Before she disappeared, he thought he saw another silhouette embrace Teresa's soul. Then the light began to sweep across the yard in its regular pattern.

"Clear?" Vince asked, and Mrs. Kleyn nodded her head.

"I thank the Morrigan for their protection, and I remain their humble servant. Until we meet again. Hail, farewell, and blessed be."

"Blessed be," the assembled witches responded automatically, and Shaun smiled.

"Cool," Shaun said under his breath, and Maggie smiled at him.

Back in the cottage, Shaun found a first aid kit while Sinthia brewed tea and coffee for those gathered in the cottage's kitchen. Antiseptic and gauze were administered between sips of caffeine as everyone sat quietly, trying to absorb what they had just experienced.

Once the injured were bandaged, Shaun drew a deep breath and began. "Normally, I'd give each of you a pad of paper and have you write your experiences to keep from cross-contaminating your memories, but I'm just too drained." Shaun's statement made Maggie smile, and she reached out to hold Shaun's hand in support.

"Instead, why don't you tell us what happened in the manor, and we'll go from there," he said.

Vince assumed the role of a storyteller with interjections from Annie and Mrs. Kleyn. However, when Vince hit the point in his tale where Teresa's whirlwind had attacked him in the manor, Shaun stopped him.

"Wait, I have a question. I saw what you did at the base of the lighthouse; why didn't you do that in the manor?"

"The attack happened so quickly I didn't have time to focus. All I could do was try and keep from being strangled or thrown through the window," Vince answered. Shaun nodded in understanding.

Annie picked up the tale. "Mrs. Kleyn had figured out the limitations of the talisman, and she told Vince to keep quiet and move away from the window. Then she tried to explain to Teresa that Mark was dead and that she was free to cross over. But, instead of calming her down, she became even more agitated. That's when the lights began to flash on and off."

Everyone turned to look at Mrs. Kleyn, who sat quietly, cradling her black mirror in her lap as gently as a sleeping child.

The expression of sorrow on her face stabbed at Shaun's heart. "Can you fix it?" he asked gently, and Mrs. Kleyn lifted her sad eyes to his and shook her head no.

"It's ruined," she said and sighed. "I'll spend the next dark moon releasing what energy it still contains and then begin the long process of creating a new one. The worst part is that this mirror has served me well for over a decade." She glanced back into the mirror, and her hand began to move gently over the smooth surface as her eyes took on a faraway look. "All that stored energy is gone." Then she seemed to shake off her melancholy. She wrapped the mirror in its black silk cloth and placed it back into her tote out of sight. "Many of us sacrificed tonight to help Teresa cross over. Thank you," she said with a small smile for each of those gathered. Then she drew a deep breath and sighed. "It's late, and my bones are aching with exhaustion, so if you don't mind, I'd like to begin the journey back to Crescent Bay."

"Of course," Vince said as he stood up and offered a hand to Mrs. Kleyn.

"Wait a minute," Maggie said. "How is Shaun going to explain the mess?"

"I've been thinking about that, and I have it covered," Shaun said.

"You're sure?" Maggie asked.

"Completely. Do you feel up to driving back down the mountain?"

"I do. Tomorrow will be a little rough, but I have enough steam to get us home," Maggie assured him as everyone stood up and trooped out to the cars.

Shaun and Maggie's cars drove down the long driveway to the large wrought iron gates that protected the driveway of Madeira Manor.

Shaun sprinted up to Maggie's car to give her one last kiss and then settled in to surf on his phone to delay the next step in his plan. He had decided to call the police and tell them that he had gone out earlier for dinner. Upon his return, he noticed the broken glass on the grass behind the manor. He would tell the police that he couldn't be sure if anyone was still inside, so he had decided to wait by the gate for the police to come and check it out. If the police checked the gate log, they would see that the gate had been opened twice since the construction crew had left for the day. Once when he had opened it for Maggie and one more time when she left. Those times would mirror the story he would tell the cops and hopefully act as evidence to support his tale.

When the patrol car arrived, the policeman asked him to wait for them by the gate while they searched the manor. Shaun handed them the keys to the manor and settled into his car seat to await their return.

He must have drifted off because he was awoken by a sharp rapping. He opened his eyes to see the policeman had returned and was knocking on his car window. When the policeman saw that Shaun was awake, he stepped back so that Shaun could open his door and step out.

"What did you find?" Shaun asked.

"The manor appears to be empty, but you're right. Someone was inside and vandalized a couple of the rooms on the third floor," the policeman said.

"What did they vandalize," Shaun said, hoping that he sounded uninformed but concerned.

"They broke one of the windows, which explains the glass you found on the ground. Tore up some drapes, and they moved some furniture around. Nothing expensive. It's possible that you returned and disturbed them before they could do any real damage," the policeman said, and Shaun nodded in mute agreement. He figured that the less he spoke, the better.

"I will have to take your statement and write up a report. Let's get this done so you can get back to sleep."

Chapter Twenty-Three

Crescent Bay, Foghorn Tavern

Maggie sat in her car and breathed a sigh of relief. She had just finished dropping off her passengers, and she was relishing a moment of solitude. Her mind raced as she thought about everything that had transpired, and she knew that as tired as she was, she wouldn't be able to fall asleep easily.

She was tempted to sneak upstairs without interacting with anyone, but she had to retrieve Anne Bonny and Jack from Suzy, who had looked after the dogs while Maggie was away. It was late, and the only part of the tavern still open was the bar, so that was where Maggie went in search of her furry pirates.

She unlocked the delivery entrance of the bar and stepped into its cool depths.

"You're back," a man's voice rang out, and Maggie turned to smile at her bartender Max.

"Yep. Is everything okay?" she asked.

"No problems. Pretty much just locals tonight," Max said.

"This weekend, we'll see some fresh faces," Maggie said.

"Here's to the season," Max said, referring to the village's most lucrative time of year, the Halloween season. In Crescent Bay, the season ran from mid-September to just past Halloween.

"Agreed. Where are the pups?" Maggie asked.

"Wait until you see," Max said with a big grin, and Maggie cringed, wondering what was up. She followed him to the bar and laughed when she saw Anne Bonny and Jack curled up on a dog couch designed to look like a pirate throne. The wooden back had been carved with a large skeleton head sporting an eye patch and a red and white striped bandanna. Raised carvings of golden coins and brightly painted gems covered the rest of the dark-colored wood. The pad on the couch was a silver-colored fleece.

When the dogs saw Maggie, they yapped joyfully and rushed across the bar to where she stood. She knelt down to pet their wiggling bodies as she tried to avoid their enthusiastic puppy kisses. Once they had settled down, she turned to Max with a questioning look.

"Where did this come from?" she asked.

"Charles J came by earlier to drop it off," Max said.

"Charles J?" Maggie asked in shock. Charles J was a reclusive artisan who lived on the outskirts of the village. His artwork was much sought after, and Maggie stared at the couch in wonder. "A Charles J original."

Maggie had often walked the dogs by Charles J's studio as it was on the walking loop that went past the lighthouse and onto the cliffs by the beach. She never intruded on him, but if he heard the puppies, he would come out to give them snacks and a few pats. Of course, those interactions generated future interactions as the dogs began to bark when they approached his studio, anticipating treats.

"Amazing," Maggie said as she ran her hands over the carvings. Anne Bonny and Jack jumped back up onto their throne and groomed themselves. "You two are thoroughly spoiled," Maggie told them.

"They deserve it," Suzy said as she entered the bar from the restaurant side of the tavern.

"Suzy, thank you for watching the puppies," Maggie said.

"Glad to do it," Suzy said. "They're such sweethearts."

"When was the last time they went for a W-A-L-K?" Maggie spelled out the word walk to keep the dogs from causing a ruckus.

"About an hour ago," Suzy said.

"Then I think we'll take one more before I head upstairs for the night. You okay locking up?" Maggie asked, and both Max and Suzy nodded.

"Suí," Maggie said to the dogs, who stood up and walked over to sit at attention by Maggie's feet. When Suzy pulled the dog's leashes out from behind the bar, their little bodies vibrated as they struggled to stay still. Maggie clicked the leashes onto their collars and said, "Sted." The dogs stood up to take a position by Maggie's right-hand side. "Okay, we're off. I'll see you all tomorrow."

Maggie stepped out of the tavern and paused to breathe in the crisp ocean-scented air. A low fog had begun to crawl up from the beach to fill the village's streets. Maggie smiled. She loved her life and the little village. *Life is good*, Maggie thought.

The moon in the sky was a slender sliver of silver in the night sky and looking at it reminded Maggie that she had a life-altering decision to make. She decided to take a walk on the beach to clear her head.

The trio continued their slow stroll through the village until they reached the lookout point above the lighthouse. Maggie sat on a bench to watch the dark ocean and the sweeping light from the lighthouse, which exposed the low-lying fog that rode upon the waves of the incoming tide. After scouting the area, the pups settled down at Maggie's feet to keep her company.

She ran her hands over their soft fur and murmured words of love to them, which they returned with adoring eyes and wet tongues. Then, finally unable to keep her thoughts to herself, she spoke to Jack.

"What am I going to do, Jack? No matter which choice I make, my life will be changed. If I say no, I'll never be offered this opportunity again. If I say yes, I step into the unknown. I don't want to upset Sinthia by turning her down, but I'm scared." Jack whined and put a paw in her hand to offer her comfort, and she smiled wistfully.

Her life had changed so much over the past handful of years. Before Shaun, she had been a wild and carefree woman who bravely took what she desired. Her main concerns had been the success of her business and enjoying her life. Now she had a husband and two furry dependents. She had sacrificed her self-focused lifestyle to partner with Shaun, and she didn't regret that decision. She had been concerned that her marriage to Shaun would impact her freedom. But instead of tying her down, Shaun's love had encouraged her to fly. Plus, she knew that he would be there to catch her if she fell.

Her heart filled with love for Shaun, and tears sprung to her eyes as she remembered how helpless he had looked with that whirlwind of debris and glass swirling around him. She thought about her vision of a Goddess and the odd sensation of watching her body move without conscious thought. *A goddess*, she thought. But, had she really seen a goddess? She asked Jack his opinion, "What do you think, Jack, was that a real goddess?"

"A goddess?" a male voice asked, and Maggie jumped off the bench, spun around, and saw Charles J standing behind her on the path. He raised his hands in a gesture of peace when he saw her reaction.

"I'm sorry, I didn't mean to startle you," he said. Maggie thought Charles J looked like an old-time whaling captain. He was a man in his 70s with piercing blue eyes and a full head of silver hair that tended to get long when he was focused on one of his projects. His lush beard and mustache were also silver. Although his shoulders were more curved than they may have been in his youth, his body reflected his active lifestyle. His clever hands, which he used to create beautiful art pieces, were often covered in paint and small scratches. He carried a walking stick made of very dark wood carved with Celtic knots, fairies, and other whimsical creatures.

Maggie clutched her hand to her chest and watched as the dogs raced over to greet their benefactor. Charles J knelt down to greet the dogs, who shamelessly flipped over onto their backs to ask for belly rubs. Charles J laughed a deep-throated laugh at their antics and obliged their request. Maggie drew in a breath and forced her heartbeat to slow before responding.

"It's okay. I just didn't hear you," Maggie said.

"My fault. I was going to walk by, but I heard you talking to Jack. You saw a goddess?" he asked, and Maggie felt foolish.

"I'm not sure what I saw," Maggie said.

"Well, what did she look like," Charles J asked patiently.

"She was beautiful with long flowing red hair. She was wearing a robe of golden yellow, and she was standing surrounded by fire."

"Brid," Charles J said with a nod of his head. Maggie remembered Mrs. Kleyn had used that name too.

"Who is Brid?" Maggie asked.

Charles J made a gesture asking if he could join her on the bench, and Maggie nodded her head. The dogs pranced around Charles J's feet as he walked over to the bench and sat across from Maggie with his back to the ocean. Once he was settled in with the dogs curled up at his feet, he lifted his eyes to Maggie.

"Brid is an ancient goddess of the Tuatha Da Danann. Which loosely translates into English as The Children of Danu. Danu is an ancient mother goddess of the Celts. Brid is a fierce fighter for those she loves. She is known as the goddess of protection, healing, divination, and blacksmithing, among other things. Which is how I know her. I seek her out for inspiration when I'm working with metal."

Maggie didn't think she'd ever heard Charles J say so much in one sitting. She smiled because his speech pattern reminded her of Shaun when he became swept away with enthusiasm by some factoid or other that had caught his attention. "You work with a goddess?" she asked.

"Sure," Charles J said with a shrug of his shoulders. "I also work with the muses, nature spirits, elementals, and Gods. Whoever wants to step forward and use me as a vessel to create beauty."

Maggie thought this was one of the oddest conversations she had ever had. But who was she to judge Charles J? Especially considering her experience earlier that night? "Speaking of that. Thank you for the puppies' gift. It's beautiful."

"You're welcome. Gwyn ap Nudd had a hand in that one," Charles J said.

"Who?" Maggie asked in confusion.

"Gwyn ap Nudd," Charles J repeated. When he saw the blank look on Maggie's face, he waved a hand in the air as if he could erase what he had just said. "Don't worry about it. He's another god who is partial to dogs."

"Okay," Maggie said slowly. "Well, please thank him for me because it's a beautiful piece of art."

"I'm glad you like it," Charles J said with a happy smile. "Now, tell me why you look so troubled."

The night took on an even more surreal feel as Maggie found herself discussing Sinthia's offer in obscure terms with a virtual stranger.

"I have a once-in-a-lifetime offer, but I'm not sure if I should take it," Maggie said.

"Interesting," Charles J said, and then he looked past Maggie, his eyes unfocused. "Do you trust the person who made the offer?" he asked distractedly.

"Yes," Maggie said, fighting the desire to turn around and see what he was focused on.

"How does your body react when you think about accepting the offer?" he asked in the same distracted way.

Maggie imagined accepting Sinthia's offer, and excitement rushed through her body. "Excited."

"And how does your body react to the idea of saying no?" he asked.

Maggie thought about telling Sinthia no, and her body seemed to fold in on itself, and unshed tears made her eyes burn. "It's painful," she said.

Charles J nodded in understanding, and his eyes swept away from the darkness beyond Maggie's shoulder to lock onto Maggie's eyes with a sharp focus. "Then you have your answer," Charles J said with finality.

Maggie stared back at Charles J and wondered if it could be that easy. A small voice in her mind asked when she had become such a coward? When had she stopped rushing toward what she desired?

Charles J was right. There was only one correct answer. "Thank you," she said, and Charles J nodded his head.

"You're welcome. Well, I'm going to finish my walk and see if I can find inspiration for my next project. Anne Bonny, Jack," Charles J said to the puppies as he gave them one last pat. "Maggie, enjoy the night, and if I might give you a piece of wisdom." Charles J hesitated, and Maggie nodded that he should continue. "Trust your soul. It knows which is the right choice."

Charles J stood up from the table, picked up his walking stick, and with one last wave, he continued his stroll out to the cliffs.

A sense of peace descended over Maggie. She realized that her decision to accept Sinthia's offer had lessened her stress. But, unfortunately, it was too late to tell Sinthia her decision tonight. Tomorrow morning she'd swing by the Gnome residence to give her the good news.

Chapter Twenty-Four

Crescent Bay, California – Foghorn Tavern

The morning after the necromancers' visit, Shaun had finished his preliminary work at the Madeira lighthouse and happily headed home to Crescent Bay.

Now he was enjoying a cup of afternoon tea while listening to Maggie tell him about her discussion with Charles J and her decision to tell Sinthia yes.

"Wow," Shaun said as he stared at her in wonder. "You had quite a night last night."

Maggie laughed, "No kidding. Fighting a ghost. Possessed by a goddess. Deciding to become a witch. Yep, I'm wiped."

"I just bet you are," Shaun said as he shared her smile. "How did Sinthia take your response?"

"I don't know. I swung by the Gnomes this morning, but Mr. Gnome said that Sinthia was out running errands. So I'll pull her aside after tonight's ghostbuster debriefing."

Shaun smiled at the idea of the ghostbusters sitting down for a debriefing. But, they had booked the back room of the tavern to do just that. He looked forward to discussing last night's adventure over good food and drinks.

"Are you nervous about your decision?" Shaun said as he watched Maggie fold and unfold a napkin.

"What do you think?" she responded sarcastically but gave him a little smile to lessen the bite.

"I think you're going to be great," Shaun said as he stood up to press a kiss to the top of her head. The phone rang, and Shaun answered it, "Hello. Yes. No, that's fine. Send her up," Shaun said into the receiver before he hung up to look at Maggie's questioning face. "That was Max.

Sinthia is downstairs and asked if she could come up and speak with you."

"What?" Maggie said in a strangled voice as she jumped up and looked frantically around the room as though looking for a place to hide.

"Maggie," Shaun crooned. "You'll be fine." Then he enfolded her in his arms for a gentle hug. "Sinthia loves you, and she would never do anything to hurt you."

"I know," Maggie said in a voice muffled by his shirt before she pulled back to search his face. "This is just such a huge deal."

"It is," Shaun agreed, "but you're up to the task." A knock on the door kept Maggie from replying.

When Shaun opened the door, he saw that Sinthia looked as stressed as Maggie, and on impulse, he hugged her too. At first, Sinthia froze in shock, then she melted into his embrace, accepting the comfort.

"You two have a lot to discuss," Shaun said. "I understand there is a work of art in the tavern that I need to check out. Anne Bonny, Jack, Suí." The dogs trotted over and stood still as Shaun clipped their leashes to their collars. "I'll see you downstairs in about an hour," Shaun said as he kissed Maggie. "Lean," she said to the dogs, and Maggie closed the door behind them.

"Would you like something to drink?" Maggie asked as she moved over to the kitchen table and picked up Shaun's empty teacup.

"No, I'm good," Sinthia said as she followed her across the apartment. Sinthia could tell that Maggie had made her decision, and Sinthia's heart beat rapidly. She had already decided that if Maggie said no, she wouldn't let it negatively impact their relationship. She loved Maggie too much to let that happen.

"I've been doing a lot of soul searching, and I've decided to say yes," Maggie said in a rush.

Sinthia stood in shocked silence, unsure that she had heard Maggie correctly. "Yes?" she asked in a hopeful whisper.

"Yes," Maggie said in a firm voice.

Sinthia made a joyful noise and swooped in to gather Maggie into her arms for a rambunctious hug. The two women held each other tight, laughed, and dried each other's tears before settling down at the table to grin at each other.

"So, what's next?" Maggie asked.

"We have a few more days until the full moon. We'll have to find somewhere for the ritual," Sinthia said.

"Because of Mr. Gnome?" Maggie asked, and Sinthia nodded her head yes. "How do you do this around him and still keep it a secret?" Maggie asked.

"I tell him that the moon is full or that I need to go do some woo-woo, and he makes himself scarce. That's easier during the warmer months because I work outside, and he avoids the backyard. It's tougher during the cold months because I prefer working inside, and I feel guilty about kicking him out of the house."

A slow smile filled Maggie's face. "You've thought of something," Sinthia said.

Maggie nodded, "I have an attic."

"Your attic. I forgot about that. Can we check it out?" Sinthia asked excitedly.

"Yep, let me grab my keys," Maggie said as she stood up to retrieve her keys.

Epilogue

Bountiful, California – The Madeira Estate – Lighthouse

Shaun stood on the lighthouse gallery and listened to the sounds of the crew working on the lighthouse.

The state had accepted the bid from Renovation 1906, and the lighthouse renovation was fully underway. The crew was working double shifts to complete the job before the first snow of winter.

Shaun had told Mrs. Kleyn that he would let her know if anyone had any paranormal encounters, but so far, the site had been quiet, ghost-wise anyway. When Shaun had returned to the site, he noticed the men were more boisterous—joking and whistling as they worked. No one had reported any odd occurrences, and Shaun was sure that Teresa was gone.

Back home, Maggie was preparing for the first step in her training with Sinthia. The two of them were having a good time cleaning and decorating the attic of the Foghorn Tavern. Shaun was dying with curiosity, but the space was off-limits to anyone except Sinthia and Maggie, so he would have to cope. He loved how animated Maggie became when she shared something Sinthia had said. He would smile in understanding when Maggie stopped talking mid-sentence, uncertain if she was about to share a secret. Shaun knew it would get easier as her instruction progressed.

The village of Crescent Bay was diving into the Harvest season as tourists began to pour in to fill the streets and businesses. In a couple of weeks, the decorations of corn stalks and bales of hay would be expanded to include ghosts and other Halloween icons.

Shaun loved the Halloween season, which for him started on October 1st and ended at the last stroke of midnight on the 31st. Shaun was looking forward to hosting a new mid-week ghost tour at the lighthouse.

Sarah Gnome hosted Ghost Stories and Cocoa events at her B&B. On those nights, Sarah would light the fire pit behind her B&B, Gnome's Rest, serve hot cocoa, and everyone would tell ghost stories. Usually, the event was just for guests, but sometimes there was room for a couple of friends. Maggie said it was a lot of fun, and Shaun hoped there would be room for them to attend this year.

Shaun put a gentle hand on the shoulder of the statue of the faceless lighthouse keeper. He said a quiet prayer to the universe for the soul of the man murdered by Davis. Shaun thought of the silhouette he had seen in the lighthouse beam, the one embracing Teresa's soul as she crossed over. He hoped that it had been Teresa's long-lost lover. He smiled when he imagined Maggie's reaction to such a romantic thought, but it was just who he was. Teresa had been treated horribly; she had earned an afterlife of love.

Deciding it was time to head back to Crescent Bay, he checked in with his construction lead and then got into his car to drive around the manor to the front gate. He paused in front of the manor and climbed out of his car to look up at the large structure. Although the energy had shifted, it was still an imposing building. Shaun wondered if a building could develop a spirit of its own, one that you couldn't cross over. He resolved to ask Annie that question the next time he saw her. A curtain twitched in a third-floor window, and Shaun froze like a deer in headlights. A fine mist covered the window, followed by a hand with a rag. A face appeared, and Shaun laughed and waved at the worker cleaning the window. Enough spooky for one day, Shaun decided as he climbed back into his car and headed home to Crescent Bay.

The End

Don't miss out!

Visit the website below and you can sign up to receive emails whenever Robin Wainwright publishes a new book. There's no charge and no obligation.

https://books2read.com/r/B-A-JWBB-ICZZB

BOOKS 2 READ

Connecting independent readers to independent writers.

Also by Robin Wainwright

Haunted Happenings
Silver Hart
Raven's Rest

The Widow's Walk Trilogy
Adrift
Becalmed
Capsized

Traditional Family
Traditional Family Values

Standalone
Cat's Meow
Traditional Family Secrets

Watch for more at www.robinwainwright.com.

About the Author

As a child, Robin Wainwright's Irish mother filled Robin's active imagination with stories of magic and the wee people.

Her days were filled with other worlds where magic and the paranormal were an accepted way of life. As soon as Robin learned how to write, she continued her mother's tradition of storytelling. She shared her stories with her mother but no one else.

In 2013, Robin decided to begin sharing her stories with a broader audience, so The Widow's Walk trilogy was born.

Robin lives in Southern California with her wonderful husband.

She loves the rain, thunder, and lightning (although she doesn't see much of it where she lives), chocolate, coffee, and Halloween.

She continues to write while sitting in her recliner, appearing to look out her window into her green yard, while in reality, her vision is focused on other locales.

Read more at www.robinwainwright.com.